To Swim Across the World

To Swim Across *the* World

a novel

FRANCES PARK
and
GINGER PARK

talk miramax books
HYPERION
New York

Library of Congress Cataloging-in-Publication Data

Park, Frances.
    To swim across the world : a novel / Frances Park and Ginger Park.
    p.   cm.
    ISBN 0-7868-6733-7
    1. Korea—Fiction.   I. Park, Ginger.   II. Title.
PS3566.A6732 T6 2001
813'.54—dc21   2001016812

Book design by Christine Weathersbee

10 9 8 7 6 5 4 3 2 1

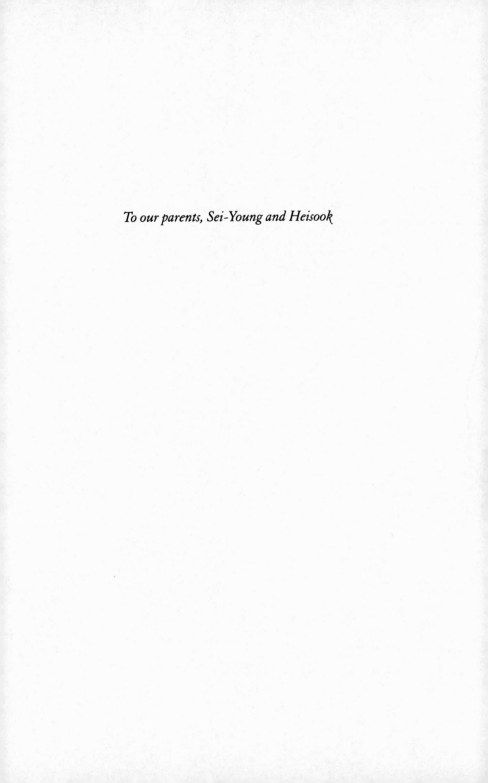

To our parents, Sei-Young and Heisook

ACKNOWLEDGMENTS

Deepest gratitude goes to our parents who grace the cover of this book. Without their lives, there would be no story to tell. Dad in heaven, mom on earth, we love you both so much.

And to our agent, the wonderous Molly Friedrich, who has a way of making dreams come true.

Also to our editor, Jonathan Burnham, for guiding our manuscript to its perfect place in the universe.

A special thanks to Tina Brown for launching the dynamic Talk Miramax Books.

Many thanks to the talented people at Talk Miramax who helped put it all together: Andrea Knebel, Kristin Powers, Farley Chase, Hilary Bass and Kathy Schneider.

Gratitude, too, to Rose Marie Morse and Paul Cirone.

And to Justin, for the joy he brings us.

ONE

SOUTH, 1941
Sei-Young

"Voices were hushed, dreams of freedom crushed."

I WATCHED FATHER HOBBLE down the mountain with his rickety cart. It was morning and he was off on the two and a half-hour journey to the capital city of Seoul. Father was a peddler of fine wooden works of art which he carved and which Mother painted while the moon rose and fell over Nabi, our mountain village. In Nabi—our word for butterfly—we accepted each passing day as a blessing in our palms, for it meant we had survived on what little food we could afford. Now summer was here and it brought a burst of butterflies, good omens for a better tomorrow.

"Good luck, Father!" I called out.

My words were lost down the mountain. Despite the butterflies and the brilliant dawn light, the hopeless feeling of the night before came back to haunt me.

I had been asleep, tucked inside my floor bedding, when

1

something startled me awake. Maybe it was hunger or a bad dream or an omen of things to come.

Our hut was lantern-lit. My one-year-old brother Kwan-Young was asleep in his bedding next to me. Grandfather was reading his Bible, lips silently moving. And then there were my parents, hunched over at work. Father sat cross-legged, his tin cup of rice wine within reach, sculpting a block of wood into an oval-shaped box with his carving knife. The base was finished and now he moved onto the lid. He smoothed out its surface, letting the wood shavings fall where they might. Then he began the soulful process of etching flowers on the top of the lid. This was when art took over labor, for Father seemed to fall into a spell of ancient flutes and songs. That is, until Mother murmured—

"*Yobo,* we have only a handful of rice left."

Father shrugged, too confidently. "Don't worry. Tomorrow will be sunny, a good day for selling our wares. At least enough to buy us a small sack of rice."

"I went to visit Sunja today." Mother spoke of her older sister. "The word in the village is that the price of rice has gone up again."

Father's knife grew still. His dark bony face stiffened.

"And without rice"—she shook her head—"my milk for Kwan-Young will dry up."

Grandfather closed his Bible. "It is not just rice. Soybeans, cabbage. Everything we put into our mouths."

"Even the air we breathe," Mother lamented, painting with a delicate hand that belied her exhaustion. "Every sprout belongs to the Japanese. I once believed we would wake up one day and they would be gone. But that was a long time ago."

It *was* a long time ago. In 1910 Imperial Japan colonized

Korea. Slowly, day-to-day life changed for Koreans. Voices were hushed, dreams of freedom crushed. I remember overhearing Mother say that it felt like wearing *comoshins* too small for one's feet. Not until that night would I begin to understand what she meant.

Father grew more hunched. Like a deformed beast, he moaned. His hands began to tremble. His knife fell; the wooden box fell. His empty hands reached for his tin cup and he drank his rice wine wretchedly, wanting more. Mother kept painting, not looking up, dreading the crash that followed.

"Aigoo!" Father wailed as he tried without luck to crush his cup with one fist. He shook with failure, then blindly threw it across the hut. Kwan-Young woke up with a loud cry. My parents looked at each other. In that moment too much was said, and Father left the hut.

Father was a moody man; one wrong word and his high spirits would sink. This happened almost every day. But tonight something was different. Maybe it was the cursed moon and the broken stars. Maybe it was Father's violent display. I was eleven now, almost a man. And I was First Son in the Shin family. It was my duty to leave my bedding and go after Father. Mother covered her face with shame, realizing what I had witnessed.

But Grandfather took my arm in the doorway. "Leave him be, Sei-Young. Leave him to his own thoughts."

"But Father needs us," I said.

Grandfather held me. "No, your father needs to be alone."

I could have easily broken away from his arms, but I believed Grandfather to be the embodiment of strength—like a spirit or a guardian angel—that would guide me through life. As a young man in Seoul, he had served as a minister in a small Methodist church. But preaching to me was not his way. "I have faith in everything you do," he would tell me, just to bring a smile to my face. And Grandfather's faith was something that was always there, like the magic glow of the sun.

But did he have faith in his son, my father?

We stood in the doorway as Father cast his arms to a sky whose vastness dwarfed him. With clenched fists, he cursed the Japanese: "Damn those monkeys for taking our land! Damn them for holding their sword over us! Damn them for taking the food from our children's mouths! For all our sweat, we are spit upon!"

Then he fell to his knees and wept.

Inside the hut Mother wept, too. Her pretty face hardened with fatigue as she brought Kwan-Young up to her breast and sang a lullaby. *"Cha jung cha jung, uri Kwan-Young, cha jung cha jung . . ."* Kwan-Young's eyes fell shut but he kept sucking for one more drop of milk. Finally, his lips gave up. Mother gently pulled him off her breast, then blew out the lantern with purpose.

"Do not remember your father in such a shameful light," she begged her baby, then prayed: "God, keep him young and innocent."

Grandfather reached for his wooden cane, a birthday present from Father. Father and I had spent days searching for the sturdiest branch, one with bend and beauty. We came upon it in the Valley of Spirits, just below our village. The people of Nabi believed that the first autumn winds to pass through the Valley of Spirits during Chusok, our harvest holiday, were the spirits of our ancestors here to bless the earth.

"Stay with your mother," Grandfather said as he labored outside. With each halting step he came closer to comforting his tortured son.

Mother's presence crept up behind me. The sound of her steady breathing soothed me and for a split second I envied Kwan-Young, drifting in dreams, so unaware.

"Go to sleep, Sei-Young," Mother finally spoke. "In the morning things will seem brighter."

I crawled back into my bedding, but sleep would not come. Sleeping space was always tight but tonight every muscle in me cramped with the curse of being born Korean. For all my life—like Father's trusty tin cup—the Japanese had been here; their presence was as natural as the sound of faraway streams. *Faraway* streams because while the Japanese lived on our land, they did not live in our world. Two people, two worlds. Koreans lived in one-room huts while the Japanese lived in palatial homes. Koreans dressed in rags while the Japanese wore garments of silk. Koreans farmed the land while the Japanese owned the land. Almost every last acre.

Now the words that Father had cried sounded across the skies. But who was listening to the words of a man who had suffered a lifetime under the Japanese sword? The man who had lost his vision first to fear, then rice wine? Not only had the Japanese taken away our land and food, but they spit upon the dignity of good men who could cry for eternity and never be heard, men who had to live with the look of hunger in their children's eyes.

Until tonight I never questioned hunger. Hunger was just a way of life, like waking up and hoping for a bowl of rice soup and soy sauce, perhaps with ferns, for the morning meal.

The last time I could remember eating treats was on Kwan-Young's *paegil-nal,* his one-hundredth day birthday. Many Korean babies did not survive their first hundred days, so the day was great cause for celebration. There were almond cookies and peanut crackers and sweet sticky rice studded with lima beans. Mother had even given me two strips of *bulgoki*. The flavor of grilled seasoned beef lingered on my lips for a long time.

The next cause for celebration would be in the following year on Grandfather's sixtieth birthday. In Nabi we believed that on one's sixtieth birthday the moon settled in the exact position in the sky as the day one was born. In Nabi, to live sixty years was to have attained all the wisdom in the universe.

But Grandfather's wisdom stretched much further than the universe. Grandfather was all things. Dreamer. Thinker. Holy man. Every night with the light of a candle flickering between us, Grandfather would sit me down in a corner of our hut and say, "Always remember, you are not Shuzo Nabano."

Under Japanese rule, every Korean was forced to relinquish his or her Korean name and register under a Japanese name. In my Japanese-supervised school, I became Shuzo Nabano, an obedient pupil who spoke only Japanese. Every morning I walked two miles to the Tanake School wearing the cotton Japanese uniform Mother had sewn for me, a gold Imperial signet pinned to my collar. Our school was designed to turn my forty classmates and me into loyal Japanese subjects. As Shuzo Nabano, I bowed before the Shinto shrine that stood outside the one-room school as an imposing symbol of Japan's dominance. As Shuzo Nabano, I recited the Pledge of Allegiance to a god-size portrait of Emperor Hirohito.

But Grandfather reminded me of who I truly was. Night after night he would recite, "Your name is Sei-Young, which means 'to swim across the world.' Someday you will do just that."

I closed my eyes and let my imagination swim far away from our hut and from the image of Father's broken spirit in the moonlight.

"To swim across the world," I repeated until I finally dreamed myself to sleep.

Today—the first morning of my three-week long summer vacation—the sun came out and brightness followed, just as Mother had promised.

After Father hobbled out of sight, I, Sei-Young Shin, son of poor peddlers, tilted my head to the sky. The sun flooded my eyes with hope. The Japanese and their Almighty Emperor Hirohito may have owned the land and my people. But they did not own the sun that crowned my head so magnificently this morning.

"Good luck, Father!"

TWO

NORTH, 1941
Heisook

"Do you hear the secrets of the waterfall?"

I STOOD WITH MY big brother Changi at the foot of Heavenly Mountain. The summer air was warm, fragrant with jasmine. I could almost hear the earth moving as a thousand shades of green sang across the countryside.

Last year during our winter break, the earth was cold and still—only the smoke from my breath brought warmth. The lush beauty of Heavenly Mountain was gone. If someone told me that vultures had picked at the mountain until it was nothing but a dry old bone, I'd believe it. And Mother had fallen ill, far worse than in winters past. For weeks she had been unable to keep food down. Her skin sagged off her bones and turned yellow. No one knew what was wrong with her, only that death might come before spring.

So Father had brought her to our country home, perched high among the clouds. He was certain she would heal here, twenty-two miles from the noise and pollution of our city home in bustling Sinuiju. She would heal here, where God's fingertips touched the sun.

Up Heavenly Mountain Changi and I had followed Father. He was carrying Mother's frail body to our home, praying "Gracious God, please heal my wife's ills...." I had never seen Heavenly Mountain so gray, so frozen. I could hear angels sing the song of death.

But Father heard faith's song. Every morning he would go to a natural spring that traveled in a sweet, peaceful rhythm down the mountain. There he would await the rising sun. When the sun's rays finally glistened upon the water, he would kneel against the bank's ancient rocks and scoop up a flask of icy, bubbling water, and declare—"The warmth of God has blessed the spring. This holy water will purify your mother's body and revive her."

Mother never once summoned me to her bedside, as she was a woman of veiled emotions. But I would often sit with her and hold her hand, waiting for some kind of reaction—a faint smile or a deep breath—to let me know that a part of her wanted me there. But there were no faint smiles or deep breaths. Still, I would remain by her side, nurturing her with the prayers I had been taught.

Before I was born, when Changi was a baby, our parents were missionaries in China. Behind the Great Wall, they tried to spread the word of a Christian God. It was hard work in a land where Buddha ruled. Whether Catholics or Methodists or Presbyterians, Christian families like ours were in the minority.

So my parents were people of great faith. They believed God had blessed the natural spring and, in doing so, would bless Mother. And it seemed to be true. In a month's time, a rose color returned to her face. She was miraculously cured.

"God has touched upon the earth," Mother said, looking out at the whole frozen world outside her window. "God has healed me."

Whenever our parents' words embraced the notion of God, Changi scoffed, sometimes to himself, sometimes not. My fifteen-year old brother only worshipped his own ideas.

But I drank their words; I believed God could heal every living thing. The first signs of spring were proof of that. And what about the spray of purple wildflowers growing between those rocks wedged at the foot of the mountain? That had to be God's doing.

And now it was summer. Songbirds and flowering trees resurrected Heavenly Mountain. Again, God had touched upon the earth.

"Quit daydreaming and start moving!" Changi yelled.

I was bewildered, suddenly aware of my footing. This was not our usual route, the *san* trail. That trail I knew by heart. Every stone in the ground, every tree trunk. My favorite willow that welcomed me when the breeze blew. And at the trail's end—our country home, basking in the shade of chestnut trees.

"Where are we going?" I asked him.

"Follow me." Changi signaled and skirted ahead. "I want to show you something."

Changi sensed my disapproving eyes boring through him. Though I was a mere girl of ten, he swung around defensively. "Okay, what's wrong?"

I stood my ground. Exploring unfamiliar territory frightened me. "I'm not taking one more step, until you tell me where we are and where we're going."

"My poor lost little sister," Changi joked.

I refused to smile.

"Look," Changi said, "if you don't trust me, then don't come with me. I will happily go alone."

"Why should I trust you? You might get me into trouble."

"What trouble?"

How could Changi ask me such a question with a straight face? Trouble followed him like his own shadow. Just the other day he sneaked into our parents' private quarters and took a wad of *yen* from Father's chest. He had sworn me to silence.

"I am just borrowing the money," he had said. "I will put it back before Father even notices it missing."

But Father noticed the money missing right away. At supper his face was swollen with disappointment. He had confronted us, his children. "Do either of you know where the money went?"

"No," Changi had replied, while I just sat there and said nothing.

"What about the money you stole from Father's chest?" I now reminded Changi.

He groaned. "Oh, no, not this again."

"How long do you expect me to hold my tongue?"

"Do you tell me this to make me feel bad, Heisook? Because I don't. Father's holy chest is filled with church money. And with that money he could feed the homeless on the streets. He could send me to school in China. But do you think he cares about you or me or Mother or the beggar he passes on his way to church? Our welfare comes second to his godless God. The Honorable Reverend Pang in his finely tailored suit would rather build a bigger church for his congregation."

Changi was wrong. Father had no reason to build a bigger church. The Sacred Heart Church was as big and beautiful as any church could be. Everyone knew it was the most impressive church in all of Sinuiju. An outside staircase led to a grand hall that led to a nave where stained-glass windows brought in the presence of God. There were four private rooms, each on a separate tiny floor, meant for times when only a one-on-one prayer with God would do. Mother would spend hours on the top floor, alone with God. Who she was praying for, and why she was praying, was a mystery.

"That's not true, Changi," I argued. "Our church is big enough."

"It is true, Heisook! You're just brainwashed like all dumb daughters."

Changi set off marching up the mountain.

It was not my nature to disobey Father, who had told us never to wander off the *san* trail. But my brother could read my mind. He picked up a rock and hurled it into the valley with great satisfaction.

"Grow up, Heisook. Don't be afraid to think for yourself. If you are afraid you are lost, then you *are* lost."

As I followed Changi, my eyes settled on the scar visible under his crew cut.

"My medal of honor," he would sneer to anyone who might be listening—for that made him feel as empowered as any king, *"I wear it proudly."*

Changi was a good student, not so long ago. Then signs of trouble, like a restless shadow, crept into his life. He began to skip school, refusing to tell us his whereabouts. When he did attend class, he was disruptive. One morning, when his *sensei* was conducting roll call, Changi would not respond to his Japanese-assigned name of Mifune Okawa. Instead, he stood before his classmates and condemned the Japanese Emperor.

"Death to Hirohito! Crush his Imperial Army!"

His *sensei* whipped him across the back of his head with a ruler until blood oozed down his neck and stained his white shirt. But Changi just grinned. He was as proud of the stain on his Imperial uniform as he was of the scar forming on the back of his neck. He hated everything and everyone Japanese.

Such thinking, such behavior, put fear in my parents' hearts that Changi would become a Korean patriot, someone who challenged the Japanese by advocating Korean independence. Such dangerous activities could lead to a swift death. Father had pleaded with him.

"Changi, why must you cause trouble in school? Trouble in school brings trouble to our home."

"They teach me nothing but Jap history. I do not need their education," Changi coolly replied.

"But we must obey the law of the land," Father tried to explain.

Changi leaped to his feet with a rebellious cry. "I am no obeying idiot. This land we call Korea is a no man's land! I do not salute the filthy Japs! I salute my own gods. Someday I will return to my birthplace of China where I belong."

Mother winced. This happened whenever Changi spoke of China. I did not know why—another mystery.

Despite Father's pleas, Changi abandoned his Japanese school for the streets of Sinuiju, where defiant boys like himself marched in public denouncement of the Emperor. And when Changi wasn't on the streets, he would often disappear to escape the frowns of our parents at home.

"Your brother is like a wild animal who must be set free," Father would explain to me. "I cannot control the wind and rain. I cannot control Changi."

But a cold world could tame even the wildest animal. After a day or two, Changi would always return home where a steaming bowl of *tooboo chigae* awaited him.

"Slow down, Changi!" I cried.

But Changi kept moving. Slowing down was a sign of defeat. Only when I slipped on a rock did he stop and turn around.

"Are you okay?" he asked, checking my ankles and elbows.

"I think so," I said.

"Do you feel any swelling?"

"No."

"Do you feel any bruises coming on?"

"No."

Changi wiped away beads of sweat on his forehead. A smile broke out on my face, so I turned away—he wouldn't like that. Deep down my brother had a delicate touch, one that had produced a wall of morning glories on the iron gate of our city home. On a dewy day, the morning glories seemed to climb above the gate and into the open sky.

After we'd hiked for a lifetime, it seemed to me, I asked again: "Where are we going?"

"To my secret place," he replied.

Whenever Changi felt trapped, he would escape to somewhere I imagined as mystical, musical, full of light.

Now we were going to see it together.

We came upon a great chestnut tree whose limbs stretched out like arms reaching for heaven.

Changi hugged it honorably.

"My two-hundred-year-old friend, if only you could talk. Then we could hear the truth about Korea's history. Not the stinking garbage the Japs feed girls like Heisook at school. Great kings and great leaders once ruled our land. But we'll never hear about it from Japs in Jap History class."

I shuddered. "Don't call them that."

"Call them what, little sister?"

"You know."

"Say it. Say *Japs*."

"I will not."

"Heisook, even when you gaze into the clearest pond, remember something: You see things backward. The Japs are not our friends. They are our enemy."

I fell silent and tried to turn a deaf ear as Changi kept talking: "Look, here is the definition of Jap colonialism: We speak Jap at school and Korean at home and end up nothing but tongue-twisted dimwits!"

Why was it always this way? How could Changi—who knew the name of every wildflower cluster and every constellation in the sky—be so wrong? The Japanese were not our enemy. What about my *sensei*? She was so kind and soft-spoken. Her name was Hanako, and what I loved most about her was the way her voice would drop to a loving whisper when we were alone and talking about my flute-playing or our favorite *haiku* and *tanka* poems. In private, she addressed me as Heisook, not by my Japanese-assigned name of Yoshiko Okawa. Of course, I kept our friendship a secret from Changi. If he knew that saluting the Imperial flag was as natural to me as talking to my *sensei*, if he knew I didn't mind my Japanese name at all, he would abandon me right here, right now. Where would I go?

"Up here I am free!" he now shouted while climbing the great chestnut tree. "Liberated from all bondage!"

Changi reached the top of the tree. He peered north and bellowed: "Hello, Manchuria! And hello, China, beyond the mountain range!"

All I saw was endless mountains and sky. "Come down from there," I pleaded.

"Ha! Ha!" Changi hollered again as he plunged downward, hit the ground, and rolled into a ball of laughter. The sight of his bloody knees made him laugh even harder.

"There's nothing funny about blood," I said.

"Heisook, pain is a part of life! Sometimes pain can feel good if it is felt for the right reason," Changi declared, moving on like a fearless soldier.

Now I was following my brother through a dark tunnel of trees. The sounds of strange animals swallowed me up. With each forbidden step I was afraid something wet and slimy might snatch me and carry me away to the center of the earth. But to my surprise, the tunnel opened up to a sun-blinding sky. And below, a vision glittered in my eyes.

It was a waterfall surrounded by majestic rocks carved for kings and queens and gods. Water splashed off the rocks like diamonds shattering. A faint rainbow arced over us. I was in awe.

Changi bowed. "Welcome to my secret place."

After a long cool drink of mountain water, Changi led me to a giant quartz rock that sparkled behind the waterfall. Then he lifted me up on the rock like a princess to my throne. "This is where I sit and think," he said.

"And what do you think about?"

"Oh, sometimes I think about the universe," he said, hopping up to join me. "About how the stars are blinking all the way out in eternity."

"What do you mean by eternity?"

"The universe has no beginning or end, Heisook. We could fly through space forever and ever and never reach the other side. And you know why? Because there is no other side. There is only eternity."

"But what about heaven?" I challenged him.

"Christ! There is no heaven!"

"How do you know that?"

"Look, when we die, we turn to dust. Dust. Don't plug your ears, Heisook! Hear the truth before you go permanently deaf."

I wished Changi wouldn't say such horrible things. If my brother had a little faith in God and the hereafter, perhaps he wouldn't need to feel so much pain to feel alive.

"Heaven is above the stars," I insisted. "I know it is, just like I know my prayers by heart. *Our Father who art in heaven . . .*"

"Amen," Changi said. "So you know all your prayers along with all your silly church choir songs. You sing your heart out when there is nothing to sing about. I pity your soul, little sister. But time will surely change your way of thinking. If not time, then surely death."

It was no use arguing with Changi.

"Close your eyes," I heard.

I closed my eyes.

"Listen," he whispered.

I listened. An orchestra of rushing water fell upon my ears.

"Do you hear the secrets of the waterfall?" he asked me.

I shook my head.

"Then listen with all your heart, Heisook. If you don't hear its secrets, then you're not listening."

"What am I listening for?"

"The truth."

I closed my eyes and listened more carefully this time. Again, I heard only rushing water. I would hear no secrets that day.

"Changi, what does the waterfall tell you?"

My big brother closed his eyes as though he were hearing chimes in the wind and whispered, "The waterfall tells me that the world is changing and we must change with it."

Before I could ask Changi what he meant by that, his mood abruptly changed. His face darkened as if thunder only he could hear was rolling in. Suddenly I felt unwelcome, not at all like a princess on her throne. I was sure Changi regretted bringing me here and was wishing he had left me behind. He didn't trust me to keep his secret. No matter what I said before, I would never tell Father who took the money from his chest and I would never tell anybody about this secret place. I would hold my tongue forever. Besides, I liked it here. Perhaps I could not hear the secrets of the waterfall but I could hear its beauty splashing and singing in my ears. When Changi leaped off the rock, the music ended.

"Let's go, Heisook," he said.

Without a word, Changi led us back to the familiar *san* trail. The silence was unsettling. Finally, I spoke up. "Changi, when you say the world is changing, what do you mean?"

As if he was alone, Changi wandered off the trail until he spotted what he was looking for: an azalea shrub in brilliant bloom. In all the times I had passed this way I had never noticed it before. But Changi's eyes were different from mine; they saw things differently and saw different things. After plucking off several white flowers and placing them in my hands, he began to talk to the shrub. "You bloom, then wither, and you never bother a soul, sweet peaceful plant. That's a noble way to live. People are not so noble. And that's why we cannot stand still like you."

Darkness was gathering when we finally reached home. In the doorway we could hear our parents.

"We can not give him one more *yen*," Mother was saying. "He must go to work and earn his own money."

"But we must give to those less fortunate," Father insisted.

"To those less fortunate. But not to worthless lazybones."

They were speaking of Father's nephew, Ilgo. Our mother saved her harshest voice for him. Every so often, Ilgo, the son of Father's long-lost brother, would appear out of nowhere, here at the door of our country home on Heavenly Mountain or at the gate of our city home in Sinuiju. All I could ever make out was a scraggly beard and a pair of cruel eyes squinting for money—our parents forbade us to meet him. Not even our God-loving Christian parents would allow this man in our home.

"If he were a leper or a beggar I would have mercy," Mother continued. "But he is a bum who would rather take the rice out of a child's mouth than lift one lazy finger in the fields. He does not deserve even a crumb of kindness, much less the wad of *yen* you give him whenever he shows up at our door."

"You are right, *yobo*," Father admitted.

When our parents spotted us in the doorway, they quickly hushed up.

It had been a day of secrets.

"Grandfather spoke to the sky . . ."

A POT OF SOYBEAN soup simmered over the hibachi stove for our morning meal. Mother unfolded the meal table and set down four tin bowls. Father had pushed his cart all over Seoul that week and his sweat had paid off handsomely. Five keepsake boxes, four Japanese dolls, eight miniature Shinto shrine sculptures—all sold. That meant enough *yen* to purchase a large sack of rice. Enough *yen* to fill each tin bowl with soup and rice and pickled vegetables. There was a smile on Father's weathered face as he crossed his legs on his straw mat and settled down to eat.

I sat down with a smile, too. Whenever Father was happy, I was happy. The warmth of the *ondal* floor made me wish that this morning, this meal, our smiles, would last forever.

"First we must pray," Grandfather insisted.

Respectfully, Father put down his chopsticks and joined hands with the family. Our sacred circle prayed.

"Bless this food and this home," Grandfather prayed.

"*Neh,*" Mother prayed.

"Bless our Sei-Young and our Kwan-Young," Grandfather prayed.

"*Neh, neh,*" Father prayed.

"Bless this moment when the love between us flows through our hands like water through a river. When we are touched by the love of God, we are linked forever, together," Grandfather prayed.

"Amen," we prayed.

At the morning meal the whole family was present. This time was especially sacred to Father who, during the supper hour, was still trudging back from Seoul. Whether soup or scraps, a quiet morning meal was his reward.

Aunt Sunja stormed through the hut. My heart sank, for her outbursts ruined many a meal for us.

"Those Japanese demons beat a man to death!" she wailed.

Normally I would close my ears and keep eating. But I was grown up now. It was time to listen.

Mother was feeding Kwan-Young. She squeezed her breast in the hopes that more milk would come. "Who? Where?"

"This morning at Suka's farm. The man was just a farmhand. He'd taken a few rotten ears of corn to keep his family alive one more day."

"And they killed him? Are you sure?"

"Killed him for corn they wouldn't feed their own dogs. We have to do something."

"What can we do?" Mother kept feeding as she caressed Kwan-Young's head. "We're just one small family."

"It's just that way of thinking that enslaves us to the Japanese," Aunt Sunja retorted.

Father mumbled into his bowl, "Talk, talk, talk. What good is talk? Words cannot challenge the sword."

"We must fight back now," Aunt Sunja challenged him, "or our people will perish from the earth."

"Leave my family out of your war," Father warned her.

"*My* war? This is *our* war. And if your cowardly backbone weren't made of rubber, you would stand up for our people. For your family! How can you eat like such a pig while your baby sucks uselessly on your wife's shriveled breast?"

Our hut grew still, one word from collapse. Father stood up and met Aunt Sunja's eyes. His lips trembled, he was screaming inside. Oh, the things he would have said to her were it not for Mother. His hatred for Aunt Sunja was no secret but, like the soup on the stove, it usually simmered quietly. Today, despite his flaring glare, was no exception. He shot her one last angry look, then bowed good-bye to the family.

When he was gone, Aunt Sunja sneered, "Has Choon-Young finally lost his mind?"

"No," Mother replied. "But his faith, perhaps."

Aunt Sunja shrugged without a bone of sympathy. "Well, he is not alone."

"But he feels alone. That's the danger."

"The danger is his own weak character, so weak he walks with his head bent down into his tin cup."

"Sunja, please! Do not speak ill of my children's father."

Aunt Sunja balked. "The whole village speaks ill of him. *Choon-Young, the singing drunk.* Turn your head if you want, Kwangok. But children must face the ugly truth. Look it in the eye and fight back. Otherwise they'll grow up to be like Choon-Young. Drunken cowards."

"Sunja, please!"

I wanted her to leave. Even Grandfather had to bite his tongue, judging by his grave expression. Grandfather did not hate Aunt Sunja. Hate was too strong a word for a man once deemed

Reverend Shin. But he did not honor her, either. "She has no grace, no harmony," I overheard him once say to Father. Now he nudged me in an almost playful manner. It was time for our morning walk.

"Finish your soup, Sei-Young."

On a mountainside graced with rocks, I asked Grandfather, "Why did Aunt Sunja say those things about Father?"

"She is very angry at the Japanese and takes it out on everyone around her." After a few steps, Grandfather said, "It does not make it right, Sei-Young, but that is her way."

"Does that make her a bad person?" I asked him.

"No, but her good nature is buried under years of bitterness."

"Like old leaves, Grandfather?"

"Yes, Sei-Young." He smiled sadly. "Like old leaves."

"Why is she bitter?"

Grandfather bided time with a cough, then a long sigh. He would have preferred a leisurely walk with the beauty of silence and the sun on his face, which was smooth and pale, unlike Father's, even though he was taller and closer to its rays. But I was ready to hear the truth about the world around me, however dark and ugly. After all, I had already seen Father cry.

"There was a time when your aunt's nature was as beautiful as this mountainside, Sei-Young, when her loving husband walked beside her."

"Aunt Sunja had a husband?" No one had ever spoken of this man before. Just as I couldn't imagine Father without his rice wine, I couldn't imagine Aunt Sunja with a husband.

"Yes, Sei-Young, but two years before you were born, her husband was slain. It happened in a village north of here where she once lived. Her husband was beaten to death on his way home from work. Who beat him, and why, are unanswered questions, although in all likelihood he died at the hands of the Japanese. Had cholera or consumption claimed him, I believe your aunt would have accepted his death as God's will and moved on. She would be able to speak, or at least whisper, her husband's name and grieve in a normal fashion. Instead, her soul died a horrible death. She has become a vengeful creature breathing tales of Japanese atrocities toward Koreans."

I recalled Aunt Sunja's claims.

"They ransack homes, beat the men and rape the women, shoot babies to stop them from crying, then feed their tiny hearts to the vultures. I speak the truth! If you don't believe me, you are no better than a dirty Jap dancing on Korean graves."

Whether these were tales or truths, this much I knew: if not for the Japanese, Father would not be a man who had to struggle for every happy moment. My family would not be hungry. Aunt Sunja's husband would probably not be dead. And our country would belong to us.

"Grandfather," I asked him in a most respectful tone, "how do you know they are tales?"

"The Japanese have not been kind to our people, Sei-Young. That is no tale. We have been brutalized for as long as they have been here. But sometimes when one is bitter, one will say things, anything, to convince you to see the world through his or her eyes."

"Why *are* the Japanese here in the first place? Why aren't they happy to stay in their own country?"

"Sei-Young, you are full of questions today," Grandfather remarked.

"Why don't the Japanese go home and leave us alone?" I said.

Grandfather explained it to me. "Japan is a small, isolated

country with too many mouths to feed and nothing but rice fields. For many centuries Japan has hungered for our land. Our soil is rich, our position is envious."

"They should just stay home and eat rice," I muttered to myself.

A rock appeared on our path, big and flat. It was as if God set it there for Grandfather to stumble upon. I knew Grandfather would kneel in front of it and take his brush and ink stone from his pouch. He did. Such rituals were comforting to me. It may be a different rock on a different path, but it was the same safe pause from a world I was seeing more clearly every day.

Grandfather began. With slow, masterful strokes, he painted characters on the rock. *Freedom in our land,* I read. Even though learning the Korean alphabet was strictly forbidden in school, in the privacy of our home Grandfather had secretly taught me *Hangu'l.*

"Will we ever see freedom in our land?" I wondered.

With great thought, Grandfather replied, "I am an old man growing older with each season. Change does not come quickly, Sei-Young. But perhaps in your lifetime freedom will ring across our land and I will hear its bells."

Whenever Grandfather spoke of his mortality, my eyes would brim with tears. I wanted to believe that Grandfather would live forever. So what if he stood a little more hunched and moved a little more slowly than he did last spring? And his eyesight was poor. But Grandfather was like the seasons, ever changing but always returning. He would never die, that day would never come.

An airplane flew overhead; Grandfather looked up. "Look at

the silver bird, Sei-Young. Someday it will take you to a beautiful place far away."

I tried to picture such a place. A blurry image came to life in my eyes. But all at once the mountainside darkened and the image was gone. Grandfather spoke to the sky and the sky spoke back.

"We must go, Sei-Young. The monsoon has arrived."

The first drops fell, followed by hundreds more. Black ink washed off the rock and ran down the mountainside. Again I wondered: Will we ever see freedom in our land?

Grandfather and I hurried home.

We returned home just before the heavy rains began to fall. Aunt Sunja was gone and Father was home. He lifted his head from his tin cup. "I was halfway down the mountain when I saw the monsoon coming and turned around. No business today."

Drinking, always drinking.

Kwan-Young crawled across the floor and onto Father's lap. Father began to hum, then sing his favorite childhood song. *"Pul mok pal mok Seoul kata otaga . . ."*

Soon Father's voice grew so loud Kwan-Young burst into tears.

"Pul mok pal mok Seoul kata otaga . . ."

What had always seemed normal in our household—Father drinking moodily from his tin cup—now struck me as not normal at all. Aunt Sunja had called him a drunken coward, and while I did not like these words from her bitter tongue, I was afraid they were true.

"Mother, why does Father drink so much?" I asked her.

Mother wiped down the table, folded it up, then placed it

behind the stove. Every movement hurt her. No words came.

Now Father was wavering between high spirits and drowsiness. *"Pul mok pal mok . . ."* he mumbled.

What occurred to me next was almost too awful to think about. I held my breath and asked Mother: "How can Father always afford to buy rice wine?"

Mother took my face in her hands and aged before my eyes. "Shh, Sei-Young, shh . . ."

My family slept soundly that night. Maybe the steady falling of the monsoon rains lulled them to sleep. But not me. In fact, I never wanted to close my eyes again. I wanted my eyes to stay wide open so I could see everything going on around me, no matter how much it hurt. Every day Kwan-Young went hungry because Father had squandered our last coins on rice wine. When he was cursing the Japanese he should have been cursing himself. But was he the only one to blame? How could Mother watch her child suck in vain on her empty breasts? How could Grandfather, with all his worldly wisdom, not make Father stop drinking? He spoke to the sky; why not his own son?

I pressed my cheek against Kwan-Young's. It was soft and warm, a baby's cheek. More monsoon rains fell upon our hut. Had the Japanese really driven Father to such a fate? Was it their fault that he became a drunken coward, as Aunt Sunja claimed? Only one thing was clear to me tonight: my vow to my brother.

"You will never be hungry again."

FOUR

"Once you hate one person, it is easy to hate many . . ."

IT IS GOD'S BREATH *that carries the winds. It is God's tears of joy that carry the monsoon rains.* Mother and Father had told me these words long ago, delivered them like a sermon. So I loved the monsoon and believed in its goodness. God made the earth fertile and green. God made the streams blue and abundant with fish.

God was everywhere.

But today as I sat by the window of our country home and watched God's tears of joy sweep down the mountainside, I prayed for sunshine. Guilt seized me like a devil. In time of worry and fear—like whenever Mother fell ill—I had always run to God. Where would I now run?

My thoughts kept sneaking back to Changi's secret place. It was *our* secret place now, for we had gone back there together three or four times. Each time I sat by the waterfall while a rush of new ideas washed over me. What did it all mean? Did God not create this waterfall?

Changi had laughed at me. "No, silly girl. If he did, then he also created the monsoon rains that destroy homes every summer."

"What homes are destroyed?"

"Not everyone sleeps in stone houses with tile roofs. Open your eyes! Look around you. Can't you see that most Koreans live in dingy dirt huts? Their faces are nothing more than skin over skulls. They're not plump like yours from eating as many Jap pastries as your spoiled heart desires. Or soft like Mother's from a jar of expensive cream. Their faces show only starvation and misery. Do you think that is God's doing?"

"No," I had replied.

"And what about the Japs who are murdering Koreans as we speak? Are they God's creations, too? Is He to blame?"

"No, and only sinners question God."

"Then call me the biggest sinner of all. Do you think that you are a privileged Pang with a perfect fortune carved into your silky little palm because you don't question God, Heisook? Because you know your prayers by heart?"

I grew confused. "I don't know."

Changi had left home two days ago without returning. I missed him, even our quarrels, terribly. The last time we went to the waterfall, Changi had chipped off a tiny piece of the giant quartz rock and presented it to me.

"Carry this and always remember our secret place," he had said.

Now I felt for the stone in my pocket. Yes, it was there. I had a piece of my big brother with me. But the moment was over-shadowed by a sinister figure moving through the rain and up to our doorway: Ilgo.

Father met his nephew in the enclosed foyer that divided the main door from the house. Here was where we took off our shoes before stepping up and sliding open a white ricepaper door. I inched up and peeked through a tiny cracked opening.

Ilgo greeted Father with a beggar's hand. His voice was hoarse with damnation.

"The monsoon is very bad this year."

Father placed a wad of *yen* in Ilgo's hand. I couldn't help but wonder whether this was church money. If so, then it was just as well that Changi took money from Father's chest. Better in Changi's hands than Ilgo's.

"You must find work soon, Ilgo," Father said.

"There is no work," Ilgo scoffed. "Not if you are Korean, anyway."

"I will help you," Father offered.

"To be a cook? Or a farmhand? Forget it. I'd rather be a beggar."

"Look into a mirror, Ilgo, and you will see a beggar. You refuse my help because being a beggar suits you."

"I can afford no mirror. But don't worry." Ilgo spat as he crumpled the *yen* in Father's face before stuffing it into his pocket. "Someday I will repay you. You will see."

Despite Ilgo's threatening tone, Father said nothing back. When I was sure Ilgo was gone for good, I slid the ricepaper door open.

"Father," I said, "tell that horrible man to go away and never come back. I hate him!"

Father looked mortified. Changi was brash, that war was lost. But I was his daughter, meant to be as sweet as the notes floating from my flute.

"It is not that simple, Heisook. He is a poor man. He needs money to live on."

"He's ungrateful and mean!"

"Yes," he reluctantly agreed. "But he will come around. I sometimes think it is my fault that he feels so unworthy. In some ways, my helping him cripples him. He does not know how to stand on his own two feet."

"He *is* unworthy, Father! Even Mother thinks so. And he's evil, too!"

"Heisook—"

"I hate him!"

"Heisook! Pity, but do not hate, him, or anyone. Once you hate one person, it is easy to hate many. Now, your mother is preparing your lunch," he said with a loving shove. "Go eat."

My eager eyes watched Mother prepare my favorite dish for lunch, a Japanese delicacy called *sushi*. I had watched Mother prepare my *sushi* lunch countless times before. Each time was special—like now as she wrapped a sheet of seaweed around a layer of sticky rice studded with fish and egg and vegetable morsels. She rolled it into a log and sliced it up, arranging the perfect pieces onto my lacquer plate like jewels. How lovely my lunch looked to me.

To Changi, *sushi* was the enemy's food. Like an *obi* or a *kimono* or a flag waving a rising sun, *sushi* was a symbol of Japan.

"I am a proud Korean. I only eat Korean food. Do not feed me their poison," he would say.

If he were home for lunch, he would probably insist upon a big bowl of rice and a bigger bowl of *tooboo chigae,* spiced with peppers. It wasn't hot or spicy enough for Changi unless it brought tears to his eyes and a cough to his throat.

But Changi was not home for lunch today. Nor yesterday nor

the day before. Changi was never as far away as he seemed, because any minute he might just slide open the ricepaper door. That's why Mother had a pot of *tooboo chigae* bubbling on the stove, just in case. Maybe Mother would not hug Changi, maybe her manner would be cool, but the warm steam in the house meant that she was always missing him.

I used to believe Changi hated all things Japanese just to be a troublemaker. Whenever he caused a scene, he was so proud of himself. He loved the tears in his eyes as he ate his *tooboo chigae,* he loved the fire burning in his belly. It made him feel alive. Now I wasn't sure what I believed anymore. Today, like clouds and rain, doubts hovered over me.

Mother served me my lunch in the main room where Father was writing a letter. Then she knelt down and unlocked one of the drawers of the tall Korean chest that housed bundles of silk and coins and scrolls—and her transistor radio. The radio had to be kept hidden, for Japanese law forbade Koreans to read newspapers or possess radios. She turned on the radio with the volume so low I could barely hear it. That is, until a jubilant Japanese voice blared—

"Japan successfully bombs Singapore!"

In school, any Japanese victory meant the clapping of hands and shouts of *"Bonzai!"* But my parents' downcast eyes expressed no victory.

Mother had never before spoken a single word against the Japanese. But war was on the horizon, and her face was tragic.

"The Japanese will not be satisfied until all of Asia is under their control," she said.

I waited for Mother to say more, but she didn't.

"Mother, are the Japanese guilty of wrongdoing?" I asked.

Without saying yes, she confirmed my fears. "Because of

them, families lie dead as I speak. Because of them, we are no better than servants bowing to their selfish ways. Because of them, many Koreans have no means to feed their own children."

"Then why is life so good for us? Why are we the privileged Pangs?"

She looked at me and gasped. "Who calls us the privileged Pangs?"

I bit my lip, I wouldn't say.

"Heisook," Father interjected, "you are old enough to know the truth. Life is good for us because Mother inherited a good sum of money long before you were born. We invested that money well and live off its earnings today. As a minister of the church, I earn a very modest salary; not even enough to pay for luxuries like your beloved afternoon visits to the tea room. The only reason the Japanese leave us alone is because I give them money from the church."

"I don't understand, Father."

Father's sigh frightened me almost as much as the words that followed.

"I accept money from my congregation and turn some of it over to the Japanese police."

"No, that's not true, Father. Mother, tell me that it's not true!"

"I'm sorry, Heisook, but it is true," she admitted.

"That is why we are the *privileged* Pangs," Father continued. "That is why life is good for us. We quietly cooperate. But for most Koreans, life is not so good."

The small stone in my pocket grew heavy. Changi was right all along.

"But you steal money from your own congregation, Father. How could you deceive them?"

"I deceive no one, Heisook. My congregation understands

what I must do. Ministers are scarce. The work is very dangerous. Many have been tortured or murdered by the Japanese. My
congregation is willing to make sacrifices to worship our God. It
is a high price we pay, but perhaps easier to understand if we
remember this: We are Koreans. We are not Japanese."

I am not Japanese, I am not Japanese, I desperately repeated to
myself. *I am Korean!*

I wanted to be a proud Korean like Changi, eating *tooboo
chigae.* I wanted to feel a fire burning in my belly. Suddenly, I
lost my appetite for my *sushi* lunch. It wasn't so lovely after all.

FIVE

SOUTH, 1941
Sei-Young

"... could I ever swim across the world ... ?"

FOR NINE DAYS THE monsoon fell. My family had spent many hours on the *ondal* floor, forming our sacred circle, hands clasped, heads bent in prayer. We drew strength from Grandfather's words:

"Protect us from the monsoon. Keep our young ones out of harm's way."

Although rain leaked through the mud-thatched roof, we were spared the worst. It was Father's idea to build our hut here, perched high between clusters of mammoth rocks. Now these rocks served as a fortress against the monsoon, forcing its flow to either side of the hut on its way down the mountain. Still, the sounds of flood surrounded us.

On the second evening of the monsoon, Father had broken from our circle and poured himself a cup of rice wine. He sipped, going places. Where, I never knew. But wherever he went, it eventually brought him back to his art. He picked up a block of wood and began to carve with soulful deliberation. Sometimes I thought Father liked his dreamy world of wood shavings falling, of etching, better than this other world, our world. In his world, it was only he and the block of wood in his hands.

Grandfather lit a candle, lost in thought while he watched its flame smoke then burn. We were not alone, and yet it felt as if we were. His tone was low, almost a whisper. "Sei-Young?"

"Yes, Grandfather?"

"You are growing up fast. You are full of questions these days because you are questioning what you see. To answer the question I see in your eyes, your father drinks to forget that he lives a life of disappointment."

"Why can't you stop him, Grandfather?"

"His disappointment or his drinking? The truth is, I can not stop either one, Sei-Young."

"But—"

"Do not judge your father. Do not blame him for his weakness. He is a troubled but good man."

"How can he be a good man when his rice wine comes before his family?"

"That is not true, Sei-Young."

"Kwan-Young goes hungry while he takes another drink."

Grandfather seemed to draw philosophy from the candle's flame. "The monsoon can be violent, wreak havoc, yet its essence reaps rewards. In the end, your father is a good man. And in the end, the monsoon rains create a fertile earth for growing crops."

"Crops we cannot afford to buy," I argued.

The flame—like Grandfather's sigh—rose, then diminished. Something in that moment brought me sadness.

"I hope that one day you will find it in your heart to forgive your father," he said.

Grandfather slipped something into my hands. It was an English instruction book, one of his few possessions.

"Take this as my gift to your future, Sei-Young. Study it, memorize it, fly with it like the silver bird. Do not be weighed down by what troubles befall our home."

But I could not open the book that day. For a question *did* weigh me down: Was Father, as Grandfather had said, a troubled but good man? For days and nights I asked myself this question but I could not hear the answer. The monsoon was too loud. Then, on the ninth day of the monsoon, the clouds began to drift away. The rains—and my heart—began to lift.

Grandfather was right. Father was a troubled but good man. The truth was as evident as this: Father was sharpening his carving knife against a brick. Something in his manner told me what was on his mind—he was trying to decide what special token he would carve for me for my upcoming birthday. Last year he had made me a pine whistle. I remembered him saying, "My grandfather was a fisherman. He told me when the wind howled on the open sea, it made this sound." Then, with a bare wisp of breath, he blew the whistle.

For my tenth birthday, Father had given me a flute, carved from a choice bamboo reed and engraved with sparrows in flight. Mother had painted the sparrows in shades of brilliant blue and orange. I blew into the instrument, but no music came. I remembered Father saying, "Maybe someday the music will call you."

I came to forgive both Father and Grandfather. One for drinking, one for hiding the truth. One wise, one not so wise. I could never really blame Mother for anything—she already suffered so. Besides, I did not want to judge anyone anymore. How could I ever swim across the world with anger weighing me down?

Later that day I finally opened up my English instruction book. Grandfather looked very pleased. On the title page was an inscription written in English with a fine fountain pen.

"Grandfather, what does it say?"

Grandfather squinted with memory, for he could no longer translate the words. The book was a gift from an American missionary, a colleague of Grandfather's when he was a young minister.

"It says, *To my dear friend Hansoo Shin, who joins me in laughter and prayer. Matthew Cates.*" Then, with urgent focus, Grandfather turned to me. "Like my vision, my English is rapidly fading, so you must teach yourself the universal language."

The universal language. To a Korean boy forced to speak Japanese at school and hide his knowledge of *Hangu'l,* the Korean alphabet, the mere words themselves held power. *The universal language.* I clutched Grandfather's book like my very own Bible. The pages of *Speak English with Me* were torn and yellowed, but in my young eyes, every page was brand new. That night I sat next to Kwan-Young in his bedding and recited from Lesson One.

"Sir, which way to the library? Madam, which way to the museum?"

Long after Kwan-Young fell asleep, I was still reciting.

"Sir, which way to the train station? Madam, which way to the market? Sir, which way to the wharf?"

The next morning the earth was quiet. The monsoon season, more destructive than most, was at last over. We stepped outside. The sun warmed my face and my arms. In a blinding moment the sky was the ocean and I swam in its shimmering blue. Hope was renewed. That is, until I looked down and saw homeless souls seeking shelter under willow trees.

Mother cried, then shut her eyes in prayer.

"The Almighty Monsoon has spoken," Grandfather said.

The monsoon season was all part of the natural cycle in Nabi. We called it the season of death, and with good reason. Secretly fearing that lives had been lost, my family came together in our sacred circle of prayer, then broke apart.

An airplane overhead roared in my ears. Without thinking, I ran up the mountain and chased after it. I believed if I ran fast enough, I, too, could fly. I believed I could fly without wings. But the silver bird disappeared into the clouds without me.

Again, our family had been spared the worst. But we were still a poor Korean family and I remembered my vow to Kwan-Young, who was crawling about the rubble. I had to find work. Yet I knew there was little work to be found in Nabi.

After an hour on foot, I knew there was no work at all. The outdoor markets which sold straw mats and *comoshins* had been washed away. Gone, too, were the rows of peddlers in the village square selling their wares—fruits and vegetables, soybeans and jars of *kimchee*. Not even one butterfly fluttered about to soften the sight.

I wandered over to the next village, disheartened to find that it was in even worse condition than Nabi. The aftermath of the monsoon left behind the chorus of human cries. I almost gave up until I remembered Grandfather's words—*Your name is Sei-Young, which means "to swim across the world."* I then wandered to the other side of the mountain, into the valley below. By now it was well past noon.

In the midst of more monsoon devastation, I came upon Suka's farm. Suka's farm was famous in this land, tucked away on the most fertile ground this side of the Han River. Corn and tomatoes and pears seemed to grow overnight. A single sprout could bear an orchard, villagers claimed. But the monsoon had no mercy. Uprooted young pear trees told the tragic story. Among the acres of mud stood a man in a straw hat. Five aimless goats surrounded him.

The man spoke in Japanese, his voice shaken from a farm in ruins. "Boy, why do you come here?"

Humbly, I bowed my head. I knew this man to be Mr. Suka, and he knew me to be a poor Korean boy. No introductions were necessary. Obeying the law of dominance, I replied in Japanese. "I look for work."

"My farm is gone!" he shouted. "There is no work here. Go now!"

But I could not go. There was nowhere to go.

"I can help you restore your farm," I said.

Mr. Suka scoffed. "It would take an army of men to do that. Not one small, skinny boy."

"But I am a strong boy."

"You are a foolish boy. Go away!"

If only I could. If only I could walk off this Japanese farm and never look back. But Kwan-Young was hungry, my father drank. I fell to my knees. "Please. I must find work for my hungry brother."

Mr. Suka studied me on my knees, in the mud. He looked at my soiled rags better suited for a boy half my size, then said, "What a pitiful sight you are. Your thin little body would not make it to one sundown in the fields. But I will give you a chance. I have lost all of my farmhands, whom I can no longer pay." He studied me longer and squinted. "Boy, what is your name?"

My name is Sei-Young, which means "to swim across the world." How badly I wanted to say that. But I was silenced by the sword and said nothing.

"I said, boy, what is your name?"

"Shuzo Nabano," I replied.

"I can only pay you meagerly, Shuzo. You begin work today in the orchard. Pull up the fallen saplings, then saw and bundle them together."

From the muddy earth I pulled up roots, one after the other. It was a painful chore. Mr. Suka was right. I was a foolish boy, not a strong boy. Whatever possessed me to think I could help restore even one inch of this farm?

And it was a lonely chore. I felt far away from my family. I felt far away from swimming across the world. My feet were stuck here, in mud. I wondered whether my family had even noticed my absence. What were they doing at this very moment under the sun-blinding sky? Father was probably repairing our roof while Mother and Grandfather were collecting straw and bamboo to help villagers repair their huts. And Kwan-Young, what about Kwan-Young?

When the sun set over a long stretch of dead saplings on the ground, I wanted to go home. Even though I was hungry and thirsty and tired, going home was not possible. There were many more saplings to pull up. When Mr. Suka appeared with a large, flat piece of dried fish and a glass of barley tea, I thought I was seeing things. His stern face belied him.

"Eat," he said.

When the stars shone over the farm Mr. Suka reappeared. He surveyed the orchard with a slow nod.

"I have not yet sawed or bundled any of the saplings," I said, too exhausted to be ashamed.

"Come back tomorrow before sunrise," he instructed me.

On my way home, with a chain of mountains as my only witness, I fell to my knees and wept. Wept for my throbbing arms and muddied feet. Wept for what seemed like a lifetime of misery ahead of me. Wept for my fading dream. How could a Korean boy in rags ever swim across the world? When I saw my own weeping shadow in the moonlight, I mistook it for Father's broken spirit.

Then I heard something. A voice.

"Sei-Young!" Father was calling out.

"Father!" I called back.

When I broke the news to my family that I was now working on Suka's farm, Father did not say a word. This came as no surprise. But the flicker in his eyes told me he was proud.

Aunt Sunja's reaction was quite the opposite. She could not hold her tongue. But she lashed out at Mother, not me. "Kwangok! How can you let your son work the soil those Japs would not touch with their porcelain hands? He is your First Son, your honorable First Son! Does that not mean anything to you? What is happening to our heritage? I will tell you. It is being buried with the bones of our ancestors."

"Our ancestors can not help us, Sunja. My First Son can," Mother explained without apology.

"Kwangok, open your eyes. Suka is a murderer. A murderer of our people."

I knew Mr. Suka was no more a murderer than Father or Grandfather or I. But obedient Korean children did not argue with elders.

"Only you accuse this man of such a crime," Mother retorted. "No other villager speaks this way."

Aunt Sunja was having murderous thoughts, for I was certain I heard her hiss.

Each day I returned to Suka's farm. By now all the uprooted saplings had been cleared, sawed, bundled, and sold for a handsome price to Japanese families in Seoul. Finally, the rich black soil was ready for planting. The air was ripe with renewal and, with it, the fragrance of future pears. Unbeknownst to my angry aunt, Mr. Suka was often at my side, working the soil with his own calloused hands.

Although he shunned conversation, I occasionally heard him humming.

Once a traditional Korean village school called a *Sodang,* the Tanake School was back in session. But education for Korean children like us was not part of the curriculum. All traces of our colorful history were erased. Instead, we studied Japanese language and the characters of the Japanese alphabet called *Kana.* Nothing more was expected of us. We were *baka,* dumb children of Korean peasants.

Our *sensei* was an uninspiring man with a constant cough. He hovered over us every day while we practiced writing *Kana* strokes.

"A true art form," he would cough.

But my true education came from Grandfather, who explained to me that my dual identity—Shuzo Nabano at school, Sei-Young Shin at home—was a fact I must accept but separate.

"Sei-Young is who you truly are, at all times. Salute their flag with the knowledge that it is Shuzo, not Sei-Young, who honors Japan."

From Grandfather, I had learned all about Korea. I had learned about King Sejong, who founded *Hangu'l,* the Korean alphabet. And I had learned about the three ancient kingdoms —namely, Silla, Paekche, and Koguryo—which dated back to 57 B.C. As a small boy I had listened to Grandfather tell me the legendary story of T'alhae, a founding ancestor of a Silla clan, every time the moon rose. I never tired of this tale; every night I awaited Grandfather's opening line. *"T'alhae was discovered in a chest on a boat which drifted along ancient shores . . ."* Now when I thought about this tale, I would dream of being on that legendary boat, drifting to a beautiful place far away.

Autumn swept in with the smell of roasting chestnuts for sale and the upcoming harvest. With school and early nightfall, my working hours at Suka's farm were halved. Every minute of sunlight had to be squeezed into a day's work. There was still much to be done. While most of the farm would have to wait until next spring when the farmhands would return, an acre's area tilled by Mr. Suka and I was already a vision of red, ripe tomatoes.

Next year we would have a corn harvest.

"Chusok is upon your people," Mr. Suka remarked on a late afternoon dimmed by clouds.

I set down a bushel of tomatoes and looked up at Mr. Suka. My boss had never spoken a personal word to me.

Chusok was the Korean harvest holiday. Traditionally cele-brated with rice cakes, persimmons, and chestnuts, the holiday was a time to give thanks for the earth's bountiful goods and to pay respects to ancestors. Many Korean families like mine, how-ever, could not afford the delicacies and, instead, humbly blessed the holiday with a long prayer.

"Does your family celebrate?" Mr. Suka asked me.

"Only with prayer," I replied.

Mr. Suka headed toward his farmhouse, a sturdy structure with a stone foundation and a roof of rice plant straw. But inside it was empty, swept of life—no wife, no children, only a couple of straw mats on a *tatami* floor and one squat, tiny table. I often had wondered why Mr. Suka lived alone. Were his nights long? Did he bother to keep a lantern lit? But I never asked any ques-tions. That would be disrespectful.

Momentarily, he returned with a basket plump with rice cakes and persimmons and chestnuts.

"Go home to your family. Chusok is upon your people!"

With glee, Kwan-Young sucked the pulp from a persimmon. Father dreamily peeled chestnuts with his carving knife. While the family was in high celebration, I went outside. The night air moved and something about the sight of my family's shadows through the ricepaper door made me wonder why happiness was so fleeting.

I turned away from the hut and looked toward the Valley of Spirits. Images of my ancestors rose like clouds. Some of my ancestors had lived freely while others had perished under Japanese rule. I bowed and prayed for them all.

And then, from another valley below, another image moved into view. It was Mr. Suka, eating his supper by a dying light.

Contrary to everything I had heard about the Japanese, Mr. Suka was a kind man. Maybe he was a Japanese landowner on Korean soil, but he also bent down on his hands and knees and worked the land. Thanks to Mr. Suka, my family would not go to bed hungry tonight.

On this Korean holiday known as Chusok, I broke tradition and said a prayer for my lonely Japanese boss.

SIX

"Time moved slowly . . . until war became real to me."

To HONOR CHUSOK, I wore the traditional Korean dress—a *hanbok*. This was not the ordinary white cotton *hanbok* which I sometimes wore to go shopping and to the movies with my friends. This particular *hanbok,* passed down from Great-Great-Grandmother, was spun from the finest satin in shimmering colors of green and pink and gold. For me to be Korean, I had to feel Korean, and I very much wanted to feel Korean this Chusok. When I wore this *hanbok,* I was a princess from a *yangban* era. Across our main room I walked with my head held high, wearing a superior smile that would astonish even Emperor Hirohito. When I wore this *hanbok,* no Japanese would reign over me.

On the morning of Chusok, Father brought us to the burying ground to say our prayers. The burying ground was a steep mountainside of countless mounds of earth; each mound was the grave of some poor dead soul. I stood before Great-Great-

Grandmother's tombstone. She had been dead for over sixty years. Almost an eternity. Once she was a young girl draped in this very *hanbok*. Now her bones lay still in the ground.

Mother had arranged for the children of the Adol Orphanage to spend the holiday with us on Heavenly Mountain. Many church members showed up, too. Among them were my friends from school, Mihae, Ji Young, and Kyung. We made sweet Korean rice cakes studded with fruits, nuts, and beans; and we ate half of them before sharing them with the other guests. We went outside and shook the chestnut trees bare for the orphans, who squealed with such delight. It was plain to see they had miserable lives. I tried to feel sorry for the orphans, but there were so many of them. It was hard to divide my pity a hundred ways. Afterward, they gathered the chestnuts from the ground, still squealing as they tucked them safely into pouches Mother had purchased at a department store in Sinuiju.

Meanwhile Changi was leaning against a tree, watching but not engaging in any Chusok festivities. Like every year. But at least he was here; I was grateful for that. His presence made the difference between me sulking and having fun. Yes, thank goodness even Changi felt an obligation to be with the family on holidays. Korean holidays, that is. Yet it never took very long before he grew bored. I could recognize the signs—his posture was growing slumped and he seemed to be looking through us, not at us anymore. My big brother was itching to leave. Although I liked my friends enough, I saw them almost every day. So when Changi slipped away, I slipped away, too. I knew where we were going.

The waterfall's secluded beauty startled me. It was either the power of Chusok or the power of Changi. Once I hopped upon the giant quartz rock, I thought I could stay here forever, with Changi, hidden from the world. That way I wouldn't have to face all the things I was beginning to feel uncertain about. That is, everything Japanese. The Osawa School where I attended fourth grade. My *sensei* Hanako. Principal Shimmura. If I didn't have to face them I could forget about them. In our own separate ways, Changi and I embraced the waterfall.

I watched. He listened.

At the first sign of nightfall, Changi said, "Come on, now. It's time to go."

The first stars appeared in the sky by the time we made our way home.

There was Chusok on Heavenly Mountain and there was the Osawa School in Sinuiju. The very day I returned from the holiday it seemed that autumn's death drew near and the vibrance of Chusok faded like the color of leaves. And it also seemed that the minute winter blew in from Manchuria, Mother fell ill again. This time she was plagued with migraine headaches so cruel even the slightest movement pained her. Though it would do no good, I would offer to sit with her in my parents' private quarters and apply warm compresses to her temples all day.

"No, Heisook, you must go to school," she would insist, lying frighteningly still.

Sometimes I would stare at Mother and see a stranger.

"Go now," she would say.

But I could never leave without playing for Mother the only Korean song I knew on my flute, "Moogung Hwa." I would play until she finally fell asleep.

* * *

Principal Shimmura stood proudly on his podium. He was a stocky figure in a black suit and bow tie. A leaden winter sky fell upon the schoolyard where we—two thousand Korean students —assembled for the morning announcements. As he spoke, a cold gust of mountain wind ushered his voice high into the sky.

"The chosen land and its people are to be revered. Know your place in our society. Be good citizens. Study hard and remember this: Your Father and Mother are watching you."

Last year these words made sense to me. The Japanese were superior people, standing tall. Or did they only appear tall next to hunched Koreans with downcast eyes? This year nothing Principal Shimmura said rang of truth. My eyes strayed from him and settled on my surroundings. The old brick school. My classmates in their dark blue uniforms. The snow-capped mountains beyond the stone wall. Hanako, standing dutifully with all the other *senseis*.

I studied my *sensei*. She was by far the prettiest one. Her face was a perfect oval and her deep-set eyes were like sparkling black stones. But today they were fixed on Principal Shimmura; they were spellbound by his every word. If he told her to jump off a mountain and into the freezing waters of the Yalu River, surely she would obey.

"Bow to your Father and Mother," Principal Shimmura instructed his captive crowd.

Every *sensei* and every student faced east, toward the land of the rising sun, and bowed to Emperor Hirohito and his wife.

Whenever I bowed, my stomach ached. Changi would say it was the spirit of an ancient Samurai warrior driving his sword into me again and again and again. Maybe I was becoming a true Korean. To make the pain go away, I would squeeze the stone in my pocket and remember what he had said to me.

*"Heisook, even when you gaze into the clearest pond, remember
something: You see things backward . . . The Japs are not our friends.
They are our enemy."*

But now Changi was gone and all I had was a stone in my
pocket to hold on to. Like a fish in that pond, Changi darted in
and out of my life. He was never in sight long enough for me to
feel I had a big brother who would protect me from a grim
morning such as this.

Principal Shimmura continued with his oration: "On this
day—December seventh in the year nineteen hundred and
forty-one—comes word from the Motherland that we have now
entered World War Two with the American devil. Your honorable brothers successfully bombed Pearl Harbor, the American
naval base in Hawaii. Now their naval fleet lays crippled in the
Pacific waters. They gave us no choice. Perhaps if the American
devil had not interfered with our plans for a superior Asia, this
day would not mark the beginning of their end. Go to your class
with this thought in mind: Your loyal brothers traveled over the
broad seas to a foreign land to protect you! Now you must show
your gratitude. When asked, support the war effort. It is your
duty and your honor to your family."

Like silent little soldiers, we marched to class in single file. The
girls marched in one direction while the boys marched in another.

I marched with thoughts of my family. Father and Mother
and Changi. Not of the Father and Mother of Japan, not of war
brothers in the Pacific. They were not my family. If only I could
return to Heavenly Mountain. To the waterfall! Where everything in the world from a giant rock to a mythical rainbow made
wondrous sense to me.

But my marching feet led me to the same classroom I had
known for the past four years. I huddled solemnly with my

classmates around the oil-run heater at the rear of the classroom, warming my hands.

Hanako's delicate footsteps clicked down the hallway. We rushed to our assigned seats and folded our hands into neat knots on top of our desks. When Hanako entered the classroom, her face, usually alive with song, was drawn with worry.

My heart flew out to my *sensei*. A part of me wanted to run up to her side and rescue her with comforting words. *Don't worry, Hanako. Japan will win the war! Life will resume as we have both known it; as teacher and pupil and, most of all, as friends.*

I looked out the window at the crowning glory of the Osawa School. A cherry blossom tree, a gift from the Motherland. With much fanfare, on a brilliant autumn day two years earlier, we planted the tree. I remembered how the leaves whirled in the sky to a medley of flutes and violins. Now, as snow fell in bleak patches, I remembered how Hanako had whispered, *"Heisook, this tree will grow with our friendship."* With the arrival of spring and songbirds came the flowering of cherry blossoms on the tree, startling pink against the blue sky and Hanako's tender words had bloomed in my heart.

But things were different now. I could no longer give my heart to my Japanese *sensei,* no matter how hard it beat for her. The line between enemy and friend had to be drawn; otherwise I would never be a proud Korean. Otherwise, I was not fit to wear Great-Great-Grandmother's *hanbok*.

Every morning Principal Shimmura assured us that Japan was winning the war.

"Japan destroys American devil airplanes and submarine ships in the Philippines!"

"Two thousand dead American devils!"

War was not real to me. Airplanes going down. Submarines sinking. Two thousand dead. I closed my eyes and tried to picture war, but it was too terrible to picture. After all, at the Osawa School classes went on as usual. We studied Japanese language and Japanese history and Japanese art. I played lovely Japanese songs on my flute. We heard no bombs dropping on Sinuiju, we heard no gunfire. How my classmates viewed the war was a puzzle to me. Only loyal talk was permitted in the Osawa School—or anywhere—these days. My closest friends were slowly falling into the shadows.

Time moved slowly, like a never-ending gray wintry day, until war became real to me. As real as snowflakes falling. As real as icicles on the cherry blossom tree. As real as ashes in urns.

One morning so bitter cold the sky held snow, Principal Shimmura raised an urn. "These are the ashes of a local Japanese man. This brave soldier lay rotting among maggots in a field for days. He died for you, for your cause."

We were forced to pay our respects to this dead soldier at a Shinto shrine, a mile's march from the Osawa School.

And then it seemed that not a week passed without Principal Shimmura holding up an urn with yet another story of Japanese sacrifice. He spoke with punishing threat, as if to doubt him meant death. As if we were to blame for the war.

I practiced my flute every day after school even though there was no music in my heart. One day Hanako interrupted my practice session.

"Your flute-playing has become spiritless," she said, concerned.

My *sensei* was right.

"Principal Shimmura is planning an upcoming rally for the war effort," she informed me. "I would like you to play the National Anthem for the school. Please practice every night."

I placed my flute across my lap and looked down. "Please, *sensei*, I cannot."

"You must play," she insisted. Her tone reminded me that she was still my *sensei* with the last word. "It is for a good cause."

"Of course, *sensei*," I said.

"Heisook," she whispered, "what is wrong?"

I wanted to share my secrets with Hanako. But I could no longer do that. She was Japanese, the enemy. She was not my faithful friend anymore.

I bowed. "Nothing is wrong, *sensei*."

"I am your Hanako." She spoke softly in a familiar voice that nearly brought tears to my eyes. "Something is bothering you."

I backed away with a bow. "I must go now."

I ran down the steps of the Osawa School and onto the snow-laden grounds, past the cherry blossom tree, past the stone wall erected around the school. If only I could run faster and leave all this behind with my footprints. Nothing would slow me down, nothing except for a pair of strong arms suddenly wrapped around me.

"Changi!" I cried, for he had not been home for days.

He laughed. "What? Does my crybaby sister miss me?"

"Where have you been? With those Korean patriots?" Not that I knew who they were. Korean patriots. Their name alone sent chills up my spine.

"If you were so curious, you should have come looking for me."

"Where?"

"Where else? Our secret place."

"I don't believe you. It's too cold there."

"The cold does not keep me away. I walk into my white winter fantasy and dream of poking out the eyes of Japs with the most deadly icicle I can find!"

"Quiet, Changi."

"The waterfall is a magical sight this time of year. Listen! It is calling you. *Heisook, Heisook!*"

I listened for my name but heard only the stark silence of snow. "I could never find my way there all by myself."

"You know the way," Changi said, shaking his head. "Don't be afraid to take steps on your own. Don't sit still in the presence of evil."

I tried to picture myself boarding the train that I always took with Mother and Father to our country home. How daring, but . . . I would be all alone. No Father to hold my hand. No Mother to feed me sweet lemon candies from her silk pouch. No, I could not do that. I could not take the train ride by myself.

"I couldn't," I admitted.

"You can. Be independent, Heisook. Open up like a morning glory. Don't follow in the footsteps of fools. Think on your own. Explore. Change the world. Go to our secret place on your own. Let that be your first step."

How could I tell Changi that I liked the world just the way it was this very minute, next to my big brother, safe and protected? How he would love to make fun of my small dreams.

"Changi, why must you always disappear from home? I have no one to talk to. I don't know what is real and what is false anymore. Am I to trust the words of Principal Shimmura?"

Changi sighed. "You are a silly girl with silly questions."

"Don't call me a silly girl."

"You are a silly girl running in the snow. You don't even know where you are going, do you?"

We walked along the snowy streets of Sinuiju. I whispered, for the wrong words could mean trouble. "Principal Shimmura says Japan is winning the war."

"Principal Shimmura should be hung by his fat tongue! He speaks nothing but propaganda!"

"Quiet, Changi," I implored him.

"Lies, lies, lies," he muttered.

"He says the Americans are devils," I continued.

Changi broke out in uncontrollable laughter. "From the mouth of Satan himself!"

"I hear this, I hear that. Who do I believe?" I wondered aloud.

Changi gripped me, wild-eyed, terrified for my weakling soul. "You believe *me!* Not Principal Shimmura, not your ador-ing *sensei!* What, you think I don't know about her? Listen to me! If she knew you learned how to write *Hangu'l* from the Bible, she would expel you from her sight. If she heard you speak Korean instead of her beloved Japanese, she would slit your throat. To answer your silly question: Trust no Jap!"

"Shh! Keep quiet, Changi," I cried. "Otherwise, you will be arrested."

With his hands high to the sky, defying all enemies and, yes, even God, Changi confronted all of Sinuiju—

"Everyone listen to me! I do not respond to the Jap name they brand me with—Mifune Okawa!" He spat with whole-hearted disgust. "Call me that name and I'll warm your *saké* with my piss! Because I am afraid of no one. No one tells me how to think or breathe. No Jap tells me who I am."

What followed Changi's outburst was a stretch of silence so silent I could hear the snow drifting. I was grateful. I was tired of talking, tired of thinking. We passed the tea room, then the noodle house. These were my favorite spots to go to with my friends after school; we'd gossip and laugh for hours. But we had not gone for some time; there was not much to gossip and laugh about these days. If I did not have choir practice today I would step into the tea room and order a plate of sweet bean pastries, fried and sugared to perfection. If the tea room happened to be too crowded, a bowl of *kalguksoo* sprinkled with sesame seeds and scallions would do.

Changi stepped up to a toothless old peddler who was roasting his wares with long twigs.

"Two sweet potatoes, if you please."

Without looking up, the peddler said, "Drop your money in the bucket."

Changi nudged me. "Pay him."

"No, Changi," I replied.

"Heisook . . ."

"No"—I clutched my pouch—"this is Mother's donation money to the church. Father is waiting for me."

"Forget about church. Forget about God. If He is so charitable, why does He let this old peddler, practically a beggar, stand here in the cold with paper bags for shoes? Trust me, this poor Korean needs the money more than Reverend Pang's church. Don't forget what Father told you—church money becomes Jap money."

I looked at the pitiful peddler who pretended not to be listening. I played with the gold tassels of my colorful silk pouch, then slowly opened it and dropped its entire contents—two yen—into the bucket.

"Heisook!" Changi proudly exclaimed. "We must celebrate your newfound independence!"

"How?"

"The river is frozen solid. It is perfect for ice-skating. The train leaves in ten minutes."

"But Father expects me at the church any minute. And I have choir practice," I protested. "Besides, we have no skates and no train fare."

Changi patted his pocket and laughed. "Who says we don't have train fare?"

I don't remember his next words, but they must have been tempting, for in a blink's time Changi and I were gliding across that giant piece of ice—the Paengma River. Mountains surrounded us and as winter dusk fell their silhouettes resembled giant treetops. Changi's hand slipped away from mine. He raced off into the crowd.

"Changi?"

"Follow me," I heard.

"Where are you?"

"I'm right here."

My eyes darted in every direction. It was too dark, there were too many people. Perfect timing—a Buddhist temple perched high on a mountainside suddenly lit up and in that spectacular moment I saw . . . *Changi!* I steadied myself across the frozen Paengma River, guided by the fiery-looking temple until I reached him. From then on it was magic, all sky and mountains and lights. I felt like I was floating in a dream with my big brother, a dream that would never end. Who needed skates to float?

SEVEN

SOUTH, 1942
Sei-Young

"Today God silenced propaganda."

ON A SATURDAY IN early March we, the Christian villagers, flocked to the Church of Devotion. Our church was a small wooden structure, painted white. Heavenly light poured through plain windows, not stained glass. Still, our church was magnificent, along with the mountainside, now bronzed with forsythia. A hymn began.

O Father save my soul from sin,
And light the true path to heaven . . .

Today God's house would protect us from Japanese propaganda. From leaflets dropping out of airplanes that portrayed Americans as devils, slayers of women and children, spineless as snakes. And from tape recordings sounding over the mountainside, *The Almighty Japanese are winning the war for your cause! Americans are on the verge of surrender!* Our hymn grew louder.

O bless thyself with purity,
And guide me through the dark to thee . . .

Today God silenced propaganda. Because today was Grandfather's sixtieth birthday.

Following our hymn, a feast was in order. Everyone huddled hungrily around the food that was set out on a long wooden table. Although it was not as lavish as feasts in a bygone time, it was bountiful in our eyes. There were pots of beef bone soup, big bowls of sesame noodles, and tiny bowls of cold spicy vegetables. A mountain of apples and a tower of fresh figs, too. Grandfather would call these gifts from God.

One face was absent today. In fact, we had not seen Aunt Sunja since she lashed out her final words to us months ago.

"As long as Sei-Young works for Suka, you are all expelled from my heart. You commit treason to every Korean!"

"Will Aunt Sunja ever stop being angry?" I had asked Grandfather after she stormed out of our hut.

"Will she ever know a moment's peace? Bite into an apple and smile from its sweetness? Hear songbirds and hum along to earth's music? No," he said frankly. "I'm afraid these things are not possible for her, Sei-Young. Not now."

"My sister has chosen to bury her heart in the past," Mother lamented.

"We can only pity and pray for her," Grandfather said.

Even Father grunted in agreement.

I did pity Aunt Sunja, though I wished her heart wasn't buried in the past. Then she could live a happier life today. My job on Suka's farm helped provide for my family. Even if Father had no sales that day, we could still eat that night. Mr. Suka would often give me dried fish and *piji,* poor man's *tooboo,* to take home. Kwan-Young, at two, never fell asleep hungry anymore. He would spend his whole day waiting for the minute when he could see me coming up the mountain, home from work. Then he would rush toward me with a surprise in his palms.

"Hyong nim! Guess what I have for you in my hand?"

"A turtle?"

He'd giggle. "No, not a turtle."

"A bluebird's egg?"

"No, not a bluebird's egg."

"What, then? What do you have hiding in your hand?"

Kwan-Young would open his palm and proudly reveal a damp clutch of—

"Peanuts!"

And then, to the music of moon rising, the two of us would eat the peanuts, one by one.

"Speech, speech!" the congregation cried.

Grandfather stepped up to the pulpit to thank everyone, but somehow, it seemed, just being here, before a congregation he once led, caused him to step back in time. Instead of delivering a few words of thanks, a sermon sprang from his lips.

"Am I a wiser man today?" He nodded, then broke into a smile. "I pray the answer is yes, that my wrinkles count for something."

The congregation politely laughed.

"Have I learned all there is to know in a lifetime? No. But perhaps God will be so kind as to let me live as long as Moses so I will have time to learn it all."

Now the congregation broke into a hearty laughter.

Grandfather was a wise man, for he knew that laughter was healthy for mind, body, and soul when all three were worn to the bone. Laughter was a gift, like one's sixtieth birthday. Still, the serious business of making sense of our tragic lives was upon him. He closed his eyes and the mood of the church changed. From the Book of Job he recited.

"... For wrath kills the foolish man, and envy slays the silly one ... For affliction does not come forth from the dust, neither does trouble spring up out of the ground; but man is born to trouble, as the sparks fly forward ..."

To a rapt audience, Grandfather opened his eyes and redelivered the passage in his own words.

"Our lives are difficult ones. At times not even the perfume after a spring rain can move our hearts, and that seems a sin upon us. But we are Christians. And we must look upon Job, whose faith God tested throughout his life, as an example of how we must keep our faith in a society that condemns us. They take away our birth names and give us Japanese names. But our faith is ours to keep lit. No one can extinguish it, not even the Japanese. Have faith that God's light will lead us through this dark period. And when it is over ..."

A heavy-hearted sigh rippled through the church—Father's. I knew it was Father's, because I had heard it all my life. I wondered whether Grandfather's words woke up a dream he once had as a young boy, a dream so long ago put to sleep. Ever since I began to earn money, Grandfather began to share stories with me; as though I was now grown up enough to hear them. Like this: Once Father had a dream to follow in Grandfather's footsteps, to become a minister someday. But Father could never stand tall in the pulpit and inspire with great eloquence. Even Grandfather admitted this.

"Whatever spoke in his heart never made its way to his lips."

"Like rice wine?" I had asked.

"Yes, I am afraid so, Sei-Young. Somewhere along life's path, your father stumbled, lost his way, and found himself reaching for the bottle instead of the Bible. It was not a proud path to follow, Sei-Young, but it was the path your Father chose."

But I thought, too, that it was on this path that Father met Mother, whose loyal presence could quell his nerves when rice wine wouldn't do. Today he reached for her hand.

And while it was true that spoken words may have failed Father, I remembered how there were times when he would carve into wood what spoke in his heart. For my twelfth birthday, he had presented me with a teakwood plaque. On its surface he had painstakingly etched in a poem.

FIRST SON

From the earth I came,
Into the earth I will go.
But not until I watch
My First Son's spirit grow.

He is as sturdy as a tree,
He is as bright as the sun.
He is as rich as monsoon soil,
He is Sei-Young, my First Son.

Now Grandfather concluded his sermon.

". . . In our darkest moments, let us hold hands and keep the candle of our faith burning."

The celebration was over.

.h a final hymn, the congregation filed out of the church.

Look up to the sky,
Receive our Lord,
Through clouds or sunshine,
Faith is restored.
Look upon the seas,
Receive our Lord,
In silent stillness,
Our faith has roared.

The next morning, a morning so early the sky was still moonlit, I woke myself up from a dream of joyful celebration, of food and song. Once in a while, like now, I ached for this, and longed for more days like Grandfather's sixtieth birthday. But I had to go to work. There were goats to milk.

Last winter—the winter World War II broke out—Suka's farm lay in hibernation. That meant my work in the fields was done. But Mr. Suka, in an act of generosity, handed his twelve goats over to me.

"Milk them, then make deliveries. I would do it myself, Shuzo, were it not for my bad knees."

Of course, Mr. Suka did not have bad knees at all. Just a good heart.

Every morning at four o'clock, I milked the goats. Afterward, on a rusty old bicycle, I made my round of milk deliveries to wealthy Japanese families in surrounding towns.

My last stop before school was at the Imperial Police Station where Officer Akoto was in charge. The man with the pencil-thin mustache watched over his jurisdiction with an intimidating eye, as though to meet his was a threat. This intimidation earned him many fringe benefits, including free milk. Because I was on time every morning, Officer Akoto treated me decently with the same salute.

"Prompt again, Shuzo!"

After school, I would return to Suka's farm to feed the goats straw. I would walk them up and down hills and watch the sun set in their sleepy eyes.

That was my routine last winter.

Now, with spring's return, my duties remained with the goats. The farmhands were back, planting corn for a late summer harvest. There were ten farmhands in all, their names unknown to me. Though we were all Koreans working on the same farm, mountains stood between us. I sensed their scowls and their spit. Maybe my youth was an unwanted reminder of their bitter years behind them.

As dawn's first light broke through the sky, I set out on my rounds to the Japanese homes, set apart from Korean homes by their grand size and tile roofs. I delivered a bottle of milk to the Shibanos and the Yamagatas. Next were the Yamauchis and the Sakais and the Ikedas. The Ikedas had a large family and required two bottles of milk every morning.

My last stop came at the stroke of seven. I arrived at the Imperial Police Station with a bottle of milk for Officer Akoto, expecting his salute.

But the police station was in an uproar. Officer Akoto was watching his Imperial Policemen surround a prisoner who was hanging from the ceiling by his feet. The prisoner's ankles were tied with his own ragged shirt. They clubbed him repeatedly, relishing their anger. My shock turned to horror when I caught sight of the poor prisoner.

Grandfather.

In a nearby corner, another crushing sight: Father crouched in fear.

"All ministers are spies for the Americans," Officer Akoto accused Grandfather in a strangely composed fashion. "Tell me what you know."

"I am no spy," Grandfather stated.

Officer Akoto replied coolly, "I will ask you one more time. Tell me what you know."

"I am only a messenger of God."

"Lies!" Officer Akoto shouted. "You have denounced The Motherland! What were your exact words? Ah, yes. *Our faith is ours to keep lit. No one can extinguish it, not even the Japanese.*"

Grandfather bravely coughed, "Who then is the spy?"

Incensed, Officer Akoto whipped Grandfather's bare back with his own belt, shouting, "Son of a street whore! Let me swat you like a filthy fly! How dare you call *me* a spy! My jurisdiction is my business! That includes what goes on behind the doors of the Church of Devotion!"

Grandfather moaned. Father whimpered like a baby while I mutely cried out. We were father and son, both silenced by the sword.

After delivering a heartless finale of lashings, Officer Akoto cut Grandfather down with a knife whose bejeweled jade handle was surely worth more than any Korean life. Grandfather lay on the floor like a pile of rags, his spirit flown. But where did it go?

Kicking Grandfather in the ribs, Officer Akoto began shouting again. "From now on you bow to Shinto! Not God! Speak his name and I'll feed your Korean tongue to the vultures! Now go home, old man. Get out of my sight! Thank me, not God, that you are still alive."

A Korean boy like me could not stand up to the monster in the perfectly pressed gold-buttoned blue uniform. The consequences would be unthinkable. But there was revenge, even for a Korean boy. Unseen by Officer Akoto that morning, I left the police station with his bottle of milk, climbed back onto the bicycle and peddled away knowing this: I would never go back there. No milk he drank would ever be delivered by my hands.

As I peddled away, hot tears streamed down my face. Hot, guilty tears—I had deserted Grandfather. But what else could I do? My stepping in would only cause more trouble. Besides, Grandfather, my hero and wise elder, would be humiliated if he knew I had seen what happened today. Our walks, though rare these days, would lack wonder and philosophy. They would be clouded by the memory of this day. A leaf falling from the sky would just be a leaf falling from the sky.

Instead of peddling to school, I peddled to the Valley of Spirits. Here I searched for Grandfather's spirit. If it could, it would fly here to meet me. If it could not, I could imagine that his spirit was here anyway.

"Should I go home, Grandfather? Should I be with you?"

You are always with me, Sei-Young. Go to school now.

So I left the Valley of Spirits and headed for school. But when my *sensei* called out "Shuzo Nabano!" I stonily replied, *"Hite."* Because Sei-Young was who I truly was, at all times. I would salute their flag with the knowledge that it was Shuzo, not Sei-Young, who honored Japan.

After school I went to Suka's farm. I greeted the goats with a glum sigh. When Mr. Suka spotted me, all the plows and hoes and shovels in the fields went still. The farmhands scorned me with vulgar smiles. Mr. Suka approached me with a very concerned face.

"Why did you not deliver milk to the Imperial Police Station?"

Pretending not to hear him, I hummed to the goats.

"Officer Akoto paid me a visit today. He was most upset. I did not know what to tell him, Shuzo. Surely you did not forget."

He waited patiently for an answer. "Shuzo?"

I was not Shuzo and I resented my Japanese boss calling me that. I replied, "Officer Akoto is an evil man. He doesn't deserve any milk. He tortured my grandfather. He had him hung from his feet and beat him and kicked him and whipped him. He called him a spy for the Americans. But my grandfather is no spy. He is just my grandfather."

Mr. Suka was stunned. Sorrow clogged his throat. Then: "Take the bicycle. Hurry home. Go! Be with your grandfather."

Furiously, I peddled home.

I never returned to the Imperial Police Station. After that day, Mr. Suka personally delivered Officer Akoto's milk to him, as the officer refused to drink from a bottle "touched by a dirty Korean farmhand."

At home Mother was caring for Grandfather, who lay lifeless on his bedding. Father kept to himself, brooding. Kwan-Young tried to crawl on top of Grandfather, but Mother nudged him away.

"I know what happened today," I told her.

"He suffered only cuts and bruises," Mother said, applying ointment to his wounds. But her eyes were uncomfortable with that statement.

Grandfather suffered more than cuts and bruises; and the wounds to his spirit were so deep, it may have fled forever. The man who painted characters on chosen rocks and whose wise face could brighten the glow of any candle was not here, in this body. As my eyes rose above him, looking for a sign, a good omen, I saw a wooden Shinto shrine sculpture—one of Father's works—on the wall instead. As the personification of a Japanese god, it hung with menacing threat.

"Mother, why is that hanging in our home?"

Father drank from his tin cup and howled—

"The damn Japs nearly killed your grandfather! May their mothers and wives and daughters rot in hell!"

"The Imperial Police have closed our church and ordered all the villagers to openly worship Shinto," Mother mournfully explained. "Otherwise, they will burn down our huts."

I picked up Kwan-Young, who seemed puzzled by the day's events. We huddled by Grandfather's side.

"Grandfather, please wake up. Please open your eyes and talk to us," I begged him.

No movement.

"Please, Grandfather!"

Father threw his tin cup across the hut with blind rage. It knocked the Shinto shrine sculpture off the wall. A look of drunken victory crossed his face. He ambled over to join us, his two children. He took Grandfather's frail hand and felt for a pulse.

"I know I am a failure," Father gasped, "a faithless son who has amounted to nothing more than my empty tin cup. But I beg you, Father, wake up. Wake up for me."

No movement. Then, a miracle.

Grandfather's eyes slowly opened. His spirit had flown back into his body. He squeezed Father's hand. Father was moved to tears, hot, streaky tears. The kind of tears shed from too much happiness and too much humiliation and too much rice wine.

EIGHT

"I am not a child anymore . . ."

I STILL ATTENDED THE Osawa School, but I was no longer a student in any true sense. I no longer sat at my assigned desk and listened to Hanako delicately lecture on the history of the Kyujo Palace secluded behind high stone walls in Tokyo, or on the grace of ancient Japanese poetry. I no longer practiced my flute. Instead, along with my classmates, I spent my days darning socks and stitching gloves. We were performing the necessary duties called upon us.

"For the war effort," Hanako would explain, mimicking Principal Shimmura.

The days were long and monotonous. They blurred into each other like dark clouds that would never go away. Each stitch I sewed tightened the knot in my stomach.

One morning the high and mighty Principal Shimmura gallantly declared—

"Nineteen-hundred and forty-three is upon us. A new year! Koreans have much to be thankful for."

Lies, lies, lies, as Changi would say. For it was a year when our own resources of rice, coal, wood, and oil were being rationed.

"For the war effort," Hanako continued to remind us the following hour while we sat at our desks, sewing instead of studying.

If only I could be gliding across a magical sheet of ice. Or following Changi to a winter wonderland. The frozen Paengma River and the waterfall both promised things that were not to be. Because here I was at the Osawa School. The most horrible place in the whole world. Without oil to run the heaters, the classrooms were unbearably cold.

I sewed a button onto the jacket of an Imperial uniform. I watched my own breath smoke, then vanish. I wanted to be able to disappear so easily, just like that. But no, I was here, just like yesterday and just like I would be tomorrow. Cold, numb from head to toe. Not even the thick wool mittens Mother had knitted for me could protect my nearly frozen fingers while I labored *"for the war effort."*

When the bell rang at the end of the day, I ran out of the Osawa School without a single good-bye. My *sensei* knew better than to stand in my way or question my change of heart. She knew that should she whisper secrets in my ear, I would sit stone-faced, not listening. Not that she would whisper secrets in my ear anymore. She was too busy mimicking Principal Shimmura all day long. Her eyes lacked light and laughter, like the halls of the Osawa School.

The clock struck five when I got home. Winter darkness fell upon the house and seeped into every corner. My fingers groped for the lamp, and soon brightness filled our home. But not warmth.

In recent weeks Father began to stow away many of the beautiful possessions that had brought life to our main room. Now there was only minimal décor. Gone was my glass-encased doll in her holiday *hanbok*. Gone was the tall red vase with the intricate inlaid mother-of-pearl design. Gone were numerous hand-painted scrolls. So many things my eyes were used to seeing and settling familiarly upon. Father had stowed them in the cellar of our country home on Heavenly Mountain because the war rations made the Japanese nervous. Raids to seize Korean assets were not so unusual.

The cold feeling in the house made me wonder where everyone was. Most likely Father was still at church. Changi had not been around since yesterday morning. But where was Mother? Most days she welcomed me at the door with a cup of ginseng tea. After inspecting my hands, she would rub them with cream or ointment, depending on their condition. If they were just cracked, cream would do. If they were bleeding, too, ointment was in order. But today my hands—unlike my classmates' hands—would not be tended to by my mother. Surely she was at the Adol Orphanage, her second home these days.

A miserable shiver went through me, one that could only be shaken off with some tea or, better yet, a hug from Father. Mother did not give hugs, that was no secret. Her meals and hand-sewn clothing and murmuring prayers demonstrated her duty to her family. Still, were there secrets? Whenever Mother was sick, she lay under her blankets, cloaked in secrecy.

I tiptoed into my parents' private quarters; tiptoed because it was not a child's place to enter their domain alone. But I needed the cream; maybe, secretly, I needed something more. My hands and eyes explored with a mind of their own.

Mother's closet creaked open. So did the top drawer of her giant teakwood chest. Her familiar scent rose from a stack of sweaters and I held one up to my face. The collar of this brown sweater was adorned with rings of faux pearls. It was one of my favorites, though Mother rarely wore it. When I folded the sweater and put it back in its place, a small striped silk pouch fell out from the stack. I loosened the drawstring and found a single brass key. I took it out, knowing its power. My hands and eyes explored further, as if I was searching for some mysterious part of Mother I didn't know, the part that made her fall ill every winter, the part that would hug a group of orphans, but not her own children.

My eyes settled on the bottom drawer, a slim drawer locked with a brass latch in the shape of a fish. My fingers trembled. I unlocked the drawer; the brass fish hit the floor and startled me. I turned around. Thank goodness, I was still alone.

Inside the drawer were tiny treasures. Nothing the Japanese would confiscate, but treasures to Mother. Although she never shared her stories, I knew there was one behind each of these items—a blue-and-lavender pouch, a cracked hairpin, a hand-kerchief embroidered with peacocks. What caught my eye was an object I had never before seen: a clothbound book. I stared at its purple velvet binding for a long, long time. Then I knew: this was Mother's diary. At first, sadness draped over me like a winter shadow. That she had kept a diary at all said so many things. Especially this: there *were* secrets. My hands ran over its surface, its spine. I couldn't open it, could I?

Changi would say, *Of course you can, silly girl!*

But I couldn't. There were some secrets that could be held

like tiny treasures in one's hands. There were other secrets that were hidden, not meant to be in my hands—like the words in Mother's diary. To read them would be a sin.

I turned my eyes away and quickly opened another drawer, this one not locked. The scent of powder and perfume made me feel dreamy, like when I watched those love scenes at the cinema. I peeked inside to a drawer full of ladies' items: a bottle of perfume, a round box of powder, a tube of lipstick. How strange—were these Mother's? Except for rubbing special cream on her face, Mother never indulged in such fancies. Or did she once wear another face? Momentarily I found myself tiptoeing again—this time to make sure no one was home. Good, no one was home. First I dared myself to do it, and then I did it. I dabbed a powder puff into the loose powder, marveling as a fragrant white cloud *poofed* in my eyes. Then I dusted my whole face. The powder was too pale for my complexion, but I loved its silkiness on my skin and luxuriated in the feeling. The fragrance promised me that one day I would become a woman.

But then—my eyes shifted back to Mother's diary. Despite the voice of protest, my hands crept with exploration. They opened the drawer, pulled out the velvet-bound book, and opened it. I listened for stirring in the house. Good, no stirring. Then my eyes took over, pouring over every word, every page, searching for secrets.

And then her secrets were no longer secrets.

December 18, 1924

Today I buried my son. His life was meant to be a celebration. Yobo tried to console me with tender words. "Someday your heart will heal. Someday you will be reunited with your son." But my heart will never heal. Never. Changsil is in his tiny grave. I don't know how any mother could live through this. My son is an orphan in heaven without a mother to take care of him. Sometimes I weep until no more tears come, until I am all dried up like an old lonely woman. Cold, cold, I feel so cold. Only God can help me now . . .

At first I couldn't move or blink or breathe. A few words told me all there was to understand about Mother. Her illnesses now made sense to me. Terrible sense. Some winters only a nagging cough and a mild migraine bothered her. Other seasons she was much sicker. Like last winter when her migraine was so severe and her body so weak with fever she could barely hold her cup of ginseng tea. We held our breaths. Once again, the only cure for Mother was the mountain water she believed was touched by God.

Page after page, the same grief was described. But one entry was particularly chilling.

February 21, 1926

God, forgive me. For when I look into Changi's eyes, I can not help but search for his brother as though he might blink or wink and Changsil's eyes might be looking back at me. When he coos I listen for another voice, a voice that might travel through time, defeat death. This is wrong and unfair of me— but all the same I can not abandon my First Son. Yobo says we can not overshadow our Changi with his brother's death, for otherwise a dark cloud will always follow him. So I have vowed never to tell him.

The minute I closed Mother's diary, tears streaked my powdered face. Mother had secrets, and her secrets hurt Changi, her surviving son. So much made sense now. After all, hushed pain can be heard and my older brother anguished in it. How could Mother not see that a silent look or a stolen glance can carry a cloud over a mountain and make rain? Something in Mother's heart for Changi was missing. Changi was not born with a restless nature—she was the cause of it. His spirit was just searching for something lost long ago. Mother's love.

I closed the drawers, then closed the ricepaper door to my parents' private quarters behind me. Not until the middle of the night when I awoke to a crushing pain did I realize that I had forgotten to put cream on my hands.

The next day was the Eve of the New Year. Mother was waiting for me on the steps of the Osawa School. She had returned home long after I had fallen asleep the night before. Her eyes misted with guilt.

"I know life is not so easy for you, Heisook. But there are many suffering children without either a mother or father to comfort them. Come with me."

I walked with Mother through the gray streets of Sinuiju, then down the stone path from the Sacred Heart Church to the Adol Orphanage. Actually, I was following her. Mother always moved swiftly, as though something in her past might catch up with her, so swiftly her feet barely touched the stones. When she closed the door of the Adol Orphanage behind us, she sighed. It was a beautiful but broken sigh, one I had never before heard.

In moments a child lay limp in her arms, unwilling to feel her love. Mother admired his beauty, his eyes shut tight against the puffy paleness of his cheeks. How old was he? Two? Three?

Who knew? His history, like that of all the children here, was unknown.

"The orphanage is struggling to stay open, Heisook. Money is short; volunteers, too. I do not understand why more people do not volunteer their time and hearts to these poor little souls. It is such purposeful work."

Mother had volunteered her time and heart to orphans for as long as I could remember. But was she really giving them her love or was she just giving them the love she could not give to her First Son?

"Do not close your eyes. I am here to help you, to love you," Mother said, cuddling the boy in a way she had never cuddled Changi or me. She continued to nurture the boy in this fashion until finally he opened his eyes. He looked at her longingly. His eyes were so black she seemed pleasantly startled. She lavished in the moment, in his sweet smile that followed.

"Your suffering is not in vain." She kissed his forehead, "God's plan includes you."

Then Mother's eyes closed in prayer. Surely she was praying for Changsil, her dead son. But why couldn't she pray for Changi, her living son?

"Remember that poor child when I am not at home with you, Heisook," Mother later said. "Or when you are in school, sewing on a button you wish you could toss out the window. Perhaps your day will not seem so terrible."

I did pity that orphan for all that he needed, and for how little he would get. Mother's attention was divided among dozens and dozens of orphans; she could not give all of herself to a single one. Still, nothing could ever change the way I felt about the Osawa School. Not even if I had ten parents.

* * *

Over a traditional New Year's Day supper of noodle soup, I said, "Father, why must I go back to school?"

As I awaited Father's reply, I watched my noodles swim in an aromatic broth of ginger and garlic. The noodles were long, because eating long noodles promised a long life. Last New Year's Day, I had lowered each noodle into my gaping mouth with my chopsticks, eating heartily. Changi was there, good-naturedly balking at tradition. "Look at Heisook! She wants to live to be a hundred years old."

This New Year's Day I wondered whether a long life would be a gift or a curse.

A variety of small dishes accompanied the noodle soup. There was sesame-seasoned watercress, sliced boiled eggs, salted fish cakes, and *kimchi*. Nowadays such delicacies rarely graced our table. With the war rations, everyone suffered, even the Japanese— not that I cared about them. Both Korean and Japanese families were now assigned rice coupons. Each coupon was traded in daily at a Japanese-run facility for a scoop of dry rice. Mother would cook the rice and bring it to the orphanage, for Father had a secret rice supply stashed away in our country home. He had been wise enough to stock many sacks of rice two years earlier when the war broke out. Now he would travel back and forth, smuggling pouches of rice sewn inside his clothing past Imperial Police who guarded Sinuiju. If caught, Father would be punished severely. He might be thrown into jail, or have his hands cut off. But to feed us was worth the risk.

Now Father replied with a hint of impatience. "We have been through this time and time again, Heisook. I have no authority in this matter. You must go to school and honor the war effort."

I threw down my spoon and retaliated—

"First you tell me the Japanese are not my friends. Now

you say I must work for the war effort. The war effort is being drummed into my ears. I am so tired of hearing those words!"

Mother dropped a small spoonful of *kimchi* into my untouched bowl. "Not too spicy, just the way you like it. Eat, Heisook. Such good food should not go to waste. Please."

"I would give up food forever if I did not have to go back to school. I hate it there!" I sobbed.

"Heisook, please," Mother implored me.

Only an abrupt knock at the gate that surrounded our home silenced me. Ilgo? The knock came again, only this time it was louder and more authoritative.

Mother and I stood at the door as Father went to answer the knock. A bat's shadow flew across the gate and I knew something was wrong. Very wrong. Father hesitated, as though he sensed it, too. I was about to shout, "Father, don't open it!" when a third, most threatening knock came.

Father unlocked the gate; it creaked open. Standing before him was an Imperial recruitment officer. The buttons on his jacket were like a thousand buttons I had sewn on. The officer's expression was stern but his eyes were blank. My stomach hurt. Before he even finished his sentence, I was trembling.

"Mifune Okawa is to report immediately for duty," the officer stated.

"I do not know where my son is," Father truthfully replied.

Even the officer's voice was vacant. "For your son's safety, I would advise you to find him at once."

Then he turned on his heels and vanished.

Father sat before his meal, hunger gone. The noodles had grown thick and pasty and the broth was now cold. Despite this, he ate with the hope that I would not detect the worry on his face. Impossible. He knew he had to explain.

"Your brother is eighteen years old now." His voice cracked, "He is a man. And the Imperial Army is recruiting all young men between the ages of eighteen and twenty-six to fight in the war."

"To die in the war," Mother groaned.

I was unable to speak. To fight in the war, to die in the war. To fight in the war, to die in the war. There was the war, there was the waterfall. The war, the waterfall. Surely they could never be spoken in the same breath.

"You must do something!" I wailed.

"There is nothing I can do," Father said.

"The church, Father. The church can help!"

"The church cannot help your brother. But perhaps our prayers can."

"No! Not prayers. You and Mother spend your whole lives praying, and what good do your prayers do when God won't protect Changi from the Imperial Army?"

Father took my words with a heavy-hearted sigh. "Then how can the church help, Heisook?"

"The church has money."

"Money cannot stop war."

"You can pay the Imperial Army to go away," I argued. "Just like you pay the Japanese Police to let us live in peace."

"No, Heisook. That is not the answer."

Changi's words came back to haunt me.

"*. . . do you think he cares about you or me or Mother or the beggar he passes on his way to church? Our welfare comes second to his godless God . . .*"

Right then Father was no better than the enemy. He was no better than Principal Shimmura standing over me during his morning announcement. No better than Hanako who carefully inspected every pocket I stitched and every button I sewed. No better than the whole Japanese race that had condemned me to a life of slavery.

"Then I hate you, Father!"

"Heisook!" Mother harshly reacted.

I dismissed her with a hateful glare. How could a mother who spent more time at an orphanage than with her own children ever understand? Did she even love Changi? Did she ever pray for him like she prayed for her First Son?

"I do! I hate you. I hate both of you for not protecting Changi."

"I beg you not to speak this way," Father said in a resigned voice.

But Mother's tongue was much sharper. "You are just a child. You know nothing of real life."

I was only twelve but I knew much of real life. My raw, blistered hands were proof of that. Not their throbbing pain, but what they symbolized. The war. An unloving mother, too busy to care for me. Her sorry voice and her tears belonged to her beloved orphans. Her prayers and her hopes, too. So here I was, left without a mother, with nothing but a pair of ruined hands.

"I am not a child anymore, Mother," I said stonily. "The war has taken that from me. I know what is real more than you do because I know your God is not real. He would not let all these bad things happen to our country. To our family. To Changi!"

To our surprise the ricepaper door slid open, followed by Changi's chuckling voice—

"Who's calling out my name with such fire? Why, it's Heisook! Did Mother add too much *kimchi* to your soup?"

"Changi!" I cried—an excited child again.

Mother swiftly closed the door behind Changi and seated him at the table.

"So why am I the topic of conversation on New Year's Day, eh, Heisook?"

I was too heartbroken to say.

Mother balanced a big bowl of soup to the table and set it down in front of Changi. Steam danced above his favorite bowl, one painted with silver dragons and brilliant flames flecked with gold. Next she brought him ginseng tea in a matching cup. Her face was grim.

Father finally spoke. "There is news, Changi. Bad news."

"I'm hungry for good news, not bad news, Father." Changi half-laughed, hunching over his soup and digging up noodles. "Heisook, don't just sit there. It is New Year's Day! Sing to me one of your silly songs, you know, the one about the bird at the windowsill that—"

"An Imperial recruitment officer was here moments ago," Father interrupted him.

Changi swallowed, then sat up. His face was ashen. The chopsticks in his fingers began to quiver, then shake. I looked away, not wanting to shame my big brother for whom bravery was above all. But even Changi knew that recruitment into the Imperial Army was a death sentence if you were Korean.

"I am not afraid," he finally said.

Mother stunned me as she hugged Changi from behind. The very act, her very touch, stunned him as well.

Then Mother began to rock Changi back and forth, arms so tight surely they would never unlock. "I have always loved my Changi. He is such a good boy. So outspoken and independent. Oh, my Changi."

Father folded his hand over mine and began to quietly pray.

Now Mother, Eunook Yee—missionary in China, mourner of her dead son Changsil, and most importantly tonight, mother of Changi—broke down with feverish moans, moans unheard of in our household. It was a sound welling up from so deep within her it was primitive but, strangely enough, familiar. It was the sound of all her years of hushed pain cast in her eyes and her shadow as she rose from her bedding every morning. It was the sound of all her winter illnesses and the words in her diary coming together in one dreadful blow. It was the sound of profound love that, not having surfaced, hurt to hear.

"Changi, Changi, Changi," she moaned, cradling him.

Changi choked back tears until he could no longer hold them back.

"Mother," he began to weep.

I did not pray with Father. God could not answer my question. Mother's moans addressed all that I needed to know. Of course Mother loved Changi. Of course she did.

NINE

SOUTH, 1944
Sei-Young

"Let us never speak of this night . . ."

I SET OUT ON my Sunday morning walk missing Grandfather's company. To watch him kneel and paint *Hangu'l* characters on a God-glinting rock was a safe pause from the outside world that I sorely missed. Now, instead of hearing his words or his wise silence, I heard only the crunching of leaves beneath my feet.

Grandfather never completely healed from his cruel beating and could no longer enjoy even a simple walk on the mountainside. The Japanese managed to leave scars on just about every Korean. Although Grandfather's body was crooked with pain, and his eyes were failing, in prayer he climbed another mountainside, one that ascended with magnificence. And how he prayed. And this gave him true strength.

"I will not subordinate myself to the Japanese," he would now declare. "I will not surrender my soul. I will die at their hands before I will bow at their feet. Death is part of life and I will go as I came. Proudly."

At four, Kwan-Young was still too young to join me for this walk. But I would have really enjoyed my brother by my side. Big shadow, little shadow. Kwan-Young would ask so many questions, and hopefully I would have a few answers. Maybe next year . . .

It had even crossed my mind to ask Father to join me. But I knew better. The same day Grandfather rose from unconsciousness, Father threw away his tin cup. Now he sang and hummed steadily and was more conversational with the family. Still, his answer would be no. Whether in art or in sleep, Father would always be a private man. Out of the blue, he had broken the news to us that he was volunteering for the war effort.

"I am told I will be working in a factory or a coal mine. Wages are guaranteed. I do this to help the family. I will be leaving soon."

My days were divided between working on Suka's farm and on a farm by the sea planting rice with my classmates. Two activities on two farms—one for my family, one for the war effort. And even though a quiet walk among leaves was a rare thing, the pleasure of the day escaped me. Without Grandfather I was lost, without path. Where did earth and philosophy meet? On the loftiest cloud? On a fallen leaf?

Or was it in Grandfather's words?

"Your name is Sei-Young, which means 'to swim across the world.'"

The vague notion of a better life over mountains and oceans always succeeded in brightening a lonely moment such as this. Wasn't that Grandfather's role? But I missed him. I needed his message and his gift and his companionship.

Most of Grandfather's waking hours were now spent inside

the Church of Devotion, serving once again as God's messenger. That our church reopened was a testament to God's mysterious ways and the faith of His worshippers to protect them within His walls. After all, Officer Akoto had conducted ruthless inspections of Nabi homes, always in search of signs of Christian worship. Rapes and random beatings plagued our village worse than disease. One night, it was our turn.

Father was still in Seoul. Knowing he would be leaving the family soon, every minute longer on the streets meant more hope for earning more money. Noise outside our hut warned us of trouble. The noise grew closer, then closer, then—

Officer Akoto, flanked by four Imperial Policemen, crashed through our door.

"Korean pigs! Don't move or you'll be slaughtered like the filthy animals you are!"

Terror flooded our faces. Grandfather stirred—he knew who this was. Kwan-Young ran into Mother's arms, but she delivered him to Grandfather.

"Oma," Kwan-Young cried, for he wanted her arms, not Grandfather's.

"Stay still," she sternly hushed him. Not even a child's life was sacred right now.

It tortured Grandfather to do nothing, to sit helplessly in the wake of danger. Mother sensed this. "Stay still," she repeated.

The police began to search our hut but turned up nothing, for our only sign of worship—Grandfather's Bible—was buried outside, beneath our magnolia tree. Frustrated, they knocked over blocks of wood and cans of paint. Grandfather held Kwan-Young tight, praying. This outraged Officer Akoto and seemed to provoke a memory.

"You!" he sneered.

But Grandfather had entered the land of prayer.

"Open your eyes when I am talking to you, old man."

Grandfather refused.

"Stop it. Stop it, I say! How dare you not heed me. Who do you think you are, you ragged Christian corpse?"

But Grandfather did not move. He was like one of those rocks on the mountainside. Officer Akoto's fury turned to Mother.

"Stay away from her," I said.

"Go sit with Grandfather," Mother spoke unflinchingly.

"Listen to your mother, boy. Go pray with your Grandfather." Officer Akoto cruelly laughed, revealing a mouthful of gold teeth. He had no memory of me, that was obvious.

"No!" I said.

Mother silenced me with her eyes. I obeyed, but reluctantly.

Officer Akoto laughed again, then shoved Mother against the wall and began to slap her face with perverse pleasure. Monster!

"Oma, oma, oma!" Kwan-Young screamed.

Grandfather pulled Kwan-Young's face to his chest to shield the coming horror.

"You cheap slut, you lowly Korean whore," Officer Akoto was muttering—along with other shameless names—into Mother's neck as his face grew scarlet red. Then he ripped her shirt open and savagely grabbed her breasts. Mother did not scream or fight back. She stood as still as stone, strangely untouched. He looked up at her, incensed. When his eyes met hers, they met a cold, deadly stare that seemed to say, *You cannot touch me, you small Japanese man.* Slowly, his hands wilted off her breasts. After a foolish pause, he cursed himself and spat with self-disgust. A Korean woman had intimidated him.

He gave the Imperial Policemen his nod and they marched out with Officer Akoto muttering, "Dirty Korean pigs . . ."

Afterward, I expected Mother to break down and cry. But she didn't. Instead, she set about straightening up the hut.

"Mother, are you all right?"

I watched her take Kwan-Young back into her arms.

"Mother?"

She allowed herself only a moment of pity as she bowed her head and bit her quivering lip. Then she lifted her chin and her eyes to mine.

"Let us never speak of this night, Sei-Young."

Father soon returned home, whistling. An empty cart was enough to know that he felt blessed by the day. No one spoke to him of this night.

My Sunday walk led me to Suka's farm. Three years had passed since I first came upon this monsoon-ruined land and begged Mr. Suka for work. Now the farm boasted corn and tomatoes. The pear orchard was coming along nicely. There was even a chance it might bear fruit next spring. Like the land, I had changed. I was fourteen, old enough not to question certain realities, like one in particular: Most of the farm's crops were now turned over to the Japanese. The war effort, it seemed, held its sword over everyone.

The sun shone over the field of farmhands. Men so poor they toiled seven days a week, even on a beautiful Sunday like today. Whenever they caught sight of me, hatred set in their eyes. Whenever they drank—which was often—they became unruly. Mr. Suka had explained it to me this way: "All their anger goes to their fists when they drink. They are hard workers with hard lives. They have no dreams."

"Shuzo!" Mr. Suka was now calling to me.

Shuzo. An empty word. An ugly sound. *Shuzo.* It was a name without meaning, and always would be.

"Shuzo!" Mr. Suka kept calling.

I headed toward the farmhouse where Mr. Suka was waving impatiently. I hurried up. Over time, the two of us had been growing closer. To find us sitting on the edge of the moonlit fields after a day of labor was not an unusual sight. Sometimes we would sit in silence, shrouded by darkness and our own hesitance. Other times our willingness to know each other would open up like a starlit universe.

On one such evening I had asked my boss why his home was empty of wife and children. Was he lonely?

"My wife died of consumption," Mr. Suka had mourned. "Yes, Shuzo, I am lonely for the life that could have been."

On another such evening Mr. Suka had asked me what life was like for a Christian in a Buddhist society. Was my family shunned?

"We try to live in harmony among ourselves," I had replied, "unlike your people and mine."

Many evenings we would share our dreams.

"Someday, Mr. Suka, I will travel the world on the silver bird."

"What is that, the silver bird?"

"An airplane that will take me to new worlds. I was born in a poor village, but I will live where there are opportunities for a better life."

He nodded. "That is a nice dream."

"What is your dream, Mr. Suka?" I wondered.

"My dream?" He pondered over his fields until a tragic smile crossed his face. "Someday, Shuzo, I would like to find peace from my past."

Our dreams were born from opposite ends of the universe, but we drew strength and success and hope from the same flourishing patch of land.

Still, I never spoke of my Japanese boss at home, and Mr. Suka knew me only as Shuzo.

He ushered me inside his farmhouse.

"Come, come, Shuzo. Quickly!"

Mr. Suka's home was even more humble than I remembered. Aunt Sunja swore that all Japanese landowners lived in exquisite homes with teakwood tables and silk cushions.

"And they eat with ivory chopsticks!"

Not Mr. Suka.

"I am very glad to see you today," Mr. Suka said. "Sit."

I sat down on a straw mat and watched my boss pour two cups of tea from a cracked pot. He looked troubled—it was the war, of course. Despite Japanese assurance that the Americans were on the verge of surrender, the climate of the war was as bleak and dreadful as the coming winter.

"I came to this country because land was offered to me by my government at a very good price, Shuzo. Yes, I knew that I was taking land away from Koreans," Mr. Suka admitted. "But I have never mistreated my workers. I do not believe in mistreatment. Now my government is pressuring many Korean families to work in factories for war production. This is called coercion, Shuzo, and your family could be next."

"But my father has already volunteered."

"No!" he exclaimed woefully. "Those leaflets they pass out to poor Koreans promising good wages are nothing more than propaganda. Words for hungry ears. The factories are miserable and dangerous. The work is not worth the small sum for which one is paid. Shuzo, go home at once and warn your father!"

"He will not listen to me."

"Tell your father that if he goes he is no better than a dead man. Shuzo, listen to me—your family must hide."

"Hide?"

"Yes," Mr. Suka said. His voice dropped to a whisper, for anyone could be a spy. In time of war and hunger, there was no such thing as a loyal farmhand. "Until peace is declared."

"But we have no place to go."

"Your family can hide here, on my farm," he offered. "I do many favors for the Imperial Army. No one would suspect betrayal."

"What about Officer Akoto?" I asked, for I had seen him on the farm, picking out the choicest fruit.

"Especially Officer Akoto. He knows that I know the truth about him."

"What truth?"

"Soojung Kim is his birth name," he revealed to me with a look of trust. "He was born to peasant farmers. His father committed suicide. His mother, already an old woman, came to work for me before she, too, died. Not a drop of Japanese blood flows through his veins."

"So he is ashamed of being Korean, isn't he?"

"As a Japanese imposter, his life is better than that of most Koreans, Shuzo. He has an office and a shiny sword in his leather belt. His hands are smooth, not calloused like his parents'. Yes, he was ashamed of them."

I looked down at my own calloused hands, proof of my poor Korean lineage. Would I ever escape the bloodline of poverty?

"Be proud of your hands," Mr. Suka said. "They are honest,

hardworking hands. Be proud of your heritage. Now, hurry Shuzo!"

I bowed, then ran home.

My family was sitting in their sacred circle outside the hut. When Kwan-Young saw me, he broke from the circle with a squeal—

"Hyong nim!"

And into my arms he landed.

"Hyong nim, let's play hide-behind-the-rock!"

I took his hand and led him back to the circle. "Later," I said.

"Hyong nim," he persisted.

"Later," I repeated, seating him in his place. Then I turned to Father.

"Father, you can not go to work for the war effort. It is too dangerous."

Father shrugged, oddly calm, as though he was under an influence other than rice wine. "Do not worry, Sei-Young. Not a day will go by without a letter from me. I will earn big money and be back home before spring's thaw. When the war is over."

"There is no promise the war will end or you will return, Father. There is no big money. You cannot leave your family. Your place is with us."

"When I return we will celebrate," Father spoke with finality.

While Kwan-Young clung to my leg, I turned to Grandfather. But he was locked in prayer. I wished he would speak up with conviction. I wished he would speak from the mouth of God. God knew the truth. God knew the horrible fate befalling us. Why didn't Grandfather?

Later, he did. Privately, Grandfather admitted, "Your father's decision breaks my heart, Sei-Young. But it is *his* decision, a decision driven by love. We must honor it."

In the days that followed, the mood inside our hut was dismal. We had faced most all of our hardships as a family in a circle. But now Father was leaving and an empty spot would take his place.

One late evening as we lay in our bedding, I overheard Mother whisper to Father, *"Yobo,* I went to visit Sunja today."

Father murmured awake. "Eh?"

"I am riddled with guilt. Think of all the years Sunja has lived alone. So many black, lonely years. No matter what, she is family. She is my sister. When I went to visit her, I told her you had joined the war effort and would be leaving the day after next. I asked her to church and to supper. I am doubtful she will accept my invitation. She is so angry. She thinks we are at war. I told her that we are not at war but that we shunned her because black-heartedness is a contagious disease."

Mother paused for Father's reaction. When nothing came, she continued.

"Perhaps we should have listened with more caring ears. *Yobo?"*

But Father was sound asleep. Mother wrestled with her thoughts, chanted her sister's name in a prayer, then fell asleep, too.

A long chain of well-wishers sloped over the mountainside. Their hands were bound by one belief: God would protect their loved ones who were off to the war effort tomorrow morning, whether their fates lay in dark coal mines or rancid factories.

The chain led to the Church of Devotion. Tears welled in Mother's eyes when she spotted her sister among the well-wishers. Aunt Sunja was holding a hand-woven basket of wild-flowers as an offering. Overnight, her voice and posture had softened.

"Just as I lay down to sleep last night I thought I heard you call out my name—'Sunja!' My eyes shot open with realization, Kwangok. Instead of flowers I have grown weeds in my heart. This is not the life I want to live anymore."

The two embraced in a halo of warm words.

When all the well-wishers and volunteers were ushered inside, the doors of the Church of Devotion closed.

Grandfather spoke.

"Tomorrow many of you will journey to a place far from our village. My son Choon-Young will be on that journey. I will miss him. I am proud of him. He is a great man."

Father closed his eyes and swam in Grandfather's words.

I had never seen him so happy.

A fine supper was in order. Father had purchased a choice cod from the fish market. It cost more than he could afford, but some occasions called for a special stew. Mother had prepared the fish in a spicy broth with cabbage and squash and *tooboo*. Although only a modest mound of rice was placed for each person, there was plenty of stew for second helpings.

This time Father led the meal prayer. He ended the prayer with a few sobering words.

"I have not always been the son or husband or father I should have been. Rice wine was my devil; it blurred my vision. For that sin, I am sorry. But even in my darkest moments, I have always loved my family. I leave tomorrow with the hope that the day will come when each of you will forgive me."

A black sky fell over the hut. Our sad dreams put out the stars. Tomorrow, Father would be gone.

Hours later, I awoke to a stirring. The silhouette of a small figure stood in the middle of the hut, pointing toward the door. It was Kwan-Young.

"Hyong nim!" he cried.

I took his arm. "Shhh! Come back to bed."

Kwan-Young resisted. "I'm frightened, *hyong nim!*"

"Of what? There's nothing to be frightened about."

"But there's a ghost. Over there!"

A ghost? There was no ghost near the door. I hushed Kwan-Young, then lay his shivering body down in his bedding.

"You had a bad dream. Now go back to sleep."

My little brother crawled into my bedding. "But what about the ghost?"

"You did not see a ghost, Kwan-Young."

"But I did, *hyong nim,"* he said. "I did, I did," he kept saying until he finally fell asleep.

The night was starless. Only the barest light trickled through the hut. How could Kwan-Young have seen a ghost? A shiver rippled through me. There were those in Nabi who believed that to witness a ghost foreshadowed one's own death. But Kwan-Young had survived his first hundred days, not to mention his first four years. He was never sick. I finally drifted off to sleep, dismissing the notion of ghosts and deaths as no more than silly superstitions.

TEN

NORTH, 1944
Heisook

"The secrets of the waterfall fell upon my stunned ears."

CHANGI FLED. WHERE HE fled was a secret. In the nine months since his disappearance, official letters demanding the immediate recruitment of Mifune Okawa to the Imperial Army arrived on a weekly basis. Father would politely reply that his son's whereabouts were a mystery to him.

I suspected my parents knew Changi's whereabouts because in their prayers they didn't ask God to watch over him 'wherever he may be,' only to watch over him. They knew where he was, but they kept it a secret from me. Unfairly, I thought.

"Tell me where Changi is," I pleaded. "Tell me!"

But my pleas were met with authoritative silence. In time I gave up in the hope that they knew what was best. But it hurt not to ask, and it hurt not to know where my big brother was, or what he was doing. Unlike in the past, wherever he was, he was far away. There was no pot of *tooboo chigae* bubbling on the stove.

* * *

By now it had become a tradition that we celebrated Chusok on Heavenly Mountain with the children from the Adol Orphanage and from members of Father's congregation. There were the songs and the food and the shaking of the chestnut trees. There was me in my *hanbok*. Not Great-Great-Grand-mother's—I had long ago outgrown that one. No, the one I wore this Chusok was secretly tailor-made for me by a seamstress named Mrs. Lim who took my measurements and cut out a pat-tern using Japanese newspapers. Mrs. Lim made a living mak-ing fine dresses for Japanese ladies in her family's mud-thatched hut. Last year I wore one of Mother's *hanboks,* but I had out-grown that one, too.

Despite my new *hanbok* and the merriment around me, I could feel no cause for celebration. I could only feel Changi's absence. *Hanboks* were not designed with pockets; with my stone left at home, I felt more empty than ever. I needed more of Changi, even if only in memory. A deep secret part of me, so deep and secret it never even voiced in my brain, hoped that Changi was hiding out at the waterfall all this time.

When no one was looking, I slipped away from the gather-ing. I was determined to find the waterfall. I envisioned Changi sitting upon the giant quartz rock like a king on his throne, patiently waiting for me. How he would command me to do this and do that with valiant humor. But . . .

I could not find my way there. With each step the vision of Changi moved further and further away from me. I even closed my eyes and tried to re-create the scenic trail Changi had led me on, our steps, but this only took me in circles until I was lost.

"You are a silly girl..."

Changi and I had returned to the waterfall so many times. Why couldn't I remember the way?

"You don't even know where you're going, do you?"

I entered the seventh grade at the Waketake School for Girls. None of my friends were allowed to enroll in the prestigious school governed by Principal Nishimoto.

"Only special girls are accepted to the Waketake School," Hanako had confided to me on my last day at the Osawa School. "I submitted a special recommendation for you."

My former *sensei* had looked at me longingly, hoping for something, a flicker of friendship. But I did not so much as blink. I would not give in to the enemy.

That was the last time I ever spoke to Hanako. On that day, I had left the schoolyard of the Osawa School without a fond farewell for her or Principal Shimmura, or the classroom where I had sat for six years. Not even the cherry blossom tree with its delicately bare beauty deserved a sentimental look. I vowed never to return to this wretched place. It was over. No echoes from my past could call me back.

Welcome to the Osawa School.

Heisook, this tree will grow with our friendship.

Bow to your Father and Mother of Japan.

Six years of memories were now entombed behind the walls of the Osawa School.

*   *   *

A new principal, the same message. Principal Nishimoto's words were as empty as air. And it was a new school, but it was the same curriculum—one that did not include books. Our assignment? The war effort.

How many more socks would I darn? How many more gloves would I stitch together with that deadly needle I wished I could use to poke out my new *sensei's* eyes? How many more pockets would I sew onto Imperial uniform jackets? I'm not certain I believed in heaven anymore, but I believed in hell and I was in it. Every minute of every day was tedious, repetitive, without worth. Sometimes I thought if I saw one more sock, one more glove, one more pocket, I would scream so loud it might just stop the war, at least for a minute. Even that, a minute of peace, seemed too much to ask for.

Often, when exhaustion stole my grip, my rusty scissors would slip and cut into my already ravaged palm. One morning my *sensei* noticed a streak of blood on one of my assigned Imperial jackets. He inspected the garment, then me, with nothing short of pure, deep-seated hatred.

"Everyone, stop what you are doing!" he yelled.

All eyes fell upon my *sensei*.

"Do you think a fine Imperial soldier deserves to wear a bloodstained uniform? A war brother who risks his life and limb for you? Stained by a Korean girl, no less?"

All eyes turned to me. But I did not respond, for truth would only result in more punishment.

"Yoshiko Okawa, answer me!" he demanded, shaking my shoulders. "Answer me now! Do you think a fine Imperial soldier should have to wear a uniform stained by a Korean girl?"

"No, *sensei*," I lied.

He threw the jacket at me and shouted, "Shred it. Now!"

I shredded the garment with my scissors, not looking up; if I did look up, surely the tears I held back would stream down my face. For that, he might laugh at me, the weak little Korean girl. Or kill me.

When I finished shredding, he slapped my fingers with a ruler. "No lunch privileges for a week."

This was hardly punishment, considering lunch was nothing more than a single sesame rice ball—students were forbidden to bring any food to school. My lacquer lunch box, once filled with rice and egg-dipped codfish and seasoned watercress, was now stored away on Heavenly Mountain with many other family possessions.

"We are all equal subjects of the great Motherland," Principal Nishimoto insisted later that day at a war effort rally. "Together we will suffer . . . for the war effort."

A weak man with a weak voice, lost in the wind. Principal Nishimoto, *suffer?* Whenever his foolish throat grew sore, he would pop honey candies into his mouth.

This time the skin did not heal. The scissors had cut me before, but never this deeply. Mother had cleaned and disinfected the wound, then bandaged it with gauze. But it did no good; pain throbbed through the layers. I remembered what Changi once told me with such conviction.

"Sometimes pain can feel good, if it is felt for the right reason."

But this much pain? And for what reason? To help the Japanese?

When Mother took off the gauze, she was horrified to see that my wound was badly infected. She took me to a doctor who treated it with mercurochrome. In the end I missed a week of school—what good was I to the war effort with a bandaged hand?—and was left with what would become an ugly scar on my palm.

What was it Changi had said? *"Not everyone is a privileged Pang with a perfect fortune carved into her silky little palm."*

Nor was I anymore.

If only the Americans would crush the Japanese like a big ugly bug, then the war would end. Even though I didn't know any Americans, I liked them. I liked each and every one of them. They were Japan's enemy and, therefore, they were my friends.

The Waketake School was a most lonely place. I made no friends. My *sensei* filled me with more hate than I thought my heart had room for. I could not help but compare him to Hanako, who was warm and affectionate. I began to miss her.

"You remind me so of my youngest sister Suko who lives in Nagasaki with my family," she once said, her face still dreamy from a Japanese melody I had played for her. "You have the same ladylike walk and hair pretty enough for a princess. And also the same look in your eye."

"What look, Hanako?" I had wondered.

"Oh, a look both honorable and mischievous." She squeezed my hand. "When you bow to an elder and pay your respects, somehow I know you are giggling inside."

I giggled, then suddenly stopped. "Is that wrong?"

"Heisook, who you are inside is much more important than the face you show to others. Promise me you will always be true to yourself."

"I promise," I said.

"Good. Now play *Sakura* one more time for me."

*   *   *

As one of the few who lived within walking distance of the Waketake School, I did not belong to the school's coterie, the girls who lived in the dormitory. I imagined my classmates giggling and sharing secrets under the covers when the lights went out. A part of me yearned to join them but another part of me cursed them. I was lonely but I would not be like them. Obedient Koreans. The Japanese could not manipulate me anymore. I was no longer a puppet like them. When Principal Nishimoto pulled their strings this way, they would bow to the Father and Mother of Japan. When our *sensei* pulled their strings that way, they would kneel at the Shinto shrine. Even if my body did those things, my soul contested them. Friends were a thing of the past, over and done with.

On a cool autumn day while darning socks, my ears fell upon the heart-struck gossip of my classmates.

"That one looks like an American movie star with his big round eyes and wavy hair!"

"Like Gary Cooper you mean?"

"No, no, like Robert Taylor!"

They were talking about Imperial *kamikaze* pilots who were also housed in the dormitory. Their tiny airplanes were either hidden behind our school in a cluster of woods or off on suicide missions. Compared to the American B-29s that streaked over Sinuiju like lightning, *kamikaze* airplanes were toys in the sky.

"*Kamikaze* means *divine wind,*" Principal Nishimoto had addressed us one morning. The air was still. I shivered. "And these divine *kamikaze* pilots will take to the sky fearlessly, selflessly, then sacrifice their lives in suicidal crash attacks on the American devil's B-29s and submarine ships. For your cause. They sacrifice their lives for you. Carry this truth with you at all times."

Despite such frightening images, a silent belief, true or not, existed: The Americans would never bomb a church or a hospital—or a school. My classmates felt safe and protected by the stone walls of the Waketake School.

"I am in love," one girl sighed.

"Me, too," sighed another.

"They are all so handsome," sighed a third.

Handsome? Not to me. They were Japs. When their eyes stung me with their desire, the back of my neck would stiffen. How dare they? No Jap would ever touch me. Never.

How could a Korean girl possibly fall in love with a Japanese man? How could she think a Japanese man could ever love a Korean girl? A Korean girl was no more than a darner of socks. And it wasn't true. Principal Nishimoto was lying. No *kamikaze* pilot ever died for a Korean girl.

In the face of an existence so terrible sometimes I wished I were dead and buried like Great-Great-Grandmother, I did think about boys. Attending an all-girl school only reminded me of that. My mind kept skating back to last winter. There was a particular boy I had noticed. Every weekend he skated on the frozen Paengma River with a group of boys and girls. One day he had skated past me; our eyes locked; yes, I was certain they did. I gave this stranger a name—Minamja, meaning *beautiful man*. Of course, I told no one of my crush, but Changi could see it in my eyes as I watched Minamja skate around and around the river.

"He's too old for you," he had teased me. "Why, he's even older than me."

"Father is eight years older than Mother," I reminded him.

"Oh? And are we talking about love and marriage?"

Changi's tone was lighthearted, but the idea of his little sister growing up bothered him enough to also keep an eye on Minamja whenever we went ice-skating.

As slowly as time passed, it was a miracle that winter was here again. Every weekend, I went ice-skating on the Paengma River. I was looking for Minamja, of course. But he never showed up. It was foolish, naïve, and ridiculously wishful. The war took all wishes away—Minamja was undoubtedly sent off to fight.

I had no friends, no Minamja, and worst of all, no Changi. The winter was insufferable. Every day seemed a century long.

On the day Changi's morning glories bloomed, the sun beat gently down on my hair, and I knew spring had arrived. Every morning I would watch his flowers come to life and hear what he had told me long ago, so long ago it seemed like a dream.

"Open up like a morning glory. . . . Think on your own. Explore."

But one morning I heard instead the anguished moans of my parents at the gate. The cause? A letter.

"What is it?" I called out.

Father grew emotional as he read and reread the letter. Mother fell to her knees with a feverish prayer. My heart stopped.

"What is it?" I repeated.

"Changi must enlist in the Imperial Army," Father said. "If I do not escort him to the train station tomorrow morning, then you and your mother's lives are at risk."

"Where is my brother?" I demanded to know, expecting blank looks. To my surprise, Father replied without pause.

"Changi has been working in a lumber mill in the mountains. A Korean patriot took many young Korean men underground to avoid the Imperial recruitment."

"What has he been doing all this time?"

Mother choked back a tragic sob as Father helped her up. "He has been waiting for the war to end," he said.

"Why did you keep this a secret from me?"

"We had to take precautions," Father explained. "If we told you, you might accidentally tell a friend—"

"I have no friends, Father. I have no one to talk to."

"We could not take any chances. We could not jeopardize your brother's life. We had prayed he would be safe there until the war ended."

"Have you seen him? Have you spoken to him?"

My questions were met with sorry silence.

"Is Changi all right?" I angrily asked. "Can you at least tell me that?"

"There has been no communication with your brother, Hei-sook," Mother said with regret. "We could not risk that."

Changi's wall of morning glories, vibrant a moment ago, looked suddenly lifeless.

I could not stay angry with my parents. Some secrets were forgivable. They prayed for Changi all the time. Of course they did. Yet they could pray for eternity. Nothing could stop the Imperial Army. Not Mother, not Father, not even God.

Sliced scallions garnished a large pot of *tooboo chigae*—Changi's favorite. But no one was hungry tonight. My big brother was a stoic figure beside me, cockiness gone. He had come home, only to say good-bye. There was so much to say, but love lodged in my throat like a sticky rice cake, only it didn't taste good. I trembled uncontrollably, unable to speak. Time was running out. Words, where were the words? Too soon Father said—

"We must go now."

I walked with my family to the train station. Distant thunder sounded in my ears. Changi took my hand and held it. My other hand, forever scarred, squeezed the stone in my pocket. The waterfall was a world away. We were there a million years ago.

"I wish the world would stop right now, Changi," I finally spoke up under a somber sky on the verge of collapsing on every dream we ever dreamed. "If it would stop right now, I would bow to every Japanese face I saw, I would kiss the ground Emperor Hirohito walked on."

"Heisook, you would do that for your big brother who loves to tease you to tears?" Changi asked in a joking way. But his voice broke and gave his act away.

Our hands clutched in the face of war and death and darkening clouds.

At the train station an army of young Korean men was saying good-bye to their families. Rain began to fall like tragic tears. Now it was Changi's turn. He saluted our parents. "Our philosophies may differ, but I love and honor you both."

Mother and Father were stricken; their eyes empty of prayer, as though the wind and the rain had swept them away. They hugged their son good-bye, questioning God's existence, I think.

Changi kissed my forehead with a departing whisper. "Remember, Heisook, don't be afraid to take steps on your own. For otherwise, you will always be a helpless little girl."

I buried my face in his chest, unable to speak. *Changi, Changi, Changi.* After a moment, Father gently pulled me away. It was time.

Changi boarded the train. The doors closed.

He waved. "Good-bye, everyone."

Changi put on a brave smile, but I remembered how his chopsticks were shaking last New Year's Day, and how he had wept at Mother's touch.

The train slowly pulled away from the station.

"No! Don't go, Changi!" I screamed. "Changi!"

Changi peered down at me from the window. His face was pale. No trace remained of my brash brother who defied all Japanese from the top of a great chestnut tree.

"Good-bye, Heisook."

"Changi!"

I was still screaming his name long after the train was gone.

The next day I skipped school. If I were caught, so be it. They could bind and gag me and torture me—tomorrow. Because today I was going back to the train station. Alone. Changi's words led the way.

"Heisook, don't be afraid to take steps on your own . . ."

I boarded the train and sat all by myself. The train steadily chugged through the heavily guarded city of Sinuiju until it reached the open countryside.

At the foot of the mountain, I dared God to stand in my way. For I was going to a place where He was not welcome. I was going to a place that belonged to Changi and me and no one else. And this time I would not be a helpless little girl; this time I would not get lost.

Changi's voice escorted me all the way up the mountain.

"Follow me . . . I want to show you something . . . My secret place . . ."

I passed the great chestnut tree whose limbs stretched out like arms reaching for heaven, still hearing my brother's voice: *"My two-hundred-year-old friend . . ."*

Before long the woods magically parted and I found myself walking through the familiar dark tunnel of trees. I kept moving until the tunnel opened up to a sun-blinding sky. Then I saw it. The waterfall.

"Welcome to my secret place."

I climbed up on the giant quartz rock that glittered behind the waterfall.

"Listen!"

I closed my eyes and listened.

"Do you hear the secrets of the waterfall?"

I listened with all my heart, trying to hear, interpret, sing with, nature's language. Then it happened. The secrets of the waterfall fell upon my stunned ears and I heard the truth.

Changi is gone. He is gone forever.

ELEVEN

SOUTH, 1945
Sei-Young

"Then the boy named Kwan-Young Shin
drifted off into eternal dreams."

FATHER HAD PROMISED US that he would write.

"Not a day will go by without a letter from me."

He had promised us that he would return before spring's thaw.

"When the war is over."

But more than a year had passed, the war was not over, and there was no word from Father. Not a single letter or a single *yen* had made its way home to our hut. For fifteen years Father had slept under the same mud-thatched roof as me. Where he went in his fitful sleep I never knew; but at least his dreaming body lay here, next to his family, where he belonged. Where he was now was a mystery. He might be in China, dying uniforms. He might be in northern Korea, polishing boots. He might be in Japan, stocking arms. Wherever he was, whatever he was doing, Father's fate was in the hands of the ongoing war.

We would not allow ourselves to think the worst.

* * *

Imperial forces were moving toward Nabi. Many families fled the village to avoid their neighbors' fate of being seized from their homes in the middle of the night and forced into the war effort.

Worry possessed me. I could not protect my family. Even faith, the love of God, meant little now. We had to take flight or chance being shipped off to separate parts of the map. The sacred circle had been broken once before; now we had to hold on to each other tighter than ever.

Every day Mr. Suka urged me to take refuge on his farm. He could be quite argumentative.

"Please, Shuzo, do not waste even one more minute. I will challenge any and every reason you give me why you should not relocate."

I was wrong. Faith, the love of God, had brought Mr. Suka into my life. My family was able to eat three meals a day from the income I earned from my goat's milk. As a consequence of rice rations, the Japanese demand for milk was at an all-time high.

If mankind came in the form of my Japanese boss, there would be no such thing as war.

But there was a problem. Aunt Sunja was now living with us. She was a changed person, it seemed. She took her place in the sacred circle and joined in prayer and song. Sometimes we walked to and from the village square together to exchange our rice coupons at the Japanese-run facility. Not once did she mutter a hateful word toward the Japanese, or grunt when an Imperial official passed by us. But sometimes she was unpredictable, like the time she laughed and cried in the same breath when simply commenting on the weather. To live on Suka's farm, the land of a Japanese man, might be too much for her healing heart to take.

"Hostility is giving way to harmony," Grandfather had remarked. "I can hear it in the way she walks, as though on flowers instead of stones."

True, but Aunt Sunja had told me many stories of her husband, a farmhand who dreamed of more. Each story always ended with the same guttural cry:

"Why did he have to die?"

Yet there were more composed moments when she would apologize for her harsh attacks on Father.

"I was wrong to say the things I said, Sei-Young. Your father was a fine family man; he loved you and Kwan-Young and my sister."

Aunt Sunja's words were well-meaning, but I really wished she would not refer to Father in the past tense. Without saying so, it was plain to see that she did not believe he was ever coming home.

But I believed Father would come home, home to the hut he built for his family and his art. I had memorized the poem he wrote for my twelfth birthday.

First Son

From the earth I came,
Into the earth I will go.
But not until I watch
My First Son's spirit grow.

He is as sturdy as a tree,
He is as bright as the sun.

He is as rich as monsoon soil,
He is Sei-Young, my First Son.

I was convinced that Father's will to return to his family would conquer any war.

But on a morning when cold fog hugged the countryside, I recalled another morning when I stood on this exact spot and watched Father hobble down the mountain with his cart. Now I squinted, hoping to make out Father's form. What at the time was a painful scene resurrected itself as a wistful memory. Fog rose in my eyes and brought with it the vision that consumed me with grief—Father working in a filthy factory or a coal mine among rats and the moans of homesick men.

"Come home, Father!" I called out.

But my words were lost down the mountain.

Spring arrived with Kwan-Young's fifth birthday. On Saturday, the day before his birthday, I had given Mother the money to buy the ingredients to make a special birthday cake, one sprinkled with red beans.

"No. It's too extravagant." Mother had said.

But I begged her to change her mind. "Kwan-Young has never had a birthday cake, Mother."

Mother gave in. She and Aunt Sunja took Kwan-Young to the market. They came home with a sackful of rice flour, sugar, and red beans. They told me how full of joy Kwan-Young was. He was skipping and singing, *"San toki toki ya . . ."*

The next morning Mother kneaded a mixture of rice flour, sugar, and boiled water on a slab of stone. As the mixture became breadlike dough, she carefully molded it into a perfect round shape. Then she crowned the top with a spare handful of red beans.

The sight of his birthday cake in the windowsill seemed to intimidate Kwan-Young. With his eyes cast down, he hesitantly asked, "When can we eat it?"

Mother scooped him into her arms and whispered with a kiss, "After church."

Kwan-Young skipped and sang all the way home from church. "I am five years old today, I am five years old today . . ." He knew the treat that awaited him.

But when we returned, the cake sat like an offering to a swarm of flies in the windowsill. Kwan-Young frowned as he watched the flies crawl and pick at his birthday cake. Mother quickly shooed them away, hoping Kwan-Young would forget the nasty sight. Like half-rotting fruits and vegetables, food never went to waste in the Shin household. Flies gone, all was thankfully forgotten. Kwan-Young's face lit up as Mother sliced his cake into five equal pieces.

"Kwan-Young," Grandfather said, "you are a growing boy. You eat my piece."

Instead of bowing, Kwan-Young hugged Grandfather.

But the next morning the hut fell strangely still, strangely quiet. I lay in my bedding, waiting for movement, waiting for sound.

"Hyong nim!" Kwan-Young gasped.

When I touched his face, my hands turned to flames. When he began to vomit, I cried out. Mother woke up, alarmed.

"What? What is the matter?"

"Kwan-Young is sick with fever!"

"The rice cake! The larvae!" Mother moaned, then caved in with agony. "Oh, why did I let him eat it?"

Grandfather sat up and listened to the commotion around him. Mother pouring water from a pitcher into a bowl. Aunt Sunja tearing cloth from the ragged hem of her skirt. Kwan-Young whimpering while I held him in my arms.

Even if we had the means, there were no doctors available in our village. We had medicinal herbs, but none could help Kwan-Young's condition that seemed to worsen by the hour. His stools were bloody. His body shivered. His eyes opened and closed with no indication of recovery. We held a constant vigil while Grandfather prayed, one word from collapse.

The word was dysentery.

"Please Lord in Heaven, protect our little Kwan-Young."

"Neh!" Aunt Sunja wept.

"Do not let him fall victim to this cruel disease. Give him the strength to fight back and live out the long life he was meant to live."

"Neh, neh!" Mother wept. "Strike me dead instead for feeding him infested food his tiny body could not fight off. Now my poor baby fights for his life. Strike me dead instead!"

I would not weep in front of my little brother who drifted in and out of our world, occasionally gasping, *"Hyong nim!"*

Only in front of the moon did I let my tears fall. Then I remembered the ghost. I wanted so badly to believe it was nothing more than superstition, and that Kwan-Young, somehow, some way, would miraculously recover. But as the days wore on, his bloody diarrhea emptied his body of life. Not even the smallest amount of *kuk bap* would slide down his throat. A thought kept creeping to, then running from me: Kwan-Young *was* the ghost; small, pale, about to leave the door of our hut.

Outside birds chirped songs of spring, but Kwan-Young was not whimpering, not moving. Mother shuddered. She knew death was here. She strapped Kwan-Young to her back and brought him outside to feel the sun on his face one last time. *"Cha jung cha jung, uri Kwan-Young, cha jung cha jung . . ."* she sang.

Grandfather, Aunt Sunja, and I followed in somber procession. I held Kwan-Young's lifeless hand. The same hand that used to open up a palm full of peanuts to me.

"Hyong nim!" he used to cry, so excited to see me.

Now his voice faded into the morning light.

"Hyong nim?"

I squeezed his hand. "I am here, Kwan-Young."

One last time, Mother sang him to sleep. *"Cha jung cha jung, uri Kwan-Young, cha jung cha jung . . ."*

Then the boy named Kwan-Young Shin drifted off into eternal dreams.

I sprinkled a handful of peanuts over Kwan-Young's tiny grave.

"Eat them in heaven," I whispered.

If Father were here he would have made a handsome wooden casket for Kwan-Young. With painstaking but noble and necessary grief, he would have covered the casket with an engraving of angels. Mother would have painted their wings yellow and blue. In their quiet magnificence, they would have carried our Kwan-Young all the way to heaven.

Instead, we buried him into the bare earth beneath the budding magnolia tree where Grandfather's Bible now permanently rested.

Day after day grief tormented me. Kwan-Young's death was all my fault.

"It was Kwan-Young's time to die, Sei-Young," Grandfather said, trying to convince us both.

Aunt Sunja's swollen eyes deformed her. "Sei-Young, do not blame yourself. Please! Dysentery is a death sentence."

"But I insisted Mother make the rice cake," I repeated over and over so that God would hear and punish me. "Kwan-Young would still be alive, if only I hadn't insisted."

"Shh! Kwan-Young is gone now," Mother abruptly said in a tone that surprised me. "Blaming yourself will never bring him back. But it is not your fault, Sei-Young. It is no one's fault. God took Kwan-Young from us because He wanted someone small and special by his side. My son, your brother."

I spoke no more of Kwan-Young's untimely death. It only served to destroy Mother; it would not bring him back. It shook Grandfather's faith and made Aunt Sunja gag with disbelief. What good would it do? Kwan-Young was gone forever. And yet . . .

This much I knew; this much comforted me. The war would end. The monsoon rains would come and go. The magnolia tree over Kwan-Young's grave would blossom year after year. And through all of this, my little brother would be there. Not in his voice or touch, but in his memory and spirit. They would expand my sky for as long as I lived. I was *hyong nim* and nothing, not even death, could ever change that.

* * *

The marching of more Imperial forces shook the ground. They had come to Nabi to seize more families for the war effort. Villagers who begged soldiers for release were beaten, then dragged into service.

I ran to the river where Mother and Aunt Sunja were washing clothes.

"Mother, there's no time to waste. We must leave now."

"We have no place to go," was Mother's stoic reply.

"No place," Aunt Sunja echoed.

"We can hide on Suka's farm," I told them.

Aunt Sunja's face took on a skullish cast, but she did not argue, hiss, resist. She looked for Mother's reaction.

Mother shrugged. "Perhaps when your father returns." Then she squeezed a rag and said nothing more.

Mother and Aunt Sunja each heaved a basket of wet laundry over their heads and steadily balanced themselves for the walk home.

"Mother, we cannot wait for Father's return," I persisted.

"What if Father comes home only to see that we have abandoned the hut? What will he do? Where will he go?"

Later Grandfather advised her.

"Choon-Young will know where we are. Common sense will lead him to Suka's farm. But Sei-Young is right. We must take refuge. Now."

Beneath a blanket of stars, some bright, some dying, we began our journey to the valley on the other side of the mountain. Two were missing from the circle. One man, one boy. My father, my brother.

Father, come back!

Kwan-Young, come back!

I was no longer an eleven-year-old boy who could fall down to the ground and cry over fate damned and dreams best forgotten. I had done that before and relied on Father's voice to carry me home. Now he was gone. I had to be strong for my family—they relied on me. Grandfather needed my help to walk. One hand on my shoulder, one hand on his wooden cane. His silhouette cast a pall over the whole mountainside.

Mr. Suka led us to a shed, one of many which dotted his farm. This particular shed, located on the farthest south side of his property, stored farm implements and was actually larger than our hut. A layer of hay was spread neatly on the dirt floor. Four straw mats surrounded a table. In a corner atop a block of cement were a hibachi stove and a lantern.

"I am sorry it is not more comfortable," Mr. Suka bowed to us, "but at least you will be safe."

"We are overcome with gratitude," Grandfather spoke. "You will be remembered in our prayers."

Aunt Sunja stepped forward with a humble bow. "I am speechless with shame, Mr. Suka. For many years I have allowed my anger toward the Japanese to distort the truth. This moment, only one truth speaks to me: A kind Japanese man is risking his life for a Korean family."

Mr. Suka's eyes shifted from my aunt to me, trying to understand an obviously tragic story. Confused but too polite to inquire, he bowed and closed the door behind him.

* * *

Our privacy was never intruded upon. Mr. Suka made certain that his presence was known only by the pail of water and the basket of corn or tomatoes he would leave outside our door once the sun went down. Three quick knocks on the door signaled Officer Akoto's presence on the farm. Three slow knocks meant he was gone.

In this way our existence was unbearable, avoiding daylight, living in fear of capture. The three quick knocks, the shadow under the door. We held our breaths when the shadow was still and when we heard that voice, the unmistakable voice of a Korean traitor, superior and belligerent. When the shadow moved on and the voice trailed off, we sighed. Even when he wasn't around for days, Officer Akoto invaded our lives.

Despite this, all of us tried our very best to make the shed feel like a home. We forced smiles throughout the day. Mother cooked over the hibachi stove, adding fresh herbs to every pot. Aunt Sunja adorned the table with a spray of wildflowers. Grandfather complimented every fine meal and shook the straw mats outside when darkness fell after supper.

Every evening I would open *Speak English with Me*. In the lantern's light I would memorize the words that Grandfather had promised would help me to swim across the world.

"It is a splendid day for a walk in the park."

"Mrs. Jones won a blue ribbon for her peach pie at the county fair."

Afterward I would listen to Grandfather recite scriptures from the Bible, scriptures he had memorized long ago. This gave us the peace in our hearts to fall asleep and dream of a better day when smiles came naturally.

But there were many times when not even the Bible could comfort Mother. Her heartbreaking moans told us that a part of her was already in her grave, too deep in the earth to hear once-loved passages.

"Even when a will is as strong as the firmest branch," Grandfather told me, "there are winds that can break it. Kwan-Young's death was one of those."

And so there were evenings when I would lie in my bedding and listen to Mother sob. I would lie still, so still.

"Keep him young and innocent, I used to pray. Now my Kwan-Young will be young and innocent forever. And what about my husband? Where is he to share in my sorrow! Where is he, God? Tell me!"

In the stillness a memory would come back to haunt me. It was the memory of one night four years ago when Father broke down in the moonlight. The image, once so tragic, comforted me now. At least Father's form was visible to me, was real to me. There he is. There! In the moonlight.

Soon I would find myself conjuring up memories on my own, always of that safe place, in a safe time. A hut in the poor mountain village of Nabi. In many ways it had been a life of despair, one fraught with hunger and disease. But at least it was a life linked by our sacred circle. I thought fondly back to Kwan-Young asleep in his bedding while Father fell into his art and a tin cup of rice wine.

TWELVE

NORTH, 1945–1946
Heisook

"I did not think we would be together on earth again!"

PRINCIPAL NISHIMOTO SUMMONED FORTH his greatest and most steadfast will to hold himself high on his podium. To look proud, honorable. He had a duty to the Motherland—even while she fell. The Americans had bombed Hiroshima. Dizzy with horror, he wavered like the weakling that he was. Not only was Japan's future uncertain, but his own future as powerful Principal Nishimoto was at stake. The Waketake School for Girls would soon close its doors indefinitely.

Forever, I hoped.

"Without a thought to the innocent, the American devil has dropped a bomb that has devastated the Motherland. One bomb has left hundreds of thousands of our men, women, and children dead. The city of Hiroshima is in ruin. Fire and ashes are all that remain. We can not hide or run from this bomb. The work of the American devil is not over yet. We may be the next victims."

Sirens ripped through Sinuiju, competing with Principal Nishimoto's final words.

"Go home to your families. The end may be near!"

I tore across the schoolyard and into the chaotic streets. Sirens rang louder and louder in my ears as I ran and ran, crying blindly and squeezing the stone in my pocket. American B-29s were soaring overhead, leaving white streaks in the sky. Was the end really near? Pandemonium struck the city. I bumped into faceless people and saw others sprawled on the streets. I passed the tea room and the noodle house, both closed, curtains drawn. In the middle of all of this, every wonderful moment of my life crumbled before me. Playing the flute for Hanako. Singing in the church choir. Eating chestnuts with Changi. Listening to the secrets of the waterfall. The meaning of morning glories.

But then the faceless crowd became familiar. One face among hundreds made all the difference—Mother's. Our eyes locked and stayed locked as we ran toward each other. The end may be coming, but at least we would be together.

Mother threw her arms around me, drowning in near-hysteria. "I did not think we would be together on earth again! I thought we would be reunited in heaven!"

Arm-in-arm we ran through the turbulent streets of Sinuiju under the threat of bombs dropping, one breath from explosion, in search of Father. Miraculously, we reached the steps of the Sacred Hearts Church.

I spotted Father in a sea of desperation—families of all faiths seeking the comfort of his words. Christians and Buddhists and Taoists. Even Shinto-worshipping Japanese families took refuge in our Korean church. But where was God? Did everyone feel His presence but me?

Hours later the sirens finally died down. The Sacred Hearts

Church quickly emptied out. People scattered in every direction. The B-29s had vanished from the sky.

By late afternoon, the earth fell back into its proper place. Sunlight danced into our home. If I learned anything in school it was that nothing was necessarily as it appeared. The sunlight might be beautiful but it might also be deceptive.

Father emerged from the *ondal* cellar. It was odd to see him holding the radio at his side instead of up to his ear.

"Father, is it true? Did the Americans really bomb Hiroshima?"

"I am afraid so," Father replied.

My heart jumped. "Does this mean the war is over?"

"Most likely it is just a matter of time before Japan surrenders. I only pray it is before America bombs Korea."

"The Americans would never ever do that, Father. And you know why? Because we are America's friend. And they know we are Japan's enemy, too. That's why they bombed Hiroshima and not us. They despise the Japanese as much as we do."

Father's somber reaction confused me. He looked into my eyes searching for any trace of the daughter who used to close her eyes and listen to his prayers.

"The entire city of Hiroshima has been wiped out, Heisook. Have you any idea the loss of life? The city is a cloud of death!"

I couldn't understand how Father could conjure up even one word of sympathy for the Japanese. What was I talking about, *one* word? He would have many prayers for them tonight and tomorrow and the day after until he was exhausted with prayers. Only faith would let him forgive the people who turned his daughter into nothing more than a slave.

"Well," I responded in a purposefully cold fashion, "I think God decided to punish them to teach them a lesson. Look outside our window, Father. I see no cloud of smoke. I see only the sun shining!"

"I beg of you"—he was horrified—"do not speak in such an ugly manner, Heisook. Please."

"If Japan had left our country alone, if they had left Changi alone, then this would not have happened to them. They deserved what they got. Don't forget, Father, under Japanese rule many Koreans have died, too. Maybe even your own son . . ."

Father closed his ears to that last remark by simply saying, "Under heaven, we are all one family, Heisook. God's family."

But Changi had once insisted, *There is no heaven.* At the time my ears stung with disbelief, but now they stung with truth. *There is no heaven.*

"There is no heaven," I said.

Father let out a tragic sigh, one that he had held back for many months. My loss of faith was a fact that hurt him too much to think about. But now it had to be addressed.

"I know you resent the time I spend spreading God's message, Heisook. Try your best to understand that when God called upon me, my heart and soul had no choice but to answer. Why must you behave as though I am a father without love for my own children? Do you not believe me when I say that it nearly killed me to watch my son go off to war?"

Yes, I believed him. The day Changi boarded the recruitment train Father's faith was tested—and nearly failed him. I remember how instead of coming inside the house, he stayed outside, taking sanctuary in the flowerless vines on the wall. He opened, then closed his Bible in a way that made me wonder whether he would ever open it again. Father thought that only God saw him in this questioning light, but in fact I was the only one who was watching. So, yes, I believed Father, but did he deserve to hear it? What sympathy, what prayers did he have for me? I turned to open the ricepaper door.

"Where are you going?" I heard Father say.

"To celebrate, Father. To behold Changi's morning glories. To feel the sun on my face. These things are real to me. And this, too: The war is almost over. Maybe now Changi will come home."

Father followed me outside. "You can lose your faith, Heisook. But don't lose sight of the truth. The war may be over, but not without consequences. Many will suffer."

"I will not feel guilty over Japan's doom," I stated. "I will not. After everything I have been through, after all *my* suffering, I believe I am entitled to one moment of joy, Father."

Father hunched over, baffled. He shook his head, his thoughts so easy to read. Changi and I were his children, his Christian flesh and blood; we were not in need of his soothing words. But he was wrong. Flesh and blood was no guarantee of bond. What happened next would prove that.

Out of nowhere, someone, having slipped through the front gate, appeared at our door. Whoever he was, his hair was long, a white knotted mess. A stranger, and yet it seemed to me I knew these eyes.

Father's neck tightened. He spoke to the stranger in an angry but familiar tone. "Why have you returned?"

The stranger spoke back through cracked, purplish-black lips. "I have aged cruelly from years of the cold and the wind and the rain on my face, Sogho, but mostly from the guilt in my heart."

"If guilt has brought you to my door, then go. That is the price you must pay for the rest of your life. Surely after all this time you can not expect forgiveness!"

The stranger paused. Then he turned to go.

Pity took over Father's anger. A man of the cloth would turn no one away. And so, Father opened our door to him. But who was he?

A little while later Mother said—

"You must be wondering why your father is sponge-bathing this man in our house, Heisook."

"Who is he, Mother?"

"He is your father's older brother, Soghil. Many years ago he abandoned his family. He is your long-lost uncle. And he is Ilgo's father."

Yes, father and son shared the same cruel, hollow eyes. That much I could see.

"His brother could not bear the responsibility of being born First Son," Mother continued in a halting voice. "The weight of poverty was too heavy for him. So the responsibility fell upon the second son—your father—to assume the First Son's duties."

"Father's family was poor?" I asked, for this was news to me.

"Your father walked in straw sandals until he was eleven years old. That is how poor his family was, Heisook."

Father was a man with *yangban* airs. His clothes were always neatly pressed, and sewn from the finest cloth. I could not picture him in a pair of straw sandals. And yet, when I thought about it, the soles of his feet had always been covered with thick calluses.

"He never talks about being poor," I said.

"To talk about it would only bring back the shame of his brother's name," Mother explained. "Instead, your father provided for his parents until their dying days, he nursed his brother's bitter, consumptive wife until she breathed her last breath, and now he continues to support his son."

After his sponge bath, this mysterious long-lost uncle sat down to supper with us. A lifetime of shame consumed him, for he made no eye contact and could not utter a word of thanks for the bowl of dumpling soup Mother set before him. Instead of wolfing down his food, he took each bite slowly, as though it hurt him to eat. Even sipping broth was painful.

"How did you find me?" Father asked him.

"You are the famous Reverend Pang," his brother replied through lips that barely parted open. "It was not so hard."

Throughout supper, I waited for Uncle to ask about his son Ilgo. But he never did. Finally, Father spoke up.

"Tomorrow I will fetch Ilgo and we will all go to church."

Father handed Uncle a *chobok,* the traditional male dress for special occasions. "You will wear this tomorrow."

Uncle accepted the chobok with a pair of hands more used to begging. The finely spun cotton brought him to his knees. Father helped Uncle to his feet, then escorted him to bed. Uncle was exhausted.

When Uncle did not rise for breakfast the next morning, Father rapped on the ricepaper door to his sleeping room. There was no response. Concerned, Father slid the door open. Uncle lay in his bedding, dressed in the *chobok.* He looked so peaceful, so at rest. Sunlight streamed through the ricepaper door and into the room. Father then realized something: Death had crossed his brother's face. What followed was a thought that would comfort him throughout life.

"My brother came home to die. His guilt would not free him of his body until we forgave him. By opening our home to him, we did."

Curiously, Father never told Ilgo that the father who had abandoned him as an infant had come home.

"I will not dig up the past when fate would not allow a reunion," was his explanation.

All these buried secrets were piling up. Like bones.

Japan sacrificed the city of Nagasaki and thousands more lives before she surrendered in defeat on August 15, 1945. My parents and I anxiously awaited Changi's return. But he did not come back.

Overnight it seemed that every last person of Japanese descent was shipped back to his homeland. A month later the Waketake School reopened as the Cheguk School. Its mission was to educate young Koreans to be Koreans. We were no longer little Japanese puppets. What was formerly taboo was now required study: Korean language, Korean history, and Korean art. When our *sunsengnim*, not our *sensei*, taught us all about the Shining Happiness Palace in Seoul, the Kyujo Palace in Tokyo floated out to sea. The lesson felt like a refreshing breeze. But not for all of my classmates. Some had been so deeply indoctrinated into the Japanese dominance that they could not read a single word of Korean.

While Koreans were jubilant over liberation from our thirty-six-year enslavement to the Japanese, we were like the children of the Adol Orphanage—left orphaned, without a leader or an established government. The United Nations had a solution, Father explained. He did not look happy about it.

"They have placed Korea under the trusteeship of several countries, Heisook. But ultimately, the two world powers— Russia and the United States—will decide our fate."

Here in the North there was talk of a young Korean general. His photograph was in the newspaper. His voice was on the radio. He was everywhere.

"We have been released from Japan's tyrannical stronghold. Now we must build our nation on our own terms!"

I could believe he was the man to guide us into the future. His face was handsome and his voice had an unusual hypnotic power that drew in all listeners, even me. That's what worried my parents.

"I do not trust him," Mother remarked, reading the newspaper over Father's shoulder. "He has nothing to offer us but a future of doom."

Father was worried, too. "His military training came from the Russians. He is a dangerous man with Communist views."

In the end the two world powers could not agree on what type of government should be established in Korea. Before we could celebrate the dismantling of Shinto shrines and Japanese flags, a line was drawn in the soil. This line was called the Thirty-eighth Parallel. The Russians established Communism in the North. The Americans established democracy in the South. Communism, democracy. In time I would learn the difference between the two.

The wave of Russian soldiers who had rushed onto our northern shores claimed to be friends. But friends did not walk the streets of Sinuiju waving machine guns. Friends did not whistle at girls like me on my way to school, making crude remarks. I didn't know their language, but I understood their tones and the looks in their icy blue eyes. Friends were not thieves who took whatever they wanted right off a person's back. It happened one afternoon while Mother and I were minding our own business, on our way home from a department store. A group of five or six soldiers had surrounded us, imitating us "rich ladies" carrying bags in a most ridiculing fashion. Then one soldier grabbed Mother's bags. When he realized their contents—nothing but inexpensive little *comoshins* for the orphans—the smile disappeared from his face. Mine were inspected next. Nothing but *comoshins,* too. This discovery made the soldiers so mad they yanked the silver pin from my hair and the gold cross from Mother's neck. When I cried out, Mother took my hand.

"Keep walking," she said.

"But my pin, it was my favorite!"

"Just keep walking. Hurry!"

To the Russians our lives were mere trinkets, worth less than their spit. They seemed to love nothing more than looting Koreans, flashing their machine guns around like they would not hesitate to use them. Like they were hungry to use them, actually. Their foreign grunts along the streets of Sinuiju sickened me.

On New Year's Day, Mother took me shopping for our dinner at the open market where barrels of apples, chestnuts, and raw fish lined the street. Mother was sizing up a row of *chogu,* dried, salted fish strung together on a rope, when three Russian soldiers began to harass a vendor of small sticky rice cakes.

Mother clutched me as we watched one of them take the liberty of stuffing his mouth with the offerings. He chewed, then began to gag. After he spat them out, he cursed at the poor vendor in Russian. The vendor—a boy not much older than me—was terrified and began to apologize to the soldier, who was also very young.

"I am sorry, I am sorry," he kept pleading.

Of course these were meaningless words to the Russian, who appeared to be both delighted and livid, judging by the strange expression on his face as he repeatedly poked the vendor with the mouth of his machine gun. At first it seemed like a game of ridicule, one he would tire of. But it wasn't a game. The Russian began to poke harder and harder. By now the whole open market was paralyzed; people were too frightened to flee from the scene, certain to be shot.

The vendor, bent over, was crying, "Please, take my money."

The Russian shrugged, turning away as if he just might let the vendor be—a cruel hoax. For in the same breath, he turned back around. With the butt of his weapon he delivered a cracking blow to the vendor's head. The boy lay still on the ground, his eyes staring blankly like fish eyes through blood. It wasn't his money the Russian took. It was his life.

Later at home I would try to make sense of what happened. But there was no sense to be made.

"Why, Mother? Why did the Russian soldier kill the vendor?"

"Perhaps to a Russian who has never eaten a rice cake, the foreign taste may have offended him," was her halting explanation.

"Offended enough to kill an innocent man?"

Mother closed her eyes. "Yes."

* * *

At the Cheguk School, my mind often wandered from my textbooks, out the window and over the Sea of Japan—to where Hanako now made her home. I began to think about her with constant grief. She used to place petals in my hair and reward my flute playing with packets of sweet red bean jelly candy. And her voice was always praising, as lovely as music. Once, under the cherry blossom tree, we composed a *haiku* together.

SPRING TREASURES

Reflecting the moon's
luster, spring waters glitter
like jewels with delight.

"This is our poem, Heisook," Hanako had declared. "It belongs to you and me and no one else."

"It is beautiful, isn't it?" I proudly breathed.

"Yes, it is—just like you, Heisook."

Where was Hanako now? A memory made me gasp sickly. Her family hailed from Nagasaki. Images of Hiroshima and Nagasaki developed like photographs in my brain. Men and women and children, all dead. My eyes opened with terror. Were all those people, were those poor little babies in the rubble, truly my enemy?

No. Of course not.

Suddenly, I missed my old life. I missed Hanako. But mostly, I missed Changi.

Months and months had passed, and there was no word from him. Each of us hoped for his swift return in our own silent way. At any given moment Father could be found praying for him.

At my desk in school, I would squeeze the stone in my pocket, then bring it up to my chest. But it was Mother whose sorrow followed her every step. Her days were spent nurturing her orphans; her nights were spent worrying over Changi's fate. She would stand at the window waiting for him to come home. Sometimes I would hear her cry, "If only I could turn back the hands of time to when Changi was a baby. I would hold him and never let him go. I would not let anyone take him away from me!"

But it was too late.

Birds were praising the sun as I stepped outside to greet our morning glories. But something caught my eye, something left at the gate. It was a letter addressed to the Pang Family. I recognized the handwriting on the envelope. My heart stopped beating. The birds stopped singing. The earth stopped moving. Changi! I ripped the letter open, disheartened at once. The date read June 26, 1944—nearly two years past.

My Dearest Family,

I have completed my military training in Seoul. As I write this letter, my train is passing through Sinuiju. I look out the window for you . . . but no luck. Please do not feel sad for me, for I am not sad. My division is on its way to China to fight the Americans! They will not tell us which province my division will be fighting in, but I am certain that once in China I will feel a great sense of freedom.

Already I feel free!

All my love,
Changi

Changi had chosen his words carefully. Very, very carefully. The letter was his . . . and yet it was not. He was no fool. Imperial officials had monitored all mail coming in and out of Sinuiju. Should Changi speak his mind, death might follow. The true meaning of the lost letter—delivered by whom, a Korean patriot?—opened up before me like his wall of morning glories: Changi's plans were never to fight Japan's bloody war with America, but to go to China where he would abandon his division.

"Someday I will return to my birthplace of China where I belong," he once declared.

"Your brother is like a wild animal who must be set free . . ." Father once explained.

Even though I had defied Mother and Father and God, I found myself praying for Changi. I prayed that he was still alive, and that somehow, some way, his dream had come true. I prayed that he had gone to China and escaped the Imperial Army. I prayed that if the secrets of the waterfall were true—*Changi is gone, he is gone forever*—that my brother had set himself free.

THIRTEEN

SOUTH, 1945–1946
Sei-Young

"Good-bye, Mr. Suka!"

THE END OF WORLD War II left me standing before Mr. Suka at
the port of Inchon, fighting tears. It seemed like only yesterday
that I was a desperate boy in search of work, looking up at an
anguished Japanese farmer. We had stared at each other—two
strangers—standing in mud, acres of ruined land spread out
before us. But it wasn't yesterday. It was a long time ago. So
much had happened.

Now the endless sea rocked with emotion. Mr. Suka looked
very distinguished today in a fine suit and hat and shiny black
shoes.

"I must return to the Motherland with dignity," he explained,
holding his head high.

Like all Japanese farmers, Mr. Suka was forced to relinquish
his land and return to Japan. In a gift of friendship, he granted
me three goats.

I bowed with these parting words: "No one has done more for my family and me. I am indebted to you, Mr. Suka. I owe you my life."

"No," he disagreed. "You owe me only one thing."

"Anything," I bowed again.

"Boy, what is your name?"

The tears of my boyhood prevented me from speaking.

"I said, boy, what is your name?" Mr. Suka repeated.

For years, as Mr. Suka and Shuzo, we had spoken of dreams and disappointments against the drama of bondage and moonlit sky, but my Korean name had never passed between us. Could I say it now, after all this time, here, at a moment of farewell? My name caught in my throat. Then I remembered something. I was a free Korean. I stood tall and said proudly, "My name is Sei-Young, which means 'to swim across the world.'"

Mr. Suka removed his hat and bowed.

"Sei-Young, sell lots of milk. Save your money and go to high school, then college. And when you swim across the world I hope there are times when you will think of me with fond memory."

With the world changing around us—American ships docking, Japanese rule dying, Korean buzzing—we embraced for the first and last time.

"Good-bye, Sei-Young!"

"Good-bye, Mr. Suka!"

It was a time of promise, tinged with peril. My people were free. But after nearly a half-century of oppression, freedom was a foreign word that was hard to understand. How were we supposed to speak and behave, how were we supposed to live when we were no longer silenced by the sword?

"As for myself, I am a carefree cloud," Grandfather said as we traveled on foot to our new home of Mapo-ku. Grinning, he added, "On a cane, that is."

A dreamy smile crossed my face. For Grandfather was with me to hear the bells of freedom ring across the land. Oh, the wise, aging prophet. How could he not see that his old bones were like the seasons, ever changing but always returning?

But soon something stole my smile. It was the thought of Kwan-Young's tiny bones, now fragments in the earth, and of Father's fate. Of course Father had perished; if not, he would have returned and found his family, the family whose forgiveness he had begged for. My brother and father were gone. Where had their spirits flown?

Faith always had an answer: Kwan-Young and Father were together in heaven, keeping each other company, watching us. Faith's answer was comforting but not all-healing. Faith's answer could not touch what was once in reach. A young hand clutching peanuts or a rugged hand carving an exquisite oval box from a crude block of wood.

Mapo-ku was a thickly populated district on the outskirts of Seoul. Unlike Nabi, where neighbors mingled and news traveled from hut to hut, Mapo-ku villagers lived anonymously among their neighbors. Father would have liked such privacy, his sufferings contained within the four walls of our home. Mapo-ku was not a lovely place blessed with orchards and swaying rice fields. There were only hills, no mountains from which to dream and cry. The sky did not seem as starry here. But after living in a toolshed for a year, Mapo-ku was a heavenly vision.

Grandfather's holy work had brought the family here. Now that the Japanese were gone, Koreans were free to worship the god of their choice. Buddhism, Shamanism, and Taoism were the prevailing religions. But in Christian circles, Grandfather's name reached far and wide. An invitation was extended to him at Mapo-ku's Church of Holy Christ. He accepted.

A welcoming party led by Mr. Kee, the church bookkeeper, escorted us to the church. The massive stone and stucco structure rose from the ground like a monument to heaven. It occurred to me that despite the Japanese Occupation, the church had remained unshaken. Later, Mr. Kee showed us to the church quarters.

"This is your new home," he said. Mr. Kee was a friendly man who also worked as a bookkeeper in Seoul. "There are four rooms and a window in each. Open them in the early morning and late evening. The breeze from the grounds is very nice those times of day."

I walked from room to room, not believing my eyes or my ears, half-expecting to walk into the next room and wake up from a wonderful dream. But I was awake, and this was real. Tonight I would stretch my legs in my sleep and smile. By my side would be my four earthly possessions: my English book from Grandfather, and my three birthday gifts from Father— my flute, my pine whistle, and my teakwood plaque.

Next Mr. Kee gave us a tour of the church grounds, plush from recent monsoon rains. I could see there was plenty of space for my three goats. These days they were still roaming on Suka's farm. Mr. Oh, the Korean farmer who had purchased the farm, was kind enough to tend them on his land until I had settled into my new surroundings. Now Suka's farm was Oh's farm.

And this was our new home.

* * *

On a seasonably warm day in early fall, Aunt Sunja claimed a sunny corner of the grounds.

"For my Garden of Life," she told me as she squatted and dug.

"Why don't I dig and you plant?" I offered.

Aunt Sunja waved me away. "I must do this alone, Sei-Young. Otherwise, this will not be *my* Garden of Life. Do you understand what I mean?"

Did I? I'm not sure that I did.

"In the spring my flowers will be born," she said, rocking with such emotion the earth seemed to crack open for her.

That day she planted her first seeds. In time I would come to understand what she meant.

For Mother, there would be no Garden of Life. While Aunt Sunja basked in the sunlight, Mother receded into the shadows. Even as she helped Grandfather usher in the newcomers to his congregation, her face was dark. The day she took out her paint-brushes, Grandfather took me aside and said, "Let us hope the healing process for your mother will begin, Sei-Young."

"By painting, Grandfather? Won't that only remind her of hard times? Remember when she would paint all night long? Her hands would become so shaky she couldn't even bring a spoon to Kwan-Young's mouth the next morning. Even then, we were never sure that there would be rice with supper."

"Yes, but they were hard times only at the time. Now they are blissful memories of when her husband was by her side and her baby was asleep a few feet away. People forget hunger before they forget love," Grandfather said. "She needs to remember who she was before all the misfortune. A wife and mother."

To our dismay, Mother's hand movements were slow and heavy. And the colors she chose were not the vibrant reds and yellows of yesterday, but muted shades of brown and blue and purple. On scrap paper, no less! The more she painted, the less she spoke, as if each stroke had stolen a little bit more of her life from her. Eventually her scraps of art appeared on the church's bulletin board, among schedules of masses. Her art always depicted a scene of a child's spirit being drawn to heaven by his father's winged arms, the mother's spirit not far behind.

Perhaps Mother did not need to speak anymore. After Grandfather asked me to describe her art to him, he said, "I am afraid her paintings speak for her."

I spent my days selling milk on the streets of Mapo-ku, peddling from one corner to the next on the same bicycle from my Nabi boyhood days. There were times when my milk supply ran out and instead of going home, my feet peddled me back to where I came from. By bicycle, Nabi was nearly an hour's ride—far enough to be tiring, but not forbidding.

On one such excursion I came across a cluster of painted rocks not far from Mapo-ku. Painted with simple black strokes, the rocks evoked images of two dead people, a boy and a man. I shuddered with recognition—Kwan-Young and Father. These were the creations of Mother's hands. Without Father, her paintbrushes no longer touched hand-carved wood. Instead, they found their way to pieces of scrap paper and to lone rocks perched on the countryside.

I never actually saw Mother paint any rocks. Her art was a mysterious journey, in the way death is.

Mr. Suka's farewell advice served me well. Every week I sold enough milk to feed all of Korea, or so it seemed. Now it was winter. My goal was to save enough money to purchase books; that is, books that would serve as study guides to help me prepare for the entrance board exam to the Christian Boys' Academy in Seoul. The academy was a private school, founded by American missionaries in the late nineteenth century. If I passed the exam, I would be allowed to transfer next year from the public school system, which was in disarray after the end of the war. Grandfather had explained to me that my first year's tuition at the academy would be waived due to his status as a minister. And if I maintained a B average, my tuition would continue to be waived the following year as well.

"Whenever I am about to fall asleep, I forget that in the waking world I can only see shadows. Because a clear vision always comes to me," Grandfather said. At least once a day Grandfather took delight in expressing this sentiment.

"What vision?" I asked, as always.

"The vision of my grandson, Sei-Young Shin, dressed in a blue uniform with shiny silver buttons and a matching cap. The vision of Sei-Young Shin entering the Christian Boys' Academy. How proud you would make me!"

With spring came the blossoming of Aunt Sunja's flowers. Occasionally, after a midday shower, a rainbow would appear over her garden and I would hear her humming along to earth's music. I wished Mother would hum along with her. I wished she would make even the smallest sound.

Traveling by train was a new experience for me. Grandfather, who of course would not miss this event, said, "Mark this day on your calendar, Sei-Young. The course of your life has changed."

But what should have been a momentous event was eclipsed by its destination. Countless times I had watched Father hobble down the mountain with his cart, his destination the same as mine today—the capital city of Seoul. Father, his rickety cart, balancing his treasures. His fate consumed me with so much grief I almost forgot the purpose of our visit. Grandfather's contented smile reminded me that I was traveling to Seoul to purchase books at a bookstore. Not just any bookstore but the Christian Boys' Academy's bookstore! Suddenly, the train conductor announced, "Next stop, the Namdaemun Gate! Seoul!"

The Namdaemun Gate was one of the walls of Seoul, the main south gate. Built in the fifteenth century, the Namdaemun Gate stood like a staunch symbol of Korea's resistance to invasion. Korean history books had failed to capture its formidability with its massive granite base and wooden structure. They also failed to capture the Namdaemun Gate's elaborate workmanship, the ornamental details provided by ancient Chosun artists. The Japanese Occupation had ended but the gate still stood.

These days the Russian presence in the North was creating an oppressive air—refugees were pouring into the South with their horror stories. A terrible situation, but I didn't want to think about that right now. I was a sixteen-year-old boy whose dreams were becoming a reality thanks to the American military in the South. The Americans and other allies were creating an atmosphere of security for Koreans in a time of reform. They supplied us with food and clothing and medicine. They helped our schools and churches prosper. They were establishing a free world for the Korean people to thrive in, a world in which we didn't feel we were wearing *"comoshins* too small for one's feet" as Mother had once lamented. I was very grateful to them, but beyond that my focus was limited to my family, my milk business, and passing the entrance board exam to the Christian Boys' Academy.

Seoul was a city of paved roads and sidewalks lined with numerous cinema houses, churches, and shops. And crowds. Every face belonged to a stranger in a hurry. Hurry, hurry, everyone was in such a hurry.

"So this is what a big city is like," I said to myself as taxis rushed by us. Bus fumes and fresh bread and garbage and yellow melons swirled in the air to compose the smell of Seoul in late spring.

What caught my eye were the faces of Korean actresses pictured on the gigantic billboards above buildings. I had never seen such faces. How did they become so beautiful? Their eyes were smoky and their lips were red.

We walked many blocks, slowly, as Grandfather tired easily. On every corner, Father materialized with his cart full of wares. *Art for sale! Best prices!*

Memories of the grim past gave way as soon as I stepped onto the grounds of the Christian Boys' Academy. The brick walkway was magical, the ivy was magical, every old stone in the building was magical. Even the sky was magical here. My eyes swam with hope.

And after I bought my books, my eyes swam with words. The words opened them to religion and philosophy and mathematics. Some subjects were more interesting than others, but Korean history was by far the most fascinating to me. Grandfather had already taught me about Korea's many great kingdoms and about the kings and queens who ruled them. Now I was learning about the society behind the colorful pageantry. Wars were won and lost, people were born and died, but class systems had always unjustly divided the population. The *sangmin* class who lived during the eleventh century Koryo Dynasty was no better off than modern Koreans under Japanese rule. To ensure a lavish lifestyle, the *yangban* class strangled the poor with excessive taxation that left them homeless and dreamless.

I was lucky. Grandfather had taught me how to dream.

After months of study, I passed the entrance board exam and won acceptance into the Christian Boys' Academy. It was the Fall of 1946; I would be entering my junior year. Grandfather's words on the train were true: the course of my life had changed. Despite that, I kept my milk business and was lucky enough to have secured accounts with several bakers in Mapo-ku. It was the only way I could afford the train fare to school. Even so, I had to walk home. Five miles was long, but Grandfather's words accompanied me with every step.

"Walk with this knowledge: Your name is Sei-Young, which means to 'swim across the world.'"

And so every day I walked home from the Christian Boys' Academy, clad in my blue uniform with shiny silver buttons and matching cap. I remember feeling as tall as the sky.

FOURTEEN

NORTH, 1947
Heisook

"Good-bye, waterfall! Good-bye, stone!"

IT WAS ALL PART of history now. Echoes from a podium. Voices in a classroom. Whispers between Hanako and me. The Japanese melodies that once piped through my flute were long-lost notes, too. Nearly two years ago my heart had found another instrument—the piano. Now I could play Korean songs and classical music from around the world. I looked forward to my lessons with our church choir pianist, Mr. Lee. Four o'clock sharp, every afternoon, at his home. Mr. Lee was a teacher of few words, but his eyes were very expressive. When they lit up, I could play forever; almost forget the days of the war effort; and a palm still scarred. The piano took me far away from those memories.

Today sunlight waltzed through the windows as I played Mozart's *Rondo alla Turca*. Mr. Lee, in a rare moment, smiled, and that was all the praise I needed. As long as I kept playing, as long as my fingers kept moving, there would be no more bad news, no disappointments, no pain. But outside, the rhythmic footsteps of over four hundred boys from the Fraternal High School were marching to a different song. My fingers stopped. Lately, the boys had been marching every afternoon to protest the newly forming government with this message:

> *The new government maintains that it is a democracy. But this is a lie! What kind of democracy forces its citizens to become Communists? What kind of democracy forbids its citizens to cross a line in the soil? Yes, cross it and you are a dead citizen, not a free one! The South is where true freedom reigns. Under the new government, our fate is to live where freedom is banished. Freedom of thought, banished! Freedom of religion, banished! Freedom of life, banished forever! Armed Communist soldiers are proof of that!*

But today a round of bullets exploded back. *Dat, dat, dat, dat, dat!*

Screaming—*"Tapulchong! Tapulchong!"*—broke out. Machine guns.

Dat, dat, dat, dat, dat!

Mr. Lee threw me to the ground and covered me with his body. *Dat, dat, dat, dat, dat! Dat, dat, dat, dat, dat!*

Three seconds of silence, then blood-curdling cries.

It was over.

Mr. Lee helped me up, but I was shaking so badly I had to hold on to the piano for support. He went over to the window and shuddered.

"Don't look outside, Heisook."

But I knew I had to look. I had seen ugliness and death face on—I would not turn away now, no matter how crippling the sight. I walked over to the window.

"Heisook, please."

I looked out. It was a gruesome sight, it was hell on earth, it was . . . a massacre.

Forty-five high school boys died that day, killed by Russian soldiers. Their blood stained the street like a Communist mark. Within days of the massacre, the charismatic young Korean general whom my parents distrusted paid our school a visit. He came to defend the actions of the Russian soldiers. But I could see right through his spotless uniform.

"They were boys, too young to die. But because they spoke untruths, the Russian Army tragically mistook them for Japanese spies." Pretending to mourn, his eyes closed and shifted with impatience.

No one said a word. We didn't know who was a Communist or not. But everyone's head was bowed. So many tears fell the floor became wet.

"I am not asking you to forget what happened yesterday. But the Russians came to our rescue, to preserve our rights. That, too, we cannot forget. Look," he said, pointing out the window to the school's raised flag, "Our Korean flag is rich with symbols of balance and harmony. There is heaven and earth, there is fire and water. For some of you, this is your first look at your own flag. Now it blows freely in the wind."

Japanese and Koreans. North and South. Russians and Americans. Communism and democracy. The war and the waterfall.

What balance and harmony was he talking about? I never played the piano again.

* * *

Like the march that ended in bloodshed, everything turned for the worse. That evening, Ilgo showed up at our house. He was here to see Father. Instead of his usual rags, he was outfitted in a Communist military uniform. Clean-shaven, Ilgo appeared even more sinister than before. Mother and I held our breaths in the background.

"Times have changed," he pointed out with a perfectly gloved hand. His eyes, once blank, flickered with spite. All those years of begging, humbling himself at our door, were over. Now he stood in the doorway, a proud member of the Communist Party. "When I look into a mirror, I see a man of great importance."

If Father was afraid, he hid it very well. "What do you want?"

After a long, grotesque pause, Ilgo said, "I once promised to repay you. Do you remember, dear Uncle? It was on a day you threw me a few measly *yen,* then cursed me away. Oh, no, not to my face, but I could hear your disgust as you shut your door on me. Do that today and—"

"State your business," Father interrupted him.

"Most gladly." Ilgo cleared his throat for the moment he had waited so long for. Revenge. "I have been assigned the duty to round up every last minister in Sinuiju, which I will do with honor for our great government."

"Your godless government!"

"Such talk"—Ilgo evilly smiled—"may cost you your head."

I could not control myself; the words burst out of me. "Get out, you ungrateful man! Get out! No wonder your—"

"Heisook!" Father cried.

Mother grabbed my shoulders. "Be quiet, Heisook!"

"Ah, my mute cousin can speak!" Ilgo laughed

"Leave my property," Father said. "Now."

"Tonight is a warning, Uncle. Be gone by tomorrow or else I

will take you in myself. I will drag you by your praying hands. If your life is worth even a few measly *yen* to you, then my debt has been repaid a thousand times over."

Ilgo turned and was gone.

After my parents exchanged grievous looks, Father sat me down.

"Heisook, you must be careful with your words."

"But how can that man come to our home and treat you so terribly, Father? After everything you have done for him."

Sometimes I thought Father could justify even murder, for he replied, "His manner was despicable, but he spared my life. As a minister whose creed challenges the Communist system, my presence in Sinuiju puts all of our lives in danger, Heisook. I am so sorry. I must leave."

"Where will you go? There is no safe place," I cried.

He gently took my shoulders and said, "I hope that the answer will come to me by morning."

But Father's faraway face told me something. He already had a plan.

The following morning, before my eyes even opened, I knew that Father was gone.

Mother was in the kitchen making *mandoo* dumplings, enough for a feast. Her hands were moving but her spirit was paralyzed.

"Father is gone, isn't he?"

She nodded without saying where. I knew better than to say anything more.

"Why are you making all this food, Mother?"

With one hand she dipped two edges of a dumpling skin into a paste of raw egg. With the other hand she plopped a spoonful of meat and vegetable filling onto its center.

"Today is the Adol Orphanage's twenty-fifth anniversary. There will be a party. Please come, Heisook."

"Of course, Mother," I consented.

As she pinched the dumpling closed, her face pinched with all the misery to come.

Yes, Father was gone.

Mother was unable to attend the party. As the morning wore on, her eyelids grew heavy and she took to her bed. I went in Mother's place, but her absence was evident on the orphans' disappointed faces. A hundred and twelve of them! There were volunteers, offering their assistance, but . . . it was Mother who sang and cuddled and kissed the orphans; it was Mother who knew each one by name and their favorite sweet to eat, bestowed at birthday time.

The children began the party with a chorus of an old Korean classic.

"*Arirang, arirang . . .*"

Brutalized by war, and still their voices were so sweet and young and harmonic. Hearing them made me feel very young and very old at once. Old because I was older than these tiny, helpless souls. In their eyes I was an adult, towering over them. I could protect them like Mother.

"*. . . arariyo arirang . . .*"

But I could not protect them. I was too young. I was just a child myself, missing my father.

* * *

For the next two months I returned every day to the Adol Orphanage, for Mother's winter migraines now lasted until spring. I read books to the children. And we played games, lots of games. Jump rope and hopscotch and marbles. We built a swing and hung it between two sturdy trees. To see their faces come alive as they swung, one by one, swinging so high they could see over rooftops and treetops; to see their smiles, changed me.

Then came the news.

"Father is in South Korea," Mother announced on a day when she seemed to be feeling a little better. "He has found sanctuary at the Seoul Presbyterian Church."

"How did he cross the border?"

"The same way we shall," was her swift reply. "We will be led by a guide across the Thirty-eighth Parallel who knows all the safe routes to escape Communist soldiers."

I was scared. I didn't believe there were any safe routes. I had heard stories at school.

"When do we leave?" I nervously asked.

"Tomorrow."

The following morning I went to the Adol Orphanage to say my good-byes. Immediately dozens of children circled me and broke into song.

"Dunpuk, dunpuk, dunpuk seh . . ."

On the former grounds of the Osawa School, I sat under the cherry blossom tree, flute in hand. Pink petals floated around me with symphonic silence. Their fragrance saddened me; so familiar, so close, close enough to snatch and yet . . . eight springs had passed since I had watched the first buds blossom with celebration. Hanako and I had stood together that day, side by side. The air was sweet; affection grew. But in time I would turn my back on my *sensei,* draw a line between friends. Between Japanese and Koreans.

Now I said good-bye to my betrayed *sensei* in the only way I could, under the cherry blossom tree. No words, not even the *tanka* I had composed, could express my grief, my regret, my love.

FOR HANAKO

Tears fall like petals
off a cherry blossom tree.
Slowly, tragically.
The blossom of our love
has no hope for renewal.

And so it was with song that I paid her homage. I brought my flute to my quivering lips and began to play her favorite, *Sakura.* I played with my whole soul, in magical counterpoint with the chirping of birds. I played and played, tears streaming, wishing my music would somehow cross the ocean and into Hanako's ears. *I am sorry, Hanako!* I ended my song, knowing I would never again play this flute.

"Good-bye, cherry blossom tree. Good-bye, Hanako," I whispered.

My next stop was the waterfall, that magnificent secret place of dreams splashing and dying. If there was one place in the world that would never change—not tomorrow or the next day or a century from now—it was the waterfall. There I sat on the giant quartz rock for so long I lost track of time, until the waning sun reminded me that I had a three o'clock train to catch home. Such a schedule seemed like a crime here, in Changi's secret place, where it was timeless, eternal, light as air.

"... *always remember our secret place.*"

The enchantment of rushing water onto majestic rocks couldn't compare to the first time Changi had lifted me up here like a princess onto my throne. I could still feel his strong hands, the gentle placing of me onto the giant quartz rock. How amazed he would be to see me now, all grown up at sixteen.

"*You are a silly girl . . . You don't even know where you're going, do you?*"

I climbed down the giant quartz rock, then felt for the stone in my pocket one last time. With great reluctance, I set it upon the rock. It belonged here, where it was safe, away from the ugly, terrifying world. On a sunny day it would glint with secrets no one could hear. Only now could I embark on my journey knowing nothing, no one, not even a Communist soldier could take away the stone Changi had once given me.

"Good-bye, waterfall! Good-bye, stone!"

That afternoon after I packed persimmons and jelly candy and sesame crackers into a burlap sack for our journey, I sipped barley tea from Changi's favorite teacup. I found myself lost in its flamboyant design, the dragons and gold-flecked flames. Like my flute and like my stone, the teacup was one of the many things I would leave behind.

Mother slipped a bundle of colorful silk into my sack.

"If you are stopped by Communist soldiers," she spoke in a wavering voice, not looking up, "offer them this silk."

Why was Mother speaking as if I was journeying alone?

"Mother . . ."

Too delicately, she placed her hand on my arm.

"I am not going with you."

I dropped the teacup on the table; it cracked loudly in two.

"No, Mother! We are going together as planned. And in a few days we will be with Father in Seoul."

"I cannot go," Mother insisted. "Not yet."

"But why not? What has changed your mind?"

She hesitated, dreading my reaction. "I have faith that your brother will return from the war. I must be here for him."

"The war has been over for almost two years, Mother. Have you learned nothing? Your faith will not bring Changi home. Either we both go, or neither goes."

Mother's tone was most firm. "You will go alone."

I gave Mother a long, hard look of disbelief. Every tear she had ever wept for her dead First Son gathered in her eyes. No, she would not lose another son. Changi was coming home. Her faith confirmed that, along with this:

"Heisook, you cannot understand until your own faith returns. And I believe that it will."

How many times had she read Changi's letter? A thousand times, at least. But his message eluded her. Her faith blinded her with false hope. Dead or alive, Changi was never coming home. But what could I say that I had not said before? Mother still believed that faith was not like a teacup—so easily shattered. But she was wrong; my faith was gone forever.

FIFTEEN

SOUTH, 1946–1947
Sei-Young

"You are the thinker, the thinker, the thinker . . ."

THE UNIVERSAL LANGUAGE CAME alive for me at the Christian Boys' Academy. On campus, English and Korean were spoken interchangeably and the struggle to understand new words and phrases ended. And the best part was this: The more fluent in English I became, the less Japanese I recalled.

Friendship also came alive for me at the Christian Boys' Academy. My classmates and I shared something very special— the dream to be college-educated in a free world. This is where Eun Ju Chun and I became fast friends.

I first met Eun Ju when I was leaving campus on a late autumn afternoon. A group of students approached me. Several were familiar; I had seen them congregating in the hallways, deep in feverish discussions. The most familiar was a tall husky student whom the others circled. He was the leader, I would soon learn.

"I am Eun Ju Chun," he brashly announced.

I could not quite put my finger on it, but there was something very unusual about him. He appeared to be both a bully and a scholar. I was both intrigued and intimidated.

"Sei-Young Shin," I replied.

"We know your name, we have been watching you. Because you seem like someone with purpose, Sei-Young, we invite you to join our group."

When I responded with nothing more than a look of surprise, he went on to explain. "We are the Korean Libertarian Youth Group. We are proindependence, prodemocracy and *anti*-Communist," he punctuated with disgust. "We are twenty strong. But we need to grow in order to silence the Communist voice. What? Don't you know? North Korean spies are slipping across the border to brainwash vulnerable South Koreans—even us students!—with their leftist ideology. Yes, they're even crawling all over this campus as we speak!"

This was news to me. But I didn't dare say, for fear of sounding foolish.

As if he could read my mind, he said, "Look around, Sei-Young. Power struggles are threatening our freedom. There are many Koreans who see the American forces as a threat. In their eyes, the Americans are no different than the Japanese, just another foreign enemy planning to colonize our country all over again. But that is not true, the Americans are our allies. Our mission is to deliver this truth."

I declined his invitation to join them. "I'm sorry, but politics is not my interest. Besides, I am very busy with my schoolwork and I have my family to take care of."

He cockily dismissed my excuses. "What are you talking about? You have your country to take care of!"

* * *

Echoes of an angry Aunt Sunja rang in my ears. And yet, did this Eun Ju Chun character have a point? As much as I cherished Father, did I want to blame others for my misery? I thought about this, and I thought about Father.

I joined the Korean Libertarian Youth Group—the KLYG—because it was committed to a free Korea. I was a free Korean now and I did not want that taken away from me. Like true brothers, Eun Ju and I were united in our efforts to fight the Communist influence in our school. We circulated our own newsletter called *A Free Korea For All*. I wrote speeches; Eun Ju delivered them in his own words. Whether there was a crowd or just a few listeners, Eun Ju always spoke with gruff conviction, like he meant every word, which he did. What he lacked in polish, he made up with fire.

"Hey, listen to me! Any other messages you hear are from the mouths of liars. We are devoted to Korea's independence. Don't be a leftist idiot. Believe in freedom and we will be free!"

My admiration for my new friend grew with each passing day. He could be quite serious one minute and a prankster the next. His many gifts included beating anyone at Chinese checkers, memorizing any book in an hour's time, and provoking a chuckle from even the sternest of lecturers. He was also a natural-born artist. When I asked him if he planned to study art in college, he scoffed, "To study art is to ruin art." Eun Ju liked to draw cartoons and caricatures of those he poked fun at. He spared no one, including me. Somehow he had managed to sneak one of his sketches into my mathematics textbook. Drawn was an oversized egg-headed student in uniform, skipping among leaves, nose up in the air, singing, "I am very very very busy, yes, just too too too busy to join your silly group."

"My mother is Buddhist," Eun Ju confided in me one crisp morning as we were passing out prodemocracy fliers at school.

"And your father?" I wondered.

"What father? He left before I could walk, but listen here, it doesn't bother me at all." There was bitterness in his shrug. "I never needed him and never will. I'm here on a scholarship, and I shall do the same when I go to college."

I didn't doubt him one bit. Eun Ju had a brilliance all his own. It was something he was born with and would die with; what would happen in between remained to be seen.

"So listen, Eun Ju, how come you attend a Christian school when you're a Buddhist?"

"I never said I was a Buddhist. I have my own mind and I have my own religion," he rather bragged.

His testiness amused me. "So you attend the Christian Boys' Academy and you are not a Christian. You *are* a boy, I hope."

"Not everyone who goes here is a Christian, Sei-Young. It is no secret that the missionary-built schools offer the best education. So here I am! But don't lose all faith in me, friend. I believe in a being much higher than you and me. I just don't believe that calling myself a Christian or a Buddhist will help me get any closer to heaven."

Meeting Eun Ju and joining the KLYG would profoundly affect my life in the way I looked at the world and at the way I looked at people. Change was necessary and there were those who sought it with their hearts and souls. Before the first semester ended, Eun Ju and I were inseparable.

* * *

The next two years passed like a wonderful dream of snow and monsoon rains and leaves falling. Every day at the Christian Boys' Academy brought new challenges and new ideas; everything seemed within reach if I kept up my studies, which I did. My family was happy for my changing life, and this happiness spread to their own smiles. Even Mother was finding treasure in everyday things. Grandfather was so thrilled he could hardly get the words out.

"Sei-Young, guess what? Your mother went into your aunt's garden and emerged with a crown of violets in her hair."

"Their perfume will affect her senses," Aunt Sunja testified. "And then her face will relax, and she will tilt her head up and accept the sunshine."

Aunt Sunja was right. I think she knew this because the same thing had happened to her.

Eun Ju and I shared the same goal: to study Political Science at another American missionary-built school in Seoul—Chosun Christian College. We were both accepted on partial scholarships. In order for me to afford the rest of my tuition, I had no choice but to sell my goats and list of clients to Mr. Oh. Truthfully, I no longer had the time to make my milk rounds anyway. But it was hard saying good-bye to my goats, for they were the last link to my rural roots. I was almost eighteen now, but what touches a boy's heart is felt forever.

We walked on the sprawling campus grounds of Chosun Christian College, Eun Ju and I, surrounded by ivy-covered stone buildings, bespectacled students, and a bustling air.

The institution welcomed the Korean Libertarian Youth

Group with open arms. Many of Chosun's alumni, living and dead, had fought for the rights of Koreans during the Japanese Occupation.

"We should post signs for a recruitment meeting," I suggested. "Maybe next week, eh, Eun Ju?"

"The sooner the better," he said, somewhat distracted. "Hey, look over there, Sei-Young."

Eun Ju was pointing across the campus grounds where they connected to another institution—Ewha Women's College. Ewha was Chosun's sister school. A small hill graced with a single willow tree separated us.

"Come on," my friend motioned me.

Equals we were, but Eun Ju was always the leader. I followed him up the hill, acknowledging this. His passion was speaking out and being noticed. Quiet pursuit was mine. So far, they both seemed to get us where we wanted to go in life. When we got to the top of the hill, Eun Ju grabbed his great big thumping heart.

"Women!"

My first semester at Chosun also brought change to the household.

It was a wonderful irony that the Japanese were responsible for resurrecting Grandfather's calling to the ministry. The day he dared to speak back to Officer Akoto was a day that nearly cost him his life. But he survived with an iron determination and a message: "The sanctity of the church must rise above the oppression of all evil powers, including Communism!"

The First Methodist Church, one of Seoul's most recognized churches, heard of the elderly minister who spoke as if he could see where heaven and earth met. The church appointed Grandfather head minister.

"Yes, I can see heaven, but help me to the door, Sei-Young," Grandfather had joked on the morning we moved from Mapo-ku.

Mapo-ku held few memories for me. For two years I had slept and studied there, but my real life, my meaningful life, had been in Seoul. I was very glad to be moving, for the commute was costly and time-consuming.

The First Methodist Church worshipped God through walls of stained-glass windows and pews of pure mahogany. Breathtaking grounds were tended to by a gardener. Though it was the end of autumn, the fragrance of all the past gardens lingered like ghosts. No room here for a Garden of Life. From time to time, Aunt Sunja would return to Mapo-ku, where her hands went back into the earth to feel their own power.

The church quarters where we now lived had sweeping *ondal* floors and many windows that brought in the character of the day. We had the luxury of a sitting room, a prayer room, an eating room, and private sleeping quarters for each of us.

The crown of violets in Mother's hair was long gone but its scent lingered. At last she was healing. It was as if one morning she awoke with a smile on her face, a miraculous smile that did not leave her that day or the next or the next. Sometimes, in the middle of studying or a lecture, I would feel her smile creep onto my own face.

"Sei-Young," she had said, rushing up to me, her face flushed with renewal, "your father would be very proud of you, his First

Son. You are the poem he carved out for you, word for word. I am proud of you, too."

Mother began to make friends at the First Methodist Church. Along with her new friends and of course Aunt Sunja, she transported food and clothing donations to peasants in the countryside. In this way, a look of peace, like another flower, gathered in her smile.

When I was not at school, I was usually studying in the church cellar. It seemed to me I had to study many more hours than Eun Ju, for whom earning good marks was as easy as winning a game of Chinese checkers, even with our course overload which we took in order to graduate a year early. So study I did, although thoughts of Kwan-Young and Father often distracted me.

My desk faced a window whose single ray of light might be an offering from the sun or the moon. I liked it down there, alone with my thoughts and my books. But I was not always alone, as I began to tutor high school students for a modest steady income. Even so, money was tight and my college expenses were mounting.

I needed a job. This time I would not have to comb a monsoon-devastated mountainside. I went directly to the bulletin board outside the president's office. Many job listings were posted and I scanned them all. Errand boy, janitor, typist. One listing caught my eye. *Office assistant position available. Good wages, flexible hours, English skills mandatory. Apply in the English Department. Professor George Stevens, Chairman.*

* * *

The English Department was cramped with tall stacks of books and papers on the desks and even on the floors. The familiar, musty smell put me at ease. There was no one sitting at the secretary's desk, but leaning against it was the American professor speaking Korean to a fellow faculty member. His Korean was nearly flawless and his emotional charge was more than pitch perfect; maybe even a bit baritone and embellished in its delivery. He shook his head with reverent expression and punctuated his lines like a true—maybe even an intoxicated—Korean. The two colleagues laughed and shook hands before parting ways.

I spoke in English. "Professor Stevens?"

He replied in Korean. "Hello, young man, what can I do for you?"

"I am here about the job, sir."

"Good, good! Come into my office."

Professor Stevens pulled up a chair for me, then seated himself behind a large oak desk. He was a pleasant auburn-haired man, not yet middle-aged, with those curious American freckles I had heard about but never seen. Behind him was a wall crowded with framed photographs and diplomas.

Our dialogue had already been established: I spoke English while he spoke Korean.

"My name is Sei-Young Shin. I would like to apply for the office assistant position, if it is still available."

"*Aigoo!* Your English is quite impressive, Sei-Young."

"Not nearly as impressive as your Korean, Professor Stevens."

"No, please. I'm still trying to master the art of Korean inflection. When a Korean tells a story he tells it religiously; with drama; his eyes shut tight; his face moves feverishly up and down." He demonstrated dramatically.

"You look and sound very authentic to me, Professor Stevens."

"I do?"

"My grandfather, who is nearly blind, would not guess you to be American."

"Are you pulling my leg?"

"Am I *what,* sir?"

"What I mean is, are you serious, Sei-Young?"

"Yes."

"Well, then, this interview is over. You're perfect for the job, in my book."

"In *what* book, sir?"

"Sei-Young Shin, you got the job!"

Though my life was ever changing, my life as a young boy working on Suka's farm stayed with me. Sweat and rain brought sprouts, then tomatoes. In some ways, God's earth was simple as a drop of rain. Water, nurture, growth. My little brother was nearby, waiting for me to come home. That seemed so long ago . . . Now I learned how to type letters and take dictation. Soon I would be grading essays where content was second to grammar and spelling. Professor Stevens and I continued our dialogue, each of us speaking in the other's native tongue. Little personal information was exchanged, but within the confines of the English Department, a four-room office with five other professors and one agreeable secretary named Mrs. Kim who introduced me to the joy of chewing gum, I was very comfortable. Professor Stevens let me use the office's carbon paper to make copies of KLYG fliers, for our group had dwindled down to a dozen members. Even Eun Ju—who himself had secured a part-time job working for Chancellor Nanjoon

Paik—and I were finding it hard to find the time to fight for our cause.

The first time I heard Professor Stevens speak English came as a surprise to me. He was on the telephone with his wife, Millie. His American voice was airy and melodic, almost feminine.

"Yes, darling, let's go for a picnic this weekend. I know of a wonderful spot on Namsan."

Amused, I kept typing.

Now I was studying such subjects as commerce and international welfare. My textbooks opened up a new world, an exciting world, but sometimes they took me too far away from my old world, a world I did not want to forget. In a twist of irony, I grew up with the dream of flying away from Nabi; but—along with the notion of the silver bird—I could see the whole picture now; how it wasn't my hometown I wanted to escape, just the poverty that cursed it. There would never be a more beautiful place in my heart than Nabi.

The image of the magnolia tree in full blossom over Kwan-Young's grave came to me on one of the first days of spring. Some things were never-changing. Season after season, the tree would blossom. And season after season, Kwan-Young would lie there forever. A small boy, too small to reach the stars, much less the branches of a magnolia tree.

He would be seven years old now.

Memories flooded me; I closed my textbook; I had to see my brother.

I don't remember the train ride. I only remember being back in Nabi and the silence of streams flowing through mountains. Not all was beautiful, though. My family's abandoned hut had been destroyed by monsoon rains since my last visit. We had always believed the fortress of rocks surrounding the hut had protected us, but perhaps it was not the rocks but our prayers. I came upon Kwan-Young's grave, a small mound of earth for a small boy. It looked just as it did the day we buried him, and the magnolia tree had flourished. Miraculous.

"Hello, Kwan-Young. I am sorry that I do not come here to visit you more often. But I think of you every day. How you hid peanuts in your tiny palm so you could share them with me. How you thought you were safe from the ghost in my bedding." I felt for Grandfather's buried Bible under the cool, damp ground. I felt frantically for it as though I might pick up its heartbeat, any heartbeat.

"My life is very different now, Kwan-Young. My future is bright. But these are still trying times. My schoolwork is very difficult and there are more books to read than hours in the day, it seems. Many nights I fall asleep at my desk. In the morning I wake up more tired than ever."

A petal drifted onto my lap with poetic statement and the whole earth changed. Who was I to complain? Why should I feel sorry for myself? Kwan-Young never even got the chance to read, or chew gum. I shut my selfish eyes with shame.

"I miss you, Kwan-Young."

After I left Kwan-Young's grave, the Valley of Spirits pulled me toward its cliff.

Your mother was right. You are the poem I carved out for you.

"Father, is that you?"

Yes, I am here. Sei-Young, do you keep the birthday gifts I made for you?

"They go wherever I go. I cherish them."

That pleases me.

"Father, what happened to you? We never got word."

Like many, I perished during the war. But that is no longer important, Sei-Young. My earthly existence is over and done with. I am happy where I am.

"Are you always here, in the Valley of Spirits?"

No, I go wherever you go.

"What do you mean?"

I am in the words of your poem, I am in the music of your flute, I am in the howling sound of your pine whistle. I am always with you, Sei-Young. Good-bye, my precious First Son.

The Valley of Spirits grew windy, then hushed. It was time to go.

Before I returned to Seoul, the memory, the lost sight, the ghost of Suka's farm called me.

The farm was just as I remembered. Seemingly untouched by the years. The tomato patch and cornfield and pear orchard could have been frozen in time. Mr. Oh and his farmhands had replaced Mr. Suka and me, but if I squinted hard enough I could make out our silhouettes in the moonlit fields.

"Yes, Shuzo, I am lonely for the life that could have been."

"Mr. Suka," I said quietly, "I hope you found a good life."

Against the peaceful backdrop of flowering hills and lush mountains, South Korean soldiers were marching. We could hear them—along with the threat of war. The year was 1947 and American troops remained in the country. Their task was to train our small Korean army in the event of war. Seoul was less than thirty miles south of the Thirty-eighth Parallel, the line that divided the country, and now the symbol of growing tensions between the North and South. We were nervous. Thirty miles from the Thirty-eighth Parallel felt like footsteps. Life was uncertain for my people as we sought an independent government. But who would come forward to lead us?

Power struggles erupted in the South, on the streets, and on college campuses. Riots prompted by zealous Communist-backed students had resulted in the shutting down of many schools. Now, as a college founded by American missionaries, Chosun was being threatened. In response, many students took to the podium to speak their minds. But they were not delivering the message of the KLYG, which unfortunately had lost its momentum. Instead, these voices shouted with the voice of Communism. On this overcast day, Eun Ju and I were just two faces in a swelling crowd.

There is a great man in the North. Under his government, there will be one class. A class of equality and freedom for all. American capitalism is just a fancy term for slavery! The Americans want to take over our country and take over our lives! We must shut down the school until every last American has left our soil!

"What a horse's ass," Eun Ju muttered.

I, too, was outraged. "This is pure propaganda. Eun Ju, get up there and speak the voice of truth!"

"Why don't *you* get up there and speak the voice of truth?"

Me? I had never spoken in public. "You are the one with the voice, Eun Ju. Not me."

"Who wrote all the speeches for the KLYG?"

"Who delivered them?"

"Handing out flyers and daydreaming at your desk will

never bring about true change, my friend. That's the life of a mouse, quietly scurrying around for a crumb or two. Tomorrow, it's the same story. Speak out, Sei-Young. Roar! Be heard!"

Eun Ju began to push me through the crowd and toward the podium. I resisted.

"Eun Ju, you are the speaker, not me!"

"But, Sei-Young, *you* are the thinker. I've known that since the very first day I spotted you walking on campus. Your big egghead was bursting with so much serious thought I laughed out loud. But I am not laughing today. Tell everyone—tell *me!*—what you are thinking."

I looked into the crowd. As drizzle fell, a sea of eyes swam in mine. *You are the thinker, the thinker, the thinker...* I thought about all of my family's sufferings, sufferings for which there was no cure; I thought about all the hard years it took me to get to this minute in time. No one was going to take that from me. No one.

The next thing I knew I was speaking into the microphone. My amplified voice competed with thunder.

"The words we have just heard are words spoken under the influence of Communism. Believe them for even one minute and we have already lost all hope for freedom." A mixed reaction rippled through the crowd. Eun Ju was pumping his fist in support. "Do not forget the rhetoric we Koreans were forced to listen to under the Japanese Occupation. Do not forget that our culture was slain. We shed our skin and became loyal Japanese subjects, deprived of even the smallest right. We lost our land, our names, our right to a Korean education. In the process, we suffered; each and every one of us. My own father perished. My grandfather was beaten. Now, for the first time in our lifetimes, we are free to choose our own destiny. Freedom is power; the power to learn how to be who we were meant to be. Educated Koreans! To listen to Communist propaganda instead of freedom is an act of suicide. If our college is shut down, we are the ones who will suffer. The Communists want to shut us down, shut all of our doors to freedom. Their definition of equality is oppression. Chosun College must stay open! Our years of sacrifice should not serve as our punishment!"

To a deafening silence I stepped down from the podium. Eun Ju jumped out of the crowd and pulled me back on.

"You have roared, Sei-Young. Now listen."

A cool rain began to fall while thunderous cheers roared back at me. I shivered. My voice had been heard.

SIXTEEN

NORTH, 1947
Heisook

". . . an angel had come for me and I
was only a moment from flight."

MOTHER HAD AN ENVELOPE in her hand. The importance of it
weighed heavily in her eyes.

"Heisook, these are the guide's instructions. Memorize them
as quickly as you can. Then we must be on our way to the train
station."

While Mother secured my knapsack, I opened the envelope
and read what felt like the fate of all my sixteen years.

"We leave on the five-fifteen train this afternoon. Do not be
late. I will not wait for you. We do not know each other; we are
strangers. I will be wearing a black suit and a white scarf around
my neck. Make no eye contact with me. Just follow me, at least
ten footsteps behind. If you fall behind, you are on your own.
There will be police patrolling the train for any suspicious-
looking persons. Take your seat and remain quiet. If you are
stopped and questioned by police, you are on your own. I am

not traveling with you. You are traveling alone. I must keep going. The train will stop in Pyongyang, our destination. A bus will be waiting for us. It will take us into the countryside. From there you will receive further instructions."

I memorized every cold, soulless word, placed the instructions back into the envelope, and handed it back to Mother. She went into her private quarters to hide the evidence—undoubtedly in that place of tragedy, her teakwood chest.

I fell behind Mother on purpose. If I missed the train, if five-fifteen came and went, then maybe I could go back home with her and we could forget all this. When Changi boarded that train three years ago, we never saw each other again.

"Heisook, we must hurry," Mother said. When I caught up with her, her face had turned grave. "If you are questioned by any-one on the train, tell them that you are traveling to Pyongyang to visit your grandmother. Explain that she has fallen ill. She may die at any moment. You are bringing her favorite treats. Do you understand, Heisook?"

Did I?

"Do you understand, Heisook?"

"Yes," I lied.

"Repeat the story back to me."

"I am traveling to Pyongyang to visit my grandmother. She has fallen ill. She may die at any moment. I bring her favorite treats."

"Good. I do not know where you will be when you cross the border, so I do not know how you will get to Seoul. But I am told there will be people who can direct you. When you arrive in Seoul, find a kind-looking person and ask where the Seoul

Presbyterian Church is. Father waits for you there. By then he will have received my letter explaining why I have not come. The money I have given you will cover the cost of bus and train fares and food for many days. One last thing, Heisook: Remember the silk in your knapsack. During your journey, it will be the most valuable possession you own. If you find yourself in a dangerous situation, it may save your life." Her words destroyed her and she choked—"God forbid!"

As we approached the train station, I hoped as hard as I could that the guide would not be there. That seemed possible. After all, even after I had hoped and wished and dreamed that Changi would be waiting for me at the waterfall, he was not there. Maybe there was this universal law that forbade anyone to be where one was supposed to be at waterfalls and train stations. But, no . . . there she was, the guide. Black suit, white scarf. Cold and soulless.

The train whistled. The guide boarded.

Under a sky of uncertainty, Mother and I clasped hands.

"It is time," she spoke.

I would not let go of her hand. Changi had slipped away, then Father. I would not let go of her hand.

"I am afraid, Mother."

Mother looked into my eyes and willed her next words to be true: "You will make it safely across the border."

"No, I am not afraid of that. I am afraid I will never see you again."

She made a promise with lips that had murmured endless unanswered prayers: "Our family will not remain separated, Heisook. Changi and I will join you and Father in Seoul."

The train whistled again. The sky summoned more clouds. Our hands unlocked.

I was boarding the train when I heard Mother cry out—

"I love you, Heisook!"

Before I could turn around to acknowledge her last words, an impatient passenger behind me shoved me onto the train.

I took a seat by the window and spotted Mother looking up at me. Her face bloomed, then withered. The train slowly moved along the tracks until she was gone.

I sat five rows behind the guide. No one sat next to me. The ride was eerily uneventful. In my thankful anonymity, I stared out the window and thought up a *haiku* in my head.

GOOD-BYE, MOTHER

Because the clouds came,
springtime is dark and lonely
and tears fall like rain.

Of course, it was too good to be true. A police officer began to pace up and down the aisle. I was scared, so scared; too paralyzed to blink, tremble, or look up. I kept my eyes to the floor as his footsteps click, click, clicked my way. My hands were clasped, my heart was pounding, and for the first time in years my lips moved in prayer. *Our Father who art in heaven, hallowed be thy name* . . . The shadow of the police officer slowly and torturously passed by. Click, click, click . . . *Thy kingdom come, thy will be done, on earth as it is in heaven* . . . Footsteps again. Click, click, click . . . *Give us this day our daily bread* . . . They slowed down. Click . . . click . . . click . . . The dreaded moment was here . . . *And forgive us our trespasses, as we forgive those who trespass against us; and lead us not into temptation, but deliver us from evil* . . .

"Who are you traveling with?"

"I am traveling alone," I replied, eyes downcast.

"Strange for such a young girl to be traveling alone. What's your destination?"

"I am going to Pyongyang to visit my grandmother."

"So late in the evening?"

"My grandmother has fallen ill. She may die at any moment. I bring her favorite treats."

"Who's coming to meet you at the train station? Surely not your old and feeble grandmother?"

I panicked. Mother had not rehearsed this question with me.

"My brother, who is already there," I blurted.

The officer breathed on my hair. "What is your grand-mother's street address in Pyongyang?"

More panic. I knew no street names in Pyongyang. I had never been there.

"Answer me!" he said.

From some place I could only describe as the place above the stars, I heard the words I would say: "731 Yak Du Road."

The officer stood over me for a merciless eternity. I felt for the stone in my pocket, only to remember that it was gone. No stone. No Changi. No Mother. No Father . . . *For thine is the kingdom and the power and the glory forever.* Finally I heard a series of fading click, click, clicks—and knew that the officer was on his way. I never saw his face. *Amen.*

* * *

Hours later the train came to a halt. Through a speaker the conductor yelled, "Pyongyang!"

The guide slipped off the train and I—ten footsteps behind—followed her to an awaiting bus. To put all my trust in a stranger was a terrifying thought, but she was my only link to my family now. There were no other choices, there was no turning back, ever.

The bright lights of Pyongyang grew dim as we slowly headed into the countryside. The bus was crowded with the smells of strangers; their unwashed flesh and soiled clothes. I closed my eyes and tried to pretend I was back home in my bedding, but the nauseating smells kept me awake. When the bus stopped, the guide got up and I followed her off. So did, one, two, three, four others; and it was then that I realized I was not traveling alone. There was a group of us, following the guide. One was an old man with a mottled complexion; the others were also men ranging from their thirties to forties, I guessed. I was the youngest, and the only female. We did not speak to one another. Now I heard the guide's voice for the first time.

"The rest of the journey we travel on foot. The ten-feet distance between us no longer applies, but I prefer to walk ahead and alone."

Cold and soulless and heartless, too.

We walked along the deserted country road engulfed in silence. We came upon a gated village of smoking rooftop huts; we followed the guide through its open entrance. Something scared me, something like that bat's shadow that once flew across the gate of our house. Everything was too quiet; we arrived here too easily, without incident. The guide stopped in front of a well-lit hut. She knocked on the door in what sounded to me like some sort of secret code. *Rap, rap, rap . . . rap, rap . . . rap.*

The door creaked open. The face behind it, at first glance, was the face of a man so old he frightened me. But no—he wasn't that old, just a weathered peasant whose eyes were crinkled from a lifetime of backbreaking work in the sun. His alarmed expression was a forecast: Something terrible was about to happen. I could feel it all around me like a shower of death. I was right—three armed police officers burst through the door, pushing the man to the ground. Their weapons glinted in the moonlight. One of them shouted, "Raise your hands! All of you!"

I did as I was told. I had no choice, I had no choice, I had no more choices in my life anymore.

Another officer, who looked too young to be armed, ordered us to line up. We did as we were told, as did the guide.

I was first in line, the first to feel his steely weapon press against my forehead. I could blink and it could all be over, but a part of me didn't care anymore. I was so tired of being scared, so weary of wanting to live and wishing to see my family as one. It would never happen.

"What is your name?" I heard him say.

"Sook Ja Chang," I replied.

His finger was poised to pull the trigger. In a moment everything would go black forever. But I was calm; didn't cry or even tremble. My mind and spirit felt light, as though an angel had come for me and I was only a moment from flight.

Go ahead, kill me. I am not afraid of you. I am not afraid to die.

But for some reason he didn't. Instead, he lowered his weapon and proceeded to torture each one in the group the same way. I never looked over but shrieks and incoherent prayers and pleas for mercy pierced my ears. When he was done, he said, "You are all going to jail. Your fates are in the hands of the Police Chief."

The three police officers led us out of the village, forcing us to march like prisoners. Despite the very late hour, villagers lined the unpaved road. To my horror, they spat and threw rocks at us as we marched by.

Traitors! Hang them!

The young police officer, now walking beside me, shouted, "Go back to your huts!"

When the villagers scattered, he addressed me in a way that was oddly both stoic and friendly. "I am sorry to put you through this. But it is my duty."

Was this a trick? I said nothing back to him. Still, he walked protectively close to me the entire length of the village. When we were outside the gate, he spoke to me discreetly.

"Why were you planning to cross the border? If you tell me the truth, everything will be fine."

I did not know who was saying the words I then spoke.

"I lived in Shanghai with my parents. Then I came to live with my sick grandmother and an elderly aunt in Sinuiju. After my grandmother died last winter, I tried to return home, but the guards would not let me leave the country. Word got back to me that my parents are now living in Seoul, and I wished to be reunited with them."

The officer listened, digested, then decided to believe my story. To believe *me*.

"Tell your story to the Police Chief in those exact words

and I will do what I can to convince him you are telling the truth."

The rural police station was crowded with many prisoners awaiting interrogation. What a godless place this was, trafficked with terrified faces and cigarette smoke. The clock on the wall indicated that it was well past midnight, but time—like a prisoner's fate—had no value here. This nightmare went on hour after hour, seven days a week.

The young officer had sat me in a section of the hall, alone. I spotted the guide far down the hall, and I made sure she was always in view. Momentarily her image was blocked by the officer. He was balancing a cot my way.

"My name is Taejun Chung," he whispered while setting up the cot for me. "Please forgive my earlier behavior, Sook Ja. But for each person I catch trying to escape across the border, I am given an allotment of rice for my family. These days, that is a generous offering from the government. Do you understand?"

"Yes, I understand," I replied.

"Sook Ja, you are a very beautiful young woman. Would you ever consider meeting me one Sunday in Sinuiju for a walk, or perhaps a tea snack?"

I would say anything he wanted to hear, especially if it meant sparing my life. "Of course," I said.

"What are your hobbies?" he eagerly asked me.

When he saw that I was too tired to make conversation, he said, "We'll talk of this another time. Get some rest, Sook Ja."

I knew I could not rest. If I fell asleep, the guide might leave without me. But I must have drifted off to sleep anyway, for it was daylight when Taejun stirred me awake.

"Sook Ja, your name is being called. Get up!"

Taejun led me into an office where the Police Chief waited for prisoners like myself behind a messy desk. Taejun bowed to his superior, then stood aside on this note: "Due to this prisoner's unusual situation, I request that she be absolved of the charges set forth, sir."

The Police Chief was a white moon-faced man with eyes like tiny tadpoles. The sneer in his voice made him even uglier. A stupid man, I could tell. "Tell me why you were attempting to cross the border illegally," he said.

Word for word I repeated my story, the story that must have rung true in Taejun's ears. When I finished, the Police Chief began to tap a pencil on his desk. He did not quite believe me.

"So you lived in Shanghai. I know that great city well. What school did you attend?"

I had never visited Shanghai, much less attend a school there. But before panic set in, the word *ichiban*—which means *number one* in Japanese—curiously popped into my head.

"The Ichiban School," I coolly stated.

Before the Police Chief could search his memory, I took a daring chance. "Surely you have heard of the great Ichiban School of Shanghai for the Musically Gifted?" I quizzed him.

A pudgy hand covered his mouth as he foolishly coughed— "Of course I have!"

I lowered my eyes in a fake show of respect. "Of course."

"Miss Chang," he began, "I will release you under one condition. Give me your word that you will return to Sinuiju and never think about crossing the border ever again."

"I give you my word."

"Next time, I promise you, I will not be so kind."

Taejun valiantly escorted me outside the police station.

"Don't be foolish, Sook Ja. What just happened is not a game. Next time you play, you will lose. Please return to Sinuiju," he implored me. "If you are caught again, I cannot help you."

"I will return to Sinuiju," I lied.

"There is a bus twenty meters from here," he pointed. "That will take you to the train station. Do you need money for bus or train fare?"

"No, thank you."

"Allow me to visit you in Sinuiju."

"Of course."

"What is your address, Sook Ja?"

"731 Yak Du Road."

He hurriedly wrote down the address, unaware that this address existed only in my imagination. But it seemed fitting at a time when nothing seemed real anyway.

His last words were said with a look of promise. "I must go. Duty calls. But I shall visit you one Sunday very soon, Miss Sook Ja!"

I watched Taejun catch up with his two comrades. He waved good-bye, then vanished from my sight. I felt sorry for him, right then, for his life and for believing me. But then my attention turned back to me.

What should I do next? What happened to the guide? Only a trickling of people were emerging from the police station, those of us with luckier fates. There was the old man. We made eye contact—*Wait for the guide*. She did appear, barely flashing her eyes—our signal to follow her. There would be no explanation of what happened to the others in the group. If they were to be eventually released, they would discover that she did not wait for them.

The old man and I followed her up a mountainside. The earth was starkly bright and unfriendly. This was nothing like the *san* trail where I had memorized the poetry of every pebble, every bush, every fork in the path—the lovely stumbling upon a great chestnut tree, a forbidden tunnel of trees, and then the glittery vision itself, the waterfall. But this, this was neither a trail nor a path. I bent branches and jumped over bushes, following a guide who never once looked back. We walked for miles to the distant barking of police dogs on the hunt. My first impression of the guide was right. She was cold and soulless, and I realized now that she was not helping anyone cross the border out of good will. This was a job for which people paid her. For which Mother had paid her, handsomely, I was sure. This was strictly business.

When we came upon a shack in the woods, the guide turned to us, her followers.

"We will rest here."

Once again, she knocked on the door in some secret code. *Rap, rap, rap . . . rap . . . rap . . . rap.*

The door creaked open. I held my breath, not knowing what to expect. A man peeked out suspiciously, then quickly ushered us inside. Anxious faces—one woman, three men—looked up at us from straw mats. One of the men kept staring at me like he was trying to remember something; a dream or a memory of which I might have been a part. My mind registered nothing. A young face, honest eyes. But his face, like all of the others, was a stranger's face.

While the guide engaged in a deep discussion with the others, I huddled close to the old man, my silent comrade, and offered him a piece of rice candy from my knapsack. He accepted it with a lost, exhausted nod. I gave him one of my rice cakes. He ate it hungrily.

There was this room, there was the waterfall.

"I have done my part," the guide informed us. What a cold-blooded creature she was. "You have a new guide now. He will lead you across the border."

The man who had opened the door for us would be the new guide. He came over to us with bedding and a smile so kind my eyes watered.

"We must wait until the sun goes down before we go on, okay? Take this time to get some sleep. The border is only five miles away, but the going is slow. A warning, my friends—this is the most dangerous part of the journey."

As a blue dusk settled over the mountain, we embarked on what the new guide had called the most dangerous part of the journey. There were seven in our group now, including the old man and myself. We traveled up a mountainside so steep all I saw was sky.

By now I felt so far from home, from Sinuiju, even the name sounded mythical. *Sinuiju.* The weight of Mother's silk in my knapsack was all I had of her now.

The old man was trailing behind the group. I feared he had used up all of his energy the day before. I kept turning around, hoping he would catch up with us, but no, he just kept falling farther behind. The guide realized this and slowed down until the old man, out of breath, finally caught up with us. I liked and trusted this guide; his words, his shadow.

"Now we should all rest," he whispered.

I remember opening my knapsack and sharing a persimmon and jelly candy and sesame crackers with the others. They, too, shared their food. I remember my hunger swelling as I took a taste of dried fish and an apple. I remember the face of the young man still smiling at me with recognition through the growing darkness. But before I knew it—

"Miss! Miss! Wake up, miss! Our rest is over!"

I had fallen fast asleep on the hard ground; the old man was trying to awaken me.

Soon I was back on my feet. We climbed, creeping our way across steep, narrow ledges. Police dogs were nearby and my ears exploded with fear. Had we come so close only to be trapped by dogs?

"Quickly," the guide was saying, "we must move quickly."

Everyone quickened his pace except for the old man. He could not keep up. Soon he collapsed with a loud, horrifying groan. I turned around to help him when the guide intercepted.

"Young lady, do not risk your freedom for an old man."

"But we can't leave him," I cried. "He will die here."

"You cannot help him. If you stop now, you risk your life. Every minute you stand here is a minute lost forever. I am moving ahead now. Please follow me. Please!"

I stood there, unable to move. There was the guide, there was the old man. There was freedom, there was freedom lost. Like my country, like my family, everything in me divided. I didn't want to leave an old man sprawled on the mountainside at the mercy of Communist police officers and their blood-sucking dogs. And yet, as I caught up with the others, I knew I had made my choice.

Freedom.

I heard and smelled the river before I saw it. When I saw it, my heart sank. The guide came to a halt and spoke with sorry candor, especially to me.

"You were not told of this last stretch of the journey. Had you known, you would not have had the strength to come this far. But here you are, only fifty meters from the border. As you have probably figured out, this last stretch is the most perilous one. For safety's sake, you must split up." The guide paused, then broke the news to us, his hushed audience. "You must crawl from here to the riverbank, then crouch in the bushes. Listen for my whistle. When you hear it, run into the river and swim—as fast as you can!—to the other side."

He pointed into the mysterious sky where dim lights flashed intermittently. "They will guide you. Look to them as the lights to heaven. Swim with all your might, for every stroke is bringing you closer to freedom. Once you are on the opposite riverbank, you are safely in the South, and you are free. But if between now and then you are caught by Communist soldiers, stop and turn around and beg for mercy. Beg. Otherwise, death may follow. Godspeed to all of you!"

With that, the guide retreated into the darkness forever.

Everyone scattered. I fell to my knees and crawled blindly, not sure where I was going. Police dogs were barking wildly from every direction. I crouched in a cluster of bushes; I waited for the guide's whistle. Time passed; I don't know how long. Then I felt a tap on my shoulder and a voice: "What's the matter with you? Did you not hear the whistle? Run!"

I did not hear the whistle but I ran toward the river anyway. For a split second I was as powerful as God. Nothing could stop me. Except for the earth-shattering sound of gunfire and the enemy.

"Halt or I will kill you!"

I froze. I had been spotted. I would be captured again. No Taejun to help me. No guide to look for. My whole body shuddered with relief when I heard the cry of another, the other woman in the group. Only hours ago she had shared her apple with me.

"Please do not kill me!" she begged him. "I have three children waiting for me in Seoul."

I heard rustling, kicking, moans. More moans and the promise of death before dawn. This would not be my fate.

I ran.

Again, gunfire.

"Halt or I will kill you!"

Either way he would kill me. I knew that like I once knew all my prayers by heart. Either way he would kill me! No, I would not do as the guide had instructed. No, I would not stop and turn around and beg anyone for mercy. I was my own guide now, unleashed by my own instincts. The only way the soldier was going to stop me from crossing the border was to shoot me. I kept running.

More gunfire.

But still I ran, looking for lights. *Lights to heaven, lights to heaven.* I reached the river and dove in with a reckless splash, oblivious to a stitch of bullets hitting the water. *Lights to heaven, lights to heaven.* I swam furiously away, away from everything I had ever known. The Osawa School. The cherry blossom tree. My home in Sinuiju. My home on Heavenly Mountain. A wall of morning glories. The stone on the giant quartz rock. My mother at the train station. My hero Changi, who was not here to say, *"Follow me"* the way he did one day on another river, lit up with different lights.

Halfway there, my legs felt heavy, weighed down by the pull of thrashing waters. How easy it would be to give up now, to go with the flow of death. At least it would be a death of my own choosing; not from the bullet of the enemy. How very easy it would almost be . . . But a wild display of flashing lights drowned all my delusions. This was my signal. I knew freedom was near. So I swam toward those wonderful lights to heaven.

SEVENTEEN

SOUTH, 1947
Heisook

"His embarrassed eyes sought out comfort in his warm drink."

WHEN I REACHED THE riverbank, I collapsed in the awaiting arms of Korean freedom patriots. They wrapped my shivering body in blankets and cheered.

My welcome was cut short when I was handed over to an American soldier. I wanted his sympathy but he had none to give me. I could not say he was evil, just following orders without a speck of emotion. And his orders were to spray my head with a blast of chemicals.

Afterward the soldier handed me back to the Korean freedom patriots. They directed me to an all-night noodle house in a nearby village where several other refugees were heading. I was tired and hungry and wet. Although it was spring, the night air was cold and my clothing froze like ice on my skin.

The noodle house warmed me up with its candle-lit lanterns

and the aroma of scallions bubbling in broth. My eyes fell upon a familiar face.

It was him. The young man from the group, the one who kept staring at me. Now I was staring at him. He sat alone at a table, drinking from a cup. He looked exhausted and deep in thought. For some reason I felt sorry for him. I approached his table.

"Hello," I said.

He looked up. "Hello! I see you made it."

Instantly I recognized his voice. "You were the one who came back for me. It was you, wasn't it?"

"Yes," he said. "But I was afraid you did not make it across the river. And yet here you are, safe and sound."

I made it across the river, but not without consequences. Not safe and sound. I did not even know where I was, or how I would get to Seoul. At that moment I was warm and with company. But whatever awaited me outside this noodle house was a mystery.

"Yes, safe and sound," I said.

Light from a hanging lantern rested on the young man's face and it suddenly occurred to me that he was very handsome. He was also several years older than I, but that was a moot observation, for my swim across the river had aged me with each stroke. I once told my mother I was no longer a child, that the war had taken my childhood from me. But that was a premature thing to say, the outburst of an angry child, I knew that now. Not until I had crossed the river did the child become a woman.

"Why did you risk your life for me?" I asked him.

The young man bit his lip with hesitation. "I used to watch you skate on the Paengma River."

"Oh?" I said, quite shocked.

His embarrassed eyes sought out comfort in his warm drink. "You never saw me."

My skating memories included only two boys, Changi and Minamja. No, I didn't remember this young man, but he could have been one of the boys gliding by me in the blur of many. Yes, he could have been.

"I think I might have seen you," I said.

"You are just saying that," he smiled.

"I am Heisook Pang," I smiled back.

"I am Sun Il Choi."

"Sun Il, did they spray your head, too?"

"Yes, with DDT. Every time I cross the border I am forced to go through their extermination. It's degrading."

"*Every* time you cross the border? Surely you don't mean to tell me that you are like the woman guide?"

"What do you mean, like the woman guide?"

"A businessperson," I said with distaste.

"Miss Heisook," he said, "not all businesspeople are impersonal, as your guide was. The guide who replaced her was a very nice man, I thought. And not everyone who crosses the border does so to leave North Korea. As for myself, I have chosen not to forsake my home."

His tone was somewhat critical, but I did not take offense. How could I? He had saved my life.

"Why do you risk your life to cross the border, Sun Il?"

"For business," he confirmed.

"What kind of business?"

Sun Il held up his knapsack, twice the size of mine. His shaky grip told me it was heavy. "I trade in machinery parts," he said.

They must have been very valuable, worth risking his life for. But then, he was an awfully brave man.

"You must be as hungry as I am. Let us eat," I said.

"I am not hungry," Sun Il said. But it was his empty pockets, not his empty stomach, speaking for him.

"Sun Il, you saved my life. Allow me to express my thanks in the only way I can. I would like to buy you a meal before we go our separate ways."

Over our big steamy bowls of noodle soup, we spoke not of politics or right or wrong, but of our past lives when we were so young we believed we could skate forever on the Paengma River.

As dawn parted the night sky, Sun Il escorted me to a train station which would stop in Seoul in less than an hour, he said. We said our good-byes, knowing that our chance meeting would be our last. All the times we shared the Paengma River without one hello. Now it was good-bye forever. I think if he said he would stay on this side of the river and if he asked me to marry him right then and there, I would have said yes. But he didn't and so I boarded a train headed for Seoul, a standing-room only train, packed with refugees like myself, alone, truly alone.

Seoul was a never-ending city of hills and tall buildings that made Sinuiju seem squat and flat by comparison. The busy streets were noisy from the honks of American cars, not the bells or whistles of bicycles and rickshaws. Historic landmarks stood proudly. But for all of Seoul's glamour, it lacked the flavor of Sinuiju where I could stop by the Bang Bakery and pick out all my favorites and run home with a boxful of treats.

I wandered the streets, lost, homeless, frightened. I opened my knapsack and peered inside to remind myself that I was not a common beggar. There was the silk Mother had given me, now wet and ruined. I walked without direction until I noticed a stately stone church with gardens. How long had it been since I had seen such things of beauty? The midmorning sun warmed my face. Faith—renewed—had brought me this far. Could this be the Seoul Presbyterian Church? My knees weakened as I drew closer, then almost gave out when I read the stone marker—the First Methodist Church. Still, like the splashes of the waterfall, its beauty overwhelmed me. Beckoned me. My footsteps carried me past the iron gate of the church and down a stone path.

At the end of the path stood a white-haired minister in a fine robe, walking with the aid of a wooden cane. I thought of the old man I left on the mountain and realized that my renewed faith was nothing short of selfish, because for all of God's glory, he was left to die, one way or another.

"Who is there?" the minister called out.

I remembered Mother's instructions. *Once in Seoul, find a kind-looking person and ask where the Seoul Presbyterian Church is.*

My soiled appearance made me blush with humility. "Forgive my appearance, Reverend. I have just traveled from the North after a long two-day journey. But I am looking for the Seoul Presbyterian Church."

The way the minister approached me, I could tell he was blind. I took his arm.

"Your kindness is most appreciated," he said in a voice so trusting my knees weakened again. "But I need no guidance. I know these steps by heart. Come this way."

I followed the minister into a courtyard, where my eyes feasted on cherry blossoms in bloom.

"Young lady," he inquired, "who waits for you at the Seoul Presbyterian Church?"

Echoes from the harrowing train episode upset me. *Who? Who? Who's coming to meet you at the train station?* Was that a lifetime or only two days ago? I grew hysterical and cried, "My father, whom I have not seen for two months! He is waiting for me at the Seoul Presbyterian Church, but I do not know where it is! Please help me!"

"Don't worry, the church is not far from here. I will give you directions. But first," he insisted, "you must have a meal."

"Thank you, Reverend, but I must be on my way. I must see my father."

The elderly minister strolled with me to the iron gate, strolled so slowly I could feel his glow warm me with the kindness of humanity. Then he honored my request for directions.

"Good luck to you, young lady!" he called out.

In the midst of statues and still fountains, I stood, not making a sound. The utter quiet of the Seoul Presbyterian Church intimidated me, not to mention its grand presence that dwarfed me. Inside, stained-glass windows etched with life-sized angels arced into the ceiling.

To an empty church hall, I whispered—"Father?"

There was no sermon to be heard or choir in practice. I could have yelled until I was hoarse, but I was afraid the glass might shatter or the angels would disappear.

"Father, are you here?"

"Heisook?"

At first I didn't recognize him. Instead of his usual fine suit, Father was draped in pious cloth. My knees gave out and I fell to the floor with a childish wail.

"Father!"

Father lifted me up so high I joined the angels in the windows, and he sang, "Thank God in heaven you made it. I knew He would bring my precious daughter to me."

Our eyes locked in a silent exchange of stories. Father knew all along that Mother was not coming with me.

Father showed me into a two-room chamber. Later I would learn that he was not the head minister at the church.

"This is my home now," he said. "Our home."

"It's so small," I commented.

"Yes, but comfortable."

Father had made it so. Every corner radiated comfort. A miniature chest supporting framed photographs of our family. A thick colorful silk cushion for praying or meditating. A writing table with a neat stack of ricepaper next to a quill pen. It was home, only smaller.

"I had prayed that your mother would come with you, Heisook. But when I saw you standing in the church alone, I knew she had not changed her mind. Your mother believes it was her calling to stay in Sinuiju and wait for Changi to come home. I have no choice but to respect her wish. But our love for each other is bonded by God; it will survive separation."

"Even a lifetime, Father?"

"It will not be a lifetime, Heisook. My faith confirms this."

Had Father spoken these words to me at another time, I would have screamed and cursed in the name of God. But now, after such a perilous journey, there was nothing left in me. No anger, no surprise. Just one question.

Was faith the answer to survival? Faith had helped Mother from her near-death illnesses. Faith—was it Mother's or mine? —carried me safely across the border in the face of certain danger, when the prospect of punishment or death seemed as imminent as my next breath. Perhaps Mother gave her faith to me, along with her silk.

After a warm sponge bath I fell into my new bedding. When I closed my eyes, I saw those lights to heaven. They guided me to a deep, deep sleep.

EIGHTEEN

SOUTH, 1947–1949
Sei-Young

*"I knew what a dream was, but a destiny sounded bigger,
like the meaning of all the dreams put together."*

THAT SPRING TERM, CHOSUN Christian College remained open.
Many students supported the message in my speech. But like a
changing sky, the threat of shutdown still loomed over our campus. At other colleges, demonstrations had led to riots, and eventually their doors were closed.

"You are no longer Mr. Egghead on campus," Eun Ju
slapped me on the back. "Everyone is talking about the famous
Sei-Young Shin."

"Who calls me Mr. Egghead?"

Eun Ju shrugged. "Me, I guess."

"And who calls me famous? I have delivered only one
speech, Eun Ju."

"It only takes one good speech to become famous. Listen, a
lifetime of hot air adds up to nothing. But you need more than
one speech to stay famous, to stay alive in the minds of your lis-

teners, your followers. You must give many speeches, each one more inspiring and delivered with more fire than the last. Sometimes it's not so much the words you say as it is the way you say them. So say them like you feel them. But don't overdo it. Never cry. Then you're a dead man."

"Why me?" I protested. "Why not you?"

"I'm happier being in the background, it gives me time to do other things, like making fun of you and chasing women. Besides"—he grew serious—"it is your destiny, Sei-Young."

My destiny. I wasn't sure what destiny was. I knew what a dream was, but a destiny sounded bigger, like the meaning of all the dreams put together. I wasn't convinced this was my destiny. But it was my duty.

There were more speeches and more cheers, but not everyone in the crowd was happy. Some yelled and booed; a few, under the Communist spell, waved knives in defiance. It wasn't too long before notes found their way into my books.

Keep your words to yourself, Sei-Young Shin. Speak out from the podium again, and they will be your last . . .

Not just notes. Death threats.

Eun Ju stepped forward with three of our former KLYG comrades and let their presence be known.

"We are Sei-Young Shin's officially appointed bodyguards. Anyone who wants to get to him has to get past us, and that will not be a pretty task."

Eun Ju enjoyed his new role of thwarting the enemy behind the scenes. It brought out the bully side of his character, which was fine as long as he was on my side. Amidst the murky political climate, we were creating anti-Communist waves on our campus, and Eun Ju rode them high. He liked a good fight when the fight was for freedom.

In the church cellar, a lantern burned beside me, casting light on my pen and paper. What more could I say that had not already been said?

We all suffered during the Japanese Occupation. Many of us lost loved ones during the war effort. The pain is greater than the sum of our souls. But after nearly forty years of oppression, our country is on the verge of being returned to us. Do we drown in our own bitter tears or do we move forward with education? Let us not sabotage what we have dreamed of all of our lives. Freedom. Our time has come, and it is our duty to decide the fate of our country. Some of you may question the American presence in our country. Are their efforts simply for their own global advancement? Perhaps. But this can only advance our people as well as we try to catch up with the enlightened age of the twentieth century. The enlightened age of freedom! Remember, many Koreans are risking their lives as they attempt to escape from the Communist regime in the North, even as I speak these words . . .

The following morning I found Grandfather standing at the gate. He seemed to be waiting for someone or listening for something.

"What is it, Grandfather?"

He looked at me, as though from a dream. "A young lady was just here, looking for her father."

"Oh?"

"Like so many, she was just another refugee. But I sensed a lovely, stricken angel."

Grandfather's choice of words surprised me. The young lady must have touched his soul.

"I also sense that I will hear her footsteps come this way again," he smiled, as though the dream was over. "On your way to school, Sei-Young?"

"Yes, I'm meeting Eun Ju before my morning class. I always read my speeches to him before I actually deliver them. He gets all heated up and that starts a fire in me."

"And you need that fire, don't you?"

"Yes!"

"You make your mother and aunt and me burst with pride, Sei-Young. For all you do, and for all you will do in the future."

Like a farm needs rain, I still needed Grandfather's words. In some respects we walked on different paths in different worlds now. But when we came together, we still walked together, in sync, on a slowly moving earth. I drank every word Grandfather spoke like a pure drop of wisdom.

"The Steps" was a gathering spot for Chosun students, located on the steps to the library. Ah, there was Eun Ju. My trusted friend was alone, oblivious to the conversations around him. He was waiting for me, as usual. At the Christian Boys' Academy, Eun Ju seemed larger than life. Eun Ju Chun, the cocky leader of the KLYG. In his presence, everyone moved aside. Now the colossal campus of Chosun diminished him and who he was. He waved at me, lost in the crowd, and I was reminded of Father, a man who was larger than he appeared. So many years Father worked the streets of Seoul without a

thought or probably a glimpse of Chosun. In all his years of peddling, he never climbed the Steps with his cart or peered into the
library. The thought of an education never entered his dreams.
But wasn't it Eun Ju who said that to study art was to ruin art?
Put that way, there was nothing to feel depressed about. Father
chose his path and he lived his life under the circumstances of
the time. Period.

Eun Ju waved."Hey. Over here!"

My friend, so eager to set me on fire, elected to stay in my
shadow. Sometimes I thought it should be Eun Ju up on the
podium, not me. He had qualities that made him unforgettable.
Charisma, intelligence, energy. But he didn't want to feel confined to writing speeches; he needed more room for other inter-
ests. That included courting an impressive number of college
women from Ewha. None had stolen his heart, he complained.
It was obvious he wasn't ready to give it away. Once he had
humorously inquired—

"Who steals your heart, Sei-Young?"

"No one," I had denied.

"What are you, a eunuch? Out of all the Ewha girls, there
must be at least one you dream of in that egghead of yours."

"Well . . ."

"Who?" Eun Ju had jumped. "Tell me who she is and I will
have her in your arms by nightfall."

I did not know her name, but I had seen her on Eun Ju's arm.
"She sometimes wears a beautiful red silk dress."

"Oh, God! Not Miyung Cho?"

"Why not? What's wrong with her?"

"She's a whore! She sleeps with any man who will have
her."

"I didn't know . . ."

"Sei-Young, you want a woman of virtue and intellect. How about Jahei Min?"

Jahei Min was certainly a woman of virtue and intellect, dictated by thick black eyeglasses and mannish shoes. "I don't think so," I said.

"Why not? Just because she wears eyeglasses?"

"No."

"Well then, is it because she is cross-eyed?"

"No!"

"Sei-Young, there is nothing wrong with a plain-faced girl. In my opinion, you and Jahei would make the perfect pair. Mr. and Mrs. Egghead," he had merrily declared.

Now Eun Ju studied my speech, grunting, shaking his fist, ready for a fight. I was on fire again.

The next two years brought many changes to the South. In the summer of 1948 the National Assembly elected Syngman Rhee into office as Korea's first President. We adopted a new name—the Republic of Korea. We had organized a new government, severing ties with the North. But we did not give up hope for reunification, even when the ROK Military was conceived. Many of my peers forsook their studies to join our dubious military. Dubious because the ROK Military lacked the necessary training to fight a real war, if it came to that. Americans wanted to leave our country as much as some Koreans wanted the foreigners gone. But they would stay until the ROK Military was strong and our security intact.

Not all Koreans were supporters of our new leader. Because the elderly politician had spent a good deal of his life in America, some Koreans questioned his loyalty to our country.

Resentment over his Austrian wife, Francesca, living comfortably in the presidential home, also known as the Blue House, made Syngman Rhee all the more controversial.

Still, I was a Rhee supporter. He was Christian and anti-Communist. He was a crusader who represented change in the right direction. Rhee had spent much of his life fighting not only the Japanese for Korean independence, but earlier on, for citizens' rights during the Korean monarchy. Sometimes I would find myself daydreaming of working for him in his office, phones ringing, urgent telegrams being received, officials in and out, all in the name of the words I was delivering.

At Chosun, where our fate had hung in a strange limbo, I had continued in my role as orator to a mixed crowd until the autumn of 1948. With Rhee in office, we saw the end of campus shutdowns.

Over the next year, both Eun Ju and I continued our part-time jobs at the college. Eun Ju might not admit it, but he thrived in the dynamic office atmosphere. Like the Ford convertible he dreamed of driving, it kept his motor running. In the office of the chancellor, it was easy to eavesdrop on the academic opinion of the day. Much like the state of our country, conflict arose between the faculty when it came to Princeton-educated Syngman Rhee. Some accused him of being less Korean and more American, all for the sake of American support. Others felt that a leader of worldly vision was better than a hermetic one.

I sat on the Steps one late afternoon taking in the glorious autumn season of 1949, along with dozens of other students. Today the sky was pure theater and we were its audience.

I spotted Eun Ju walking across the fiery-tinged campus

grounds. With him were Chancellor Paik, and a woman of unmistakable stature. Likewise, Eun Ju spotted me.

"Hey! Sei-Young!"

The eyes of Chancellor Paik and the woman were now on me. I waved with hesitation. I wasn't sure if it was appropriate for me to join them. My invitation came when the chancellor waved back.

"Nice to see you, Chancellor Paik," I said, bowing to both him and the woman.

Chancellor Paik was an amiable man with a receding hairline and a leisurely gait. Despite his position, I always felt immediately at ease with him. We had met on many occasions and he never failed to mention that I had done the school a great service by speaking out in favor of keeping Chosun open.

"Sei-Young Shin, meet the honorable Maria Park, dean of the School of Liberal Arts at Ewha Women's College," he said.

By name, Maria Park was no stranger to anyone on or off campus. Aside from her position at Ewha, she was the wife of the prominent Kibung Yi, Rhee's chief-of-staff. Her commanding character was made clear by her straight back and forthright handshake. She was frail-boned yet intimidating. Masculine, almost, except for a smattering of pale freckles that ran across the bridge of her nose. Eun Ju would later joke that Maria Park picked up this typically Caucasian feature in Boston where she attended college, and where she adopted her Western name. One could see that she had traveled abroad and returned a woman of the world.

I bowed nervously. "I am honored to meet you."

She studied my face, then said, "I have heard you speak, young man. Do you write your own speeches?"

"Word for word!" Eun Ju said.

She shot Eun Ju a rather icy look.

"Yes, I do," I replied.

"Most impressive," she nodded. "Tell me, Sei-Young, what are your goals?"

Once a farmer named Mr. Suka and I had shared our hopes, but that was a long, long time ago, when the possibility of a dream coming true was further than the moon from the fields. My goals today were more concrete, without the seduction of the night sky. With speechlike conviction, I delivered my reply. "My immediate goal is to obtain my bachelor of arts in political science, put my skills to work in President Rhee's office, and eventually become a diplomat."

Eun Ju's mouth dropped. "Huh?"

Chancellor Paik exclaimed, "Oh?"

"That is certainly a lofty dream," Maria Park said. "But working in President Rhee's office requires many qualifications."

"I have many qualifications. I write speeches, I type, and I speak English. Plus, I am well versed in foreign policy."

My assertiveness took both Eun Ju and myself by surprise.

Maria Park did not say a word. Her impression of me was hard to read. My guess was that it was either very good or very bad. Finally she said, "It was fine meeting you, Sei-Young Shin."

Two days later the English Department received a memorandum from Dean Maria Park's office addressed to me. Chairman Stevens lingered curiously while I read it.

To: Sei-Young Shin
From: Dean Maria Park
Date: October 11, 1949
Re: Appointment

*I would like to see you in my office this afternoon
at five o'clock. Be prompt.*

"You have a rendezvous with fate," Chairman Stevens said
with a flair foreign to the Korean language.

"Yes . . ." I said.

Eun Ju was overjoyed to usher me to Dean Park's office.

"You need your bodyguard, after all. These Ewha women
are animals, Sei-Young. And you're a famous man. You need my
protection. Who knows? If any woman tries to molest you,
they'll have to take me on first."

I was too nervous to joke around. Eun Ju knew I didn't need
a bodyguard right now, just his moral support. As we stepped
onto the Ewha campus, he put his arm on my shoulder.

"Kidding aside, Sei-Young, you have left an indelible impression on Maria Park. She is asking to see you for a very important
reason." A pretty student caught Eun Ju's attention. "I leave you
now, my friend," he said, following her. "Good luck!"

A secretary showed me into the dean's office. Like Maria
Park herself, the office was scholarly, worldly, intimidating.
There were countless photographs of her and her husband at
political functions. Books everywhere, authored by Americans.
Hemingway, Faulkner, Fitzgerald. Just being in this room
excited me.

"Dean Park will be in shortly," the secretary informed me.

Five minutes, ten minutes, fifteen minutes passed. Then the
dean stormed in, her posture stooped from an armload of books
and papers.

"Pardon my tardiness, Sei-Young. My interview with the

Hanguk Ilbo took longer than I had anticipated. The reporter asked too many questions, hoping he would hear the response he wanted to print. Of course, I did not give him that satisfaction. Anyway, let me get to the point." She seated herself behind her desk and folded her hands together. Despite her obvious iron will, her hands looked very delicate, as though even a pen would weigh them down. "Having listened to your speeches last year, I believe our views on the future of the Republic of Korea are quite similar. So! I am scheduled to give a speech at a faculty meeting to be held the day after next. The topic is 'Education in Our New Nation.' I would like you to write my speech and I would like it to be ready tomorrow."

"*Tomorrow?*"

"Yes, tomorrow. I'll need time to review it and make changes, possibly. I'm not going to say anything I don't want to say, after all. Are you up to the task, Sei-Young?"

When I didn't respond right away, she repeated, "Are you up to the task, Sei-Young?"

"Yes," I replied.

"Very well," she said. "I will see you in my office first thing tomorrow morning."

While Seoul slept, I worked on Maria Park's speech in the church cellar. She did not speak as I spoke; it was imperative that the words reflected this. Eun Ju's opinion was that this task was about much more than a speech, that Dean Park was putting me to a test for reasons presently unknown. I had to agree with my friend who, for all his clowning around, never strayed from the serious points in life. I was writing this speech not simply for a speech's sake. But I was in no position to ask why. And so, with no further questions, I began to draft "Education in Our New Nation."

At eight o'clock sharp the following morning I walked into Dean Park's office, speech in hand. This time she was waiting for me.

"Your promptness indicates that you are confident of your speech, Sei-Young," she said.

"Yes," I said. "But even more important is that you must be confident of it, Dean Park."

"Agreed," she said, putting on a pair of reading glasses. "Sit down."

I sat down and watched her as she read my speech. I was confident, but I was nervous, too. Her face was stone—did she like it or not? When she finished, the words of praise I had hoped for did not come. Instead, she handed the speech back to me.

"I don't understand . . ." I said.

Maria Park took off her glasses and rubbed her eyes as if the night before brought little sleep.

"Your speech is superb," she said in an understated way. "But tell me, can you translate this into English?"

"Yes," I replied. "I think I can."

Scorn crossed her face. "You *think* you can or you *know* you can? Such uncertainty is not a trait for a future diplomat, no matter how well versed you are in foreign policy. Either you can or you cannot translate this speech into English."

"I can," I said, standing up.

"Very well," she said, looking more satisfied, but not convinced. "I will see you in exactly twenty-four hours."

I bowed good-bye, once again, speech in hand.

* * *

Luckily, my schedule was light that day. Only two classes—Ancient Korean History and World Religion. I had never missed a class before, but this was for a worthy cause. Not that I even knew the cause, but I was certain it was worthy. Maria Park would not have asked me to write and translate a speech for no reason.

To translate "Education in Our New Nation" might only take an hour—but a special hour, an hour enveloped in inspiration. My task was not just a matter of translating Korean words into English words. Were that the case, I would not have to miss my classes. Yet every language had its own poetry. Where would I find the poetry for this speech?

Under a bare magnolia tree where Kwan-Young lay, all the identities I had earned up until now—college student, orator, assistant to Chairman Stevens, best friend of Eun Ju Chun—were stripped away like leaves off a tree. Here in Nabi, right now, I was merely *hyong nim*. No, not merely. Eternally. I was eternally *hyong nim*. I remembered Mother's words—*God took Kwan-Young from us because He wanted someone small and special by his side. My son, your brother.* Yes, someone small and special. Yes, that was my brother. One monsoon-plagued night when I was a boy and he was a baby, I vowed to take care of him. Now I was a man and I needed him near me. Small shadow, big shadow.

"Kwan-Young!" I called out. "Kwan-Young!" I called out again.

Then his essence—who he was then, now and forever—came to me and guided me so that together we found the poetry.

Education in Our New Nation

Four years ago, Korea divided. We lost half our land and a great many resources. Our economy was on the brink of collapse. But in the spirit of brave soldiers, we moved forward and created the Republic of Korea. Picture our new nation laid out like a vast, virginal farm. Imagine that this farm can harvest freedom.

Most of you know that I have studied abroad in America. I have tasted the fruits of freedom and they are most delicious. Very few of our generation had the luxury I was fortunate enough to have. Now it is time to look toward the next generation. Our children and young adults are our seeds of hope for freedom. But they need to be planted. They need to be watered. They need education. Only then will the farm of freedom, our new nation—the Republic of Korea—flourish . . .

Afterward, I spoke to Kwan-Young until the day grew dark and I heard him say, "*Hyong nim, it is time for you to go home now.*"

I arrived at Maria Park's office the following morning, speech in hand. She looked somewhat more refreshed than yesterday.

"I am eager to see what you have done," she said, putting on her reading glasses.

I was more nervous than ever, for it was true that one person's inspiration can make the next person yawn. People did not see the world through the same pair of eyes. My beloved brother's soul helped me breathe poetry into this speech. But who was Kwan-Young Shin to Dean Maria Park? Could she hear its poetry? Her critical expression from one line to the next worried me.

"This is fine work," she said in a tone just short of praise. She leaned forward and met my eyes. "But can you converse in English, Sei-Young? There is a world of difference between writing a language and speaking it."

Dean Park's lack of praise for my efforts made me feel bold enough to reply in English. She listened with controlled surprise.

"I chat with Chairman Stevens in his native tongue every day while he chats back in his perfect Korean. I've worked for him for about two years now and our friendship has grown. We sometimes drink English tea when the afternoon is late and most of the students have left the campus. We talk about politics and religion and philosophy. He likes a good debate and I like to watch him become hot and heated like all true Korean men. He always jokes about being raised on a Nebraska farm, but I suppose one has to be American to understand that."

Dean Park blinked with composure and said, "Thank you. That will be all, Sei-Young."

That's when she granted me her first smile. It was a tiny one, but I took it and left her office.

NINETEEN

SOUTH, 1949–1950
Heisook

"I left my flute in Sinuiju, along with my mother."

AUTUMN DELIVERED WINDS AND leaves to Seoul, but no letters from Mother.

"Heightening tensions along the Thirty-eighth Parallel have thwarted many fleeing south," Father reported to me, directly from the *Hanguk Ilbo*. Reading the newspaper was his favorite pastime these days. He would lose himself in the pages for hours, not hearing me come and go. "But Communists continue to infiltrate the South, disguised as refugees."

After the end of World War II, newpapers and radios and journals in the South became free presses. Koreans were starved for information and devoured every word.

In the two-room chamber we called home, the only privacy we had was the privacy of our thoughts. Every evening Father would be at his desk, closed up like one of Changi's morning glories at nightfall. In that state he would write to Mother. How many letters had he written? One for every day they had been apart. None were answered, or at least none were delivered to us. Like their Japanese predecessors, the Communists were monitoring all mail coming in and out of the North. In his heart, Father believed that some of his letters had eventually found their way to Mother. Still, he grew sad. He began to speak frequently of the past now. Of his and Mother's first meeting—a tea ceremony at her parents' house, for it was a planned marriage. About their life together in China; knocking at huts and visiting orphanages and praying with a hot sun beating down on their bent heads. He began to talk a lot about Changi, too. So many stories. As with his letters, there was one for every day. Like the time my parents lost Changi on the streets of Shanghai.

"We couldn't keep up with a three-year-old. How he could run. Even then he was running away from us."

"Where did you find him, Father?"

"Oh, he was playing marbles with a group of street children. Our Changi was a character before he was knee high."

No matter how many stories Father told me, they never included Changsil, the brother I never knew.

Of course, I wrote Mother, too. Details of my journey south were never mentioned.

"Word might get back to that Police Chief and officer who released you," Father said. "If so, they could seek revenge on your mother."

I would rather not think about them or my journey anymore, anyway. I would rather tell Mother how much I missed her. I held on to her ruined silk and held it up to my heart every night, remembering how emotional she became when she said, *If you find yourself in a dangerous situation, it may save your life.* I told Mother how sorry I was for once blurting out that I hated her; of course I loved her more than any daughter could love a mother. I told her how comfortable life was for me at the Seoul Presbyterian Church. I told her I sat through every one of Father's sermons, which were held on Wednesday, Saturday, and Sunday evenings—with now unwavering faith that we would see each other again. The last part was not completely true. I did have faith—sometimes.

Father hired a tutor to help prepare me for the entrance board exam to Ewha Women's College in Seoul.

"It is imperative that you continue your education," he said.

"But, Father, I have not even graduated from high school."

"There are new rules which make allowances for students like you whose studies were interrupted by forces beyond your control. Now that you have reached the age of eighteen, you will be granted freshman status at Ewha, if you pass the entrance board exam."

I obeyed Father's wishes. My tutor was Mrs. Han, a stout widow who preferred the company of anyone, even a reluctant student like me, to solitude. Six hours a day, six days a week. By noon I always felt headachy.

If only I could escape to the Korean Playhouse on Myung Street. For the past two years, the theater had been my sole source of happiness. The experience of watching a play came as close to the magic of the waterfall as I was going to get here. Like Father with his newspaper, I would lose myself in the current production, pretending it was all real, and forgetting the life I was living. My heart would pound, my eyes would water.

Every late afternoon, for an hour or two, I would come alive in the roles of the actors who painted their faces and draped themselves in lavish silk and sauntered across stage. My favorite play was *Queen Min*. Queen Min was a controversial political figure in Korean history, often remembered as a self-serving royal who wouldn't lift a jeweled finger for the plight of the commoners. Still, she was Korea's last queen and she died at the hands of the Japanese, so I considered her a half-heroine.

Father cried—"Heisook! Heisook, come here!"

In his trembling hands was a letter. We knew who it was from. The postmark was smeared.

"Open it, Father. Please!"

But he couldn't. The man who had smuggled rice past police guards at the risk of imprisonment could not open Mother's letter. There was too much at stake here.

So I did. My fingers shook so violently it seemed to take me hours to tear open the letter. Father breathed fitfully over my shoulder. Our hearts fell when we realized the date of its creation—September 2, 1947. Silently, we read Mother's two-year-old letter.

Dearest Sogho:

Every evening before I go to sleep, I write one letter to you, and one letter to Heisook. In one hand I hold my pen, in the other I hold my cross.

I pray your eyes will read these words. For I have yet to receive a single letter from you or from Heisook. But faith— the same faith that keeps me waiting for our son—tells me that our daughter is with you. For three months after I put

Heisook on that train, I spent every day at Sacred Hearts in the fourth-floor private room. That was the one closest to heaven—remember how we always said that? And I would pray and pray and pray that she made it safely across the border and found you.

Then Sacred Hearts closed down. A Communist doing, of course. When anger wells up in me, I do my best to quiet it with a warm cup of tea and let my wonderful memories of my family come back to me. And I remind myself that this is only a temporary situation. Each time the sun rises I tell myself, this could be the day our family will be reunited.

Please know that I am well, Sogho. I keep busy at the Adol Orphanage, which mercifully has remained open.

Please take care of our Heisook. Make sure that she eats well. My hope is that her faith has returned and that she will continue her studies.

Sogho, I miss you more. Be well!

> *All my love,*
> *Eunook*

Father grew infinitely sad that day. Almost like he walked into a windowless room and didn't come out. Father was not a man of conceit by any means, but in Sinuiju he was always a man of stature. Here in Seoul everything was different. No one knew him; few listened. What got him through each day was very much like Mother's sentiments in a letter that happened to slip through the Communist hands—this could be the day of reunification. But for how long could one keep living this way? Did hope die after a certain length of time?

Words written two years ago. They told me nothing about

what Mother was doing today. Who brought spring water to her bedside when she fell ill? Did she just lie there in the dark, clutching her cross?

I entered Ewha Women's College that fall semester, studying music and literature with renewed interest. I cultivated friendships and engaged in many activities like volleyball and tango dance lessons. But the sadness lingered. I kept this sadness a secret from everyone, even from my best friend Mihei Hong, a sophomore. She came from a loud, happy household of five sisters and four brothers, countless aunts and uncles and nieces and nephews coming over and making the laughter louder. She could not share in my sadness.

While I walked through a cloud of sadness, I never forgot the First Methodist Church. In the mornings on my way to Ewha, I would take the long route—that way I could pass by the church—and slow down with curious intrigue, not really knowing why. I would forget my sadness for a moment as I peered through the iron gate and into the courtyard, hoping to catch sight of the elderly minister. But when I didn't see him, the sadness would return.

Lately, a Chosun brother had made a point of meeting me each morning at the entrance to Ewha and walking me to my first class. He had introduced himself to me a few weeks earlier.

"I am Eun Ju Chun. My best friend, Sei-Young Shin, is on his way to a very important meeting with Dean Park," he said in a boastful manner.

When I reacted with no more than a disinterested stare, he said—

"You do know who Sei-Young Shin is, don't you?"

"No, why should I?"

"Because he is the famous orator from Chosun," he bragged. "When he speaks of freedom, tears form in even the angriest eyes. My association with him brings me respect, but danger too, sometimes."

His face looked contorted. Was he crazy? I didn't know whether to laugh at him or run away. Instead, I walked away with dismissive words.

"I do not listen to any orators, famous or not. My ears still sting from all the lies I've heard. No orator can help me or my situation."

After that, Eun Ju considered us friends.

Mihei shuddered with distaste every time she saw me walking with Eun Ju.

"He looks like a gangster. How can you stand him? Tell him to go away."

I think Mihei was a little jealous that Eun Ju barely said hello to her whenever our paths crossed. But I never said anything when she made her nasty comments. I didn't want to start an argument or hurt Mihei's feelings.

Not that I was interested in Eun Ju. He didn't possess the qualities I hoped for in a man. He was nothing like Minamja or Sun Il. Two attractive young men who would surely bring me flowers every day, if only fate had been kind enough to step in. Mihei had a point; Eun Ju was more the gangster than the gentleman. Still, I didn't really want him to go away. He could be amusing and I didn't mind being walked to class. I liked the company.

One afternoon Mihei surprised me from behind and hooked her arm in mine. We walked across campus.

"Heisook, have you heard?"

"Heard what?"

"Eun Ju," she whispered giddily, "visits the whorehouse."

"No!"

"What kind of bodyguard could he possibly be to Sei-Young Shin when he's busy visiting the whorehouse?"

"Tell me more about this Sei-Young Shin I keep hearing about."

"He's only the most famous man on Chosun's campus."

"Eun Ju seems to think he's a god."

"I don't know about that, but he gives a good speech."

"Mihei, why haven't I heard one?"

"Because you're only a freshman, Heisook. Last year and the year before when all the colleges were demonstrating and shutting down, Chosun was alive and buzzing with the sound of speeches. Some were from the mouths of Communists, they say, who wanted to start riots. But when Sei-Young Shin got up on the podium, everyone listened because his message of freedom made a lot of sense. Because of him, Chosun remained open. That's what everyone says."

"But why did Sei-Young Shin need a bodyguard?"

"People wanted to kill him."

"Who?"

"Communists. There was a story floating around that one student stepped forward after hearing him speak. He admitted that he had been brainwashed with Communist lies; he didn't really understand what he got himself into, he just wanted to be part of some group. Anyway, he was so moved by the speech that he came forward and admitted that he had been ordered to kill Sei-Young, but now he was joining him in the fight for freedom. Can you believe that?"

Sei-Young Shin sounded like a man of much courage, the sort of man I would like to meet and size up for myself. But his affiliation with Eun Ju Chun made me uneasy.

"Does Sei-Young Shin visit the whorehouse, too?" I asked my friend.

Mihei laughed so hard her arm unhooked from mine and she dropped her notebook.

"Sei-Young Shin? Oh, please. That egghead?"

The sun parted the clouds after a passing spring shower, and Seoul was shrouded in mist. On my way to school I stopped in front of the First Methodist Church. When I opened the gate and stepped in, the act of once sneaking into Mother's teakwood chest flooded back to me. I let out a small cry.

The urge to re-enter the church grounds, to once again walk upon the stone path, had no explanation. It was more than an urge. I felt summoned by the time of year, the memory of the elderly minister whose aura had haunted me for the past three years. Like the mist around me, I half-wondered whether I had invented him—or his aura—at a moment of postjourney trauma when he seemed to symbolize the opposite of any harm that could come my way.

Then I saw him. Yes, he was real. The sun was beaming down on his face. Only then did I remember that he was blind. He spoke out: "Who is there?"

"Hello, Reverend. I'm sure you wouldn't remember me, but

three years ago, when I had just escaped across the border, you were kind enough to give me directions to the Seoul Presbyterian Church."

"Many times I have wondered what happened to you and whether you found your father that day. Did you, young lady?"

"Yes, I did."

"Good. I am Reverend Shin," he introduced himself.

"I am Heisook Pang," I bowed honorably.

It seemed like such a natural thing to do as we strolled together into the courtyard. Spring in full bloom arced over me like a rainbow from a lustrous painting.

"On my last day in my hometown, I played my flute under my favorite cherry blossom tree," I told him. "I do not know whether I shall ever be able to go back there."

"Where is your hometown, Heisook?"

"Sinuiju—Reverend, have you ever been there?"

"No, I'm afraid not."

"Oh," I said, so disappointed.

"I hope you will once again play your flute under that very tree, Heisook. And that the music will celebrate the sovereignty of our country. In the meantime, I would be most honored if you would play for me one day."

My voice broke as I said, "I cannot. I left my flute in Sinuiju, along with my mother."

"Have faith that God will soon reunite Korea and reunite you with your mother."

Could he read my mind? For he added, "During trying times, faith will waiver. But God still lives within you, Heisook. Remember that."

"My brother Changi never returned home from war," I said, shriveling with grief at the sound of his name, for it had been so long since I had heard myself say it. *Changi, Changi, Changi.* "I may never see my mother again. I never knew the brother who died before I was born. With all due respect, Reverend, it is hard to keep faith, even when it has come to my rescue."

Reverend Shin's blind eyes watered for me and for all Koreans who had suffered personal losses. "Do not think that those who have left this world are less fortunate," he said. "You and I are no more fortunate because we are here. I have lost a son and a grandson. In life we all suffer, Heisook, whether it is for a hundred days or a hundred years. But a better place awaits us all."

"Forgive me, but I'm not sure I believe that to be true," I said.

"Wait here," Reverend Shin said. Then he crossed the courtyard and went into the church.

While he was gone, I inhaled the fragrance of cherry blossoms, closed my eyes, and remembered all that I had lost.

Reverend Shin returned. In his palms lay a most lovely flute.

"Play for me," he requested. "Play for both of us."

I stared at the flute, too afraid to touch it.

"I have forgotten how to play. It has been so long."

"Bring the instrument to your lips, Heisook. The magic will return," he assured me.

The flute in my hands felt strange at first. Surely I could no longer play. My fingers studied its ornate engraving. My eyes danced over its brightly painted sparrows. Who created such a flute? From wood to art, surely its music was magical, even without me. Slowly, I brought the flute to my lips and played *"Moogung Hwa,"* the only Korean song I knew.

TWENTY

SOUTH, 1950
Sei-Young

". . . a song flew through my window . . ."

I COULD NOT STUDY today. Down here in the church cellar the hopes for my future seemed dim. I looked out my only window, watching it close on me. Intellectually I knew spring was here and that it was a sun-flooded morning. Emotionally it was the darkest winter. Six months had passed without a word of correspondence from Maria Park. Six long months. Secretly I had believed that she would be my introduction to President Rhee's office, my window of opportunity, and that it was all part of my destiny. But that dream was dying, and my destiny would have to change.

The ones to whom I was closest tried to offer me comfort.

Aunt Sunja said, "My flowers brought me back to life. But the truth is, I should have never died in the first place. What wasted years. Do not do what I did. Soon you will graduate from college and find your place in the world."

Mother said, "Your dream will still come true. There are some things a mother knows."

Grandfather said, "Listen to them, Sei-Young. They speak from experience and intuition."

Eun Ju said, "You need a woman."

I opened my book but it was no use. All the comforting words could not comfort me right now. I was alone in my darkest winter. So I was surprised when a song flew through my window, surprised to hear music at all. The song flew in like a bird, a magic bird. All at once the world outside expanded with light and beauty and pale shades of spring.

I closed my book and followed the melody, so sad and mysterious, into the courtyard. There was Grandfather, listening intently to a young woman playing a flute. In fact, it was the flute Father had given me so long ago. When I was ten years old I had blown into it, but no music came. Today, finally, music breathed through its body.

I stood next to Grandfather and listened. The young woman kept playing. She was unaware I was here; her eyes were closed. If there were lyrics to her song, I did not know them, but I thought I could hear years of suffering whistle through the flute and into the spring air.

Maybe someday the music will call you.

Father was very wise to say that.

When her performance was over, the young woman's eyes opened with surprise.

"Hello," I said. "You play so beautifully."

"Heisook, this is my grandson, Sei-Young," Grandfather said.

She looked startled. "Sei-Young *Shin?*"

"Yes," I said. "It is very nice to meet you."

"It is very nice to meet you, too," she said.

For me to say she was a pretty and talented girl and that I was spellbound would not do her justice. That would diminish who she was, and how I felt. Her face and her song, my flute in her fingers, was literally the sum of all my dreams. I knew it immediately, and so did Grandfather.

"I believe I hear your mother calling me," he said.

Heisook bowed good-bye. "I shall visit you again, Reverend Shin."

Grandfather grinned. "We are already old acquaintances."

When he was gone, Heisook gasped. "I forgot to give your grandfather back his flute!"

"Actually, the flute is mine," I said.

"Oh! Do you play?"

"No, I do not have the talent. But my flute is very special to me. You see, my father was a woodcarver. Not just any ordinary woodcarver. He peddled the finest wooden works of art in all of Seoul." I watched her face for a reaction, for it was clear to me that she was a daughter of privilege. What would she think of the son of a poor peddler?

She examined the flute's engraved and painted magnificence. "Are you telling me that your father made this flute?"

"Yes, for my tenth birthday," I replied.

"It is by far the most lovely flute I have ever seen." She tried to give it back to me, but my eyes told her that it was now hers.

"What a talented man your father is. Does he live here, at the church?"

"No," I said, and she understood.

We crossed the courtyard to the gate. We did not discuss taking a walk; there was no need. She still carried my flute; I still carried her song. She told me she was enrolled at Ewha; I told her I was enrolled at Chosun. She told me how she met Grandfather; I did not tell her it was destiny.

"So," she said rather curiously, "are you the famous orator whom I have heard so much about?"

"I am not famous," I assured her.

"Eun Ju Chun says you are."

"How do you know Eun Ju?"

Heisook smiled. "Eun Ju knows every woman at Ewha. But seriously, Sei-Young, I have heard many impressive things about you. How you were responsible for keeping Chosun open. And how you wrote a speech for Maria Park."

The dark winter of the last hour had passed, barely recalled. The speech for Maria Park, merely an exercise. It was springtime in Seoul.

"This is not fair, Heisook. I know so little about you. Tell me something. No, tell me *everything.*" I do not know whether it was what I said or the way I said it, but something seemed to move her. She had beautiful eyes but the danger would be to misread them. She played a beautiful song, but I needed to hear her own lyrics, from her own lips.

"I try to have faith, but it comes and goes," she began.

"Like the seasons, Heisook?"

"Yes, like the seasons. I loved my brother Changi more than life itself, but I lost him; not just to war but to other things, too. I lost my mother when I left my hometown of Sinuiju. If I had true faith, absolute faith, I would believe we will be together again. But do I? Each day that passes promises only less hope, less faith. My father, like your grandfather, is a minister, but even he expresses doubt. Not in his words, but in his eyes. But then I remind myself how fortunate I was to have survived my escape across the border. When I arrived in Seoul, my eyes fell upon the First Methodist Church. I was hoping it was the Seoul Presbyterian Church and that I would find my father there. Instead, I found your grandfather there. He affected me in a way I could not explain. That is why I returned. I was drawn here to see your grandfather again, to play the flute your father carved, and to meet you. Just the sound of those words are magical, like the sounds of a waterfall. Sei-Young, do you understand what I am saying?"

I had heard the lyrics correctly.

Over the next month our two lives became one, so that one's pain and celebration became the other's. A newly formed sacred circle included both families, even the missing—Father and Kwan-Young, Heisook's brother Changi and her mother. Mother and Aunt Sunja embraced Heisook, hungry for more stories about a dreamy girl and her mischievous older brother. Grandfather and Reverend Pang enjoyed each other's company, often discussing their common creeds over cups of chilled barley tea. When our sacred circle prayed, it was powerful.

At the height of spring I took Heisook to Nabi. The train passed quiet villages, cornfields, still ponds. Like a child, she stared out the window.

"This looks very much like the ride from Sinuiju to Heavenly Mountain," she said, clutching a bouquet of flowers she had hand-picked from the church garden.

The sight of Heisook, here, beneath the magnolia tree, made me feel weak and strong at once.

"Hello, Kwan-Young," she said, laying down the flowers.

I spoke at great length about my little brother, but her tragic sobs interrupted me.

"Your brother is dead, mine is gone," she cried.

"Yes," I said, taking her shoulders, "my brother is dead, but his memory and spirit live on. And Changi may not be here with us, but you don't know for certain that he is gone forever."

"He is dead," she pronounced.

"Heisook, there is always the chance that he's alive in China. He may even have gone back to Sinuiju and is reunited with your mother as we speak. You may still see each other again."

She was both listening and lost in thought. "The other day I secretly watched your Aunt Sunja in the garden. She was captivated by the simple act of watering, clipping, and humming to a small, dead plant. I went up to her and asked, 'Why do you nurture this plant so, when it is already dead?' Your aunt pointed out a spotted green leaf lost in a cluster of withered brown ones on a lifeless branch. 'This is a sign of life,' she insisted. 'I have faith that one lone leaf will struggle and win over death.' Even though her own husband was murdered in cold blood, your aunt believes in the survival of a dying plant—and that it is all faith's doing." Her eyes searched mine. "Do you believe that, Sei-Young?"

It was a difficult question for difficult times. People were born and people died, and life was not fair, I knew that. Why Kwan-Young did not live long enough to go to school or fall in love was almost too much to bear if I thought about it too much. Still, there was only one answer.

"Yes, Heisook. Because without faith, the seeds would have never been planted in the first place."

"But once the seeds are planted, who is to say which ones will die?"

"Not all will survive, but faith promises that some will sprout."

"So you are saying that even though your brother lies dead beneath our feet and your father never returned home, you believe in faith's doing?"

"I must believe that. And I also believe that meeting you was faith's doing."

She murmured in reluctant agreement. "And yet even my father doubts the words in his own sermons these days. I sometimes wonder whether I am the only one who hears this. It is painful to watch him up there, knowing how powerless he feels."

"I am sorry," I said.

"No, I am the one who should be sorry. You brought me here to see Kwan-Young and all I have done is talk about myself." Heisook knelt down and spoke to my brother in a voice as heartbreaking as the song she had played on my flute. "Your big brother has told me all about you, Kwan-Young. You are such a special little boy and we both love you so much and will always keep you in our hearts . . ."

Reverend Pang spoke to a small gathering in his church that evening.

"As God's children, we must kneel before Him and feel his comforting embrace . . ."

Heisook was not alone, for I heard it, too. Her father's doubt, his powerlessness. Not in God, but in the outcome. I prayed our new President would reunite our country and thousands of families like hers.

* * *

In early May more change was to come my way. Chairman Stevens found me in the library, studying for my final exams.

Like a giddy Korean schoolboy, he whispered too loudly, "Chancellor Paik has news from Maria Park. Go to his office. Now! Go!"

The past seven months flew by me as I raced across campus to the chancellor's office. Eun Ju was there, putting on the finishing touches to a sketch.

"Congratulations, Mr. Egghead."

Good old Eun Ju was a tonic to my nerves. The sketch portrayed none other than me, Mr. Egghead, skipping into a building, nose up in the air, saying "Move aside, everyone, the mayor wants to see me, me, me . . ."

And indeed that was the message. Chancellor Paik came out and greeted me, exchanged a few pleasantries, then gave me Maria Park's note. Handwritten on Ewha College stationery, it read:

> *May 5, 1950*
> *Dear Sei-Young,*
> *Please report to the Mayor's office on May 19—the day after your graduation—at three o'clock in the afternoon. My husband, Kibung Yi, will be expecting you.*
>
> > *Sincerely,*
> > *Maria Park*

Eun Ju and I had dinner at a small restaurant where we each ordered *bibim bap,* a meal of rice and spicy plum sauce stirred into a bowl of well-seasoned vegetables, dried seaweed, ground beef, and a fried egg. It was a celebration of sorts, for our graduation coming up, and for whatever my meeting with the Mayor might bring.

Eun Ju toasted my glass of barley tea with his glass of beer. "Double victory!"

"Eun Ju," I began to say, then paused while the waitress set down our bowls of *bibim bap*, "I don't know why I'm being called to the Mayor's office. In two weeks I may be toasting that victory, but tonight I am only toasting our upcoming graduation."

"Don't be such a pessimist. What, do you think he just wants you to come to his office to shine his shoes? Or challenge you to a game of Chinese checkers? Hey, waitress! More beef for my friend's bowl here. He needs his sustenance—he has a very important upcoming meeting with the Mayor."

The waitress muttered, "Troublemaker," then ignored us.

"Eh," Eun Ju sneered, "she'll still be here with white hair and rickets when you become President and can order beef by the kilo."

Eun Ju was more than my best friend. He was my brother in the truest sense. Despite his charisma, he put me in the center of the world. And that center was in the President's seat. I did not have the heart to tell him that was neither my dream nor my destiny.

"And I will be your chauffeur," he said, "as long as you hire good-looking women on your staff. After all, you stole my girl."

Our graduation ceremony came and went like a dream. The audience was huge, but I focused on only a few faces. Names were called and diplomas were handed out. A proud hush, then glow, fell over the Chosun campus as the last few graduates left the stage. Then, it seemed, all of Seoul was in an uproar of cheers and clapping and caps thrown in the air.

*　*　*

When I arrived at the Mayor's office the next day, a surprising sight changed my plans. Several policemen were escorting the Mayor outside.

"Out of the way," they shouted, pushing me aside like some nuisance beggar boy.

But I was no longer a boy in rags, standing in mud. Or a milk delivery boy, afraid to stand up to Officer Akoto. I was Sei-Young Shin, influential orator at Chosun Christian College. It was I who was responsible for keeping the school open. It was I who wrote and translated Maria Park's speech. I fought my way through a clot of policemen, then held my hand out to Kibung Yi with a bow.

"Honorable Yi, I am Sei-Young Shin. I am here for our three o'clock appointment."

"Oh, yes, Sei-Young Shin," he bowed back. "I have not forgotten our appointment. But I regret to say that something very urgent has come up and I must cancel our meeting. Nonetheless, you are to report to work tomorrow at the President's office. Go inside and give my secretary your home address. A limousine will pick you up at five thirty a.m. Madame Rhee will be expecting you."

The Mayor was whisked away and all the policemen evacuated the scene. I was alone. *Madame Rhee will be expecting you. Madame Rhee will be expecting you. Madame Rhee will be expecting you.* Now I watched the speaker of those words, Kibung Yi, one of the Republic of Korea's most powerful men, drive off in a police car. Sirens screamed over Seoul. Change was coming, but almost too fast and too alarming.

Was I up to this task?

*　*　*

Heisook and her father joined my family that evening. Mother had prepared a special meal of *tangjang* soup, fried *too-boo,* and five cold spicy vegetable dishes in five different bowls.

Grandfather respectfully asked Reverend Pang to deliver a prayer before supper.

"Let us pray for those not present at our meal, but forever present in our hearts. Changi, Eunook, Choon-Young, and, of course, little Kwan-Young."

"Neh," Mother prayed.

"And let us thank the Lord for bringing us together this night, in celebration of Sei-Young's great achievement."

"Neh, neh," Grandfather prayed.

We ate.

After supper, as we drank chilled cinnamon-ginger tea, the customary beverage on such an occasion, Grandfather urged me to say a few words.

"Tomorrow I will report to the Blue House wearing my best church clothes," I said, referring to my only suit, gray with black buttons. "But I still think of myself as a young boy in Nabi."

Each member of the sacred circle held up a cup of celebratory tea and honored me.

"May your humble roots always keep you grounded," Aunt Sunja said.

"I am bursting with pride," Mother cried. *"My* son, in the Blue House!"

"My grandson in the Blue House!" Grandfather said.

"Urge President Rhee to reunite our country, Sei-Young," Reverend Pang said. "Now that you are a VIP."

"VIP?" Mother questioned him. "What is a VIP?"

I believe Heisook blushed when she replied, "Very important person."

* * *

At five-thirty a.m. a black limousine pulled up outside the First Methodist Church. Grandfather, Mother, and Aunt Sunja were so excited they walked me to the car. Inside, a silent chauffeur waited for his cue to drive. Outside, a uniformed guard waited for me.

"Are you Mr. Sei-Young Shin?" he asked me in a polite but formal manner.

"Yes."

"I am required to see some form of identification, sir."

I showed him my college I.D. card, which he carefully examined to his satisfaction. He handed it back to me along with an I.D. badge to wear around my neck. The badge read: *Sei-Young Shin, Staff Employee, The Blue House.*

My family threw their arms around me, overcome with joy. The guard grinned, then opened the limousine door. I stepped into its plush interior and looked out its spotless window. As we drove away, my mother's hands were still on the glass.

The limousine conspicuously made its way across town. Pedestrians and bicyclists peeked in for a look as though I *was* a VIP. The sun was barely visible in the sky and I felt less a VIP than a young boy delivering milk this time of day when my legs ached on a rusty old bicycle. It was the same sun, shining on the same earth, although, it was true, my world had changed. From the window I could see the Blue House in the distance, that famous sight on the hill.

It was no dream. The presidential gates swung open. The limousine slowly rode along a steep lane. There it stood, the Blue House. The limousine stopped and in one swift move, the silent chauffeur got out and opened the door for me. Once out, I took in the kingdom airs of the president's residence. The stone walls, the exotic gardens, the crowning blue sky.

"This way, Mr. Shin," the guard said and motioned to me.

Two secretaries sat at adjacent desks outside Madame Rhee's office. Both were smartly dressed American women, both fair-haired, although the one who spoke was older and heavier.

"Mr. Shin," she welcomed me. "I'm Betty and this is Emma. We've been expecting you."

"Thank you, nice to meet you both," I replied.

"It's a lovely spring day, isn't it?" Betty said as she led me into Madame Rhee's office.

"Very lovely," I said.

"May I get you a coffee or Coca-Cola, Mr. Shin?" she asked, seating me.

"I'm fine, thank you very much," I said.

"Madame Rhee will be with you momentarily."

Betty bowed before leaving me alone in a stately room that lacked personality. No place for photographs or personal mementos here. Strictly a place of business. Madame Rhee's private life with the president was kept private.

On the campus of Chosun, people were quite opinionated about the president's wife. She was referred to as a foreigner, a cold fish, an Austrian Communist. Now I would find out for myself what kind of person Madame Rhee was.

She entered her office wearing a *hanbok* of pale green and yellow—colors not in harmony with her pallid complexion. The satin Korean garment contrasted with her sharp Austrian features and rippled gray hair. Immediately I stood up. Madame

Rhee was middle-aged; discernibly younger than her husband. There was something I found charming in her stern, commanding gesture.

"Sei-Young Shin," she greeted me in an accented English and with an awkward bow, "I have been searching for an assistant who could handle some of the President's private affairs. Someone trustworthy and responsible, someone who speaks impeccable English. My dear friend, Maria Park, tells me you are that person."

My bow was long and heartfelt. "I am that person, Madame Rhee."

"Excellent," she smiled. "You begin today. Your salary will be thirty-five dollars a month, paid on the first Monday of each month. Benefits include all meals and your own car and driver. You will be chauffeured to and from work every day. How does that sound to you, Sei-Young?"

"It sounds very generous."

She smiled again, as though my reaction pleased her. But her smile now turned to serious business. "There may be times when you are sitting in on crucial meetings. Whatever goes on in those meetings, whatever is said, must stay within the confines of the Blue House. Is that understood?"

"Yes."

"Excellent. Now you will meet the President."

I followed her austere figure down a hallway lined with security guards. Her pace was quick with a slight waddle. Despite her title of First Lady and her educated presence, she struck me as born from European peasant stock. I could picture her with an apron tied around her thick waistline, kneading bread or walking from room to room with a dustpan. She was no cold fish. We walked past three Korean secretaries who respectfully acknowledged us.

Madame Rhee poked her head in the President's office. "Sei-Young Shin is here."

"Okay," issued the voice from the office, "send him in."

Madame Rhee opened the door and presented me to the President of the Republic of Korea. He stood up from behind the most immense desk I had ever laid eyes on—mahogany and glass-covered. He was much older and kinder-looking than his photographs in the newspapers.

"Welcome to the Blue House," President Rhee spoke in our native tongue.

"It is a great honor, Your Excellency," I responded with a bow.

"You know, Sei-Young, we will be passing each other countless times every day from now on. Let's just forget about this bowing business, okay? I respect you, you respect me. This old back just can't take all this bowing anymore."

My first day on the job was spent orienting myself in my new surroundings. Madame Rhee's secretary Betty took me on a tour of the Blue House. My eyes explored every room. Then she introduced me to the entire Blue House staff, who were instructed to address me as Mr. Shin. I had never been called Mr. Shin before—I felt the same way Syngman Rhee felt about bowing. But I suppose in my official capacity, I *was* Mr. Shin now.

Over the weeks I settled into my duties at the Blue House. But even among Korea's most powerful, I found my work unchallenging. I made President Rhee's appointments with his English-speaking Canadian physician. I picked up his prescriptions. I kept Madame Rhee's office tidy. Despite my I.D. badge, I was more a houseboy than an assistant. The only interesting aspect of the job was that I was privy to conversations between the President and his advisors, a group that usually included Madame Rhee.

Our men are ill-equipped to fight a war, Mr. President.

Skirmishes on the Thirty-eighth Parallel are worsening.

A mass grave of South Korean civilians was found.

We must convince the Americans that war is on the horizon.

Five weeks into my new job, everything changed.

TWENTY-ONE

SOUTH, 1950–52
Sei-Young

". . . the Korean War broke out."

IT WAS JUNE 25, 1950, a bright, warm Sunday. Grandfather's late morning sermon was in session. Normally the two families would share a meal afterward, then meet again later in the evening to hear Reverend Pang speak at his church. But on this memorable day, the Korean War broke out.

We did not hear it announced on a radio or through a loudspeaker. The congregation was deep in prayer when chaos erupted outside. Hand-in-hand, Heisook and I ran to the window, straining to see through stained glass. We could see people wild-eyed in the streets, screaming—

Communist soldiers have invaded!

They have crossed the Thirty-eighth Parallel!

With Seoul barely thirty miles south of the Thirty-eighth Parallel, the city would be a battleground within a day's time.

Heisook's hand let go of mine. "My mother," she cried. "She is all alone."

My future was with Heisook. She was my destiny. I would love and comfort her for all the years God would give us. But right now I could not comfort her. I was not part of her past, the lyrics in her song. Instead, she fell into her father's arms.

Our sacred circle huddled in the prayer room of the church quarters, listening to the incoming reports over the radio.

"North Korean soldiers have moved southward with mortar and artillery fire . . ."

"ROK Army helpless against enemy soldiers . . ."

Midday brought an urgent message from President Rhee.

"Citizens of the Republic of Korea, this is your President speaking. Help is on its way. Be assured that the free world will not be bullied by Communists. We will fight to the end . . ."

Syngman Rhee *would* fight to the end; that I believed. It wasn't only the Japanese he had fought in his lifetime. As a young independent revolutionary in turn-of-the-century Korea, his way of thinking—to give more power to the people— jeopardized the Korean Royals, who had ordered Rhee captured, imprisoned, and tortured. Even when bamboo sticks were driven under his fingernails and lit with matches, he would not relent. Only as his flesh began to singe were the burning sticks extinguished. For the rest of his life, whenever he became infuriated, he would blow on his fingertips as though they were on fire. The habit of a lifelong crusader.

The thought had occurred to me that maybe I should be at the Blue House at this time of crisis, but I reminded myself that I was only a houseboy and could serve no purpose. Besides, I belonged here, with my family.

* * *

Nightfall collapsed on us with the sounds of war. Heisook's expression turned ghostly. "Please try to rest," Reverend Pang begged his daughter.

"No, Father. If I close my eyes, I will never wake up again."

While everyone else stayed in the sacred circle, Heisook and I retreated to our corner. She had something on her mind. "Where were you when the Americans dropped the bomb on Hiroshima?" she asked me.

"My family and I were living on Suka's farm."

"Mr. Suka was a good man. I am grateful to him for treating you so well."

"I remember the horror on his face when news came that Hiroshima had been decimated," I told her.

Heisook seemed not to be listening anymore. Her eyes were glazed over, not from memories of skating or sitting at a waterfall, but from a very different kind of memory. "Principal Nishimoto told us that the end might be near. I can still hear the sirens ringing in my ears as I ran home. They were the sounds of death. But to tell you the truth, Sei-Young, I was not afraid, not really. At least, I was not afraid to die. I just wanted to see my parents one last time. Now, as an adult, it all comes back to me, like the sound of sirens. I am still not afraid of dying, but I am afraid of losing you and our life together. And I am afraid of never seeing my mother again."

I held Heisook in my arms, knowing mine had little power at a moment like this. Still, I held her for a long time. Reports continued to pour in.

"North Korean soldiers descend on Kaesong . . ."

"Train station shuts down . . ."

"North Korean soldiers move toward Seoul as civilians head toward Pusan . . ."

Only Reverend Pang was brave enough to say what we all knew was true: "We must leave Seoul tomorrow morning and head south."

Grandfather agreed. "It is too dangerous to stay here."

"We must seek shelter in Pusan," I said.

"But the trains are no longer running," Heisook reminded me.

This time, only Grandfather was brave enough to say: "We must go by foot."

In unison, the three women objected.

"You cannot make the trip," Mother said to Grandfather.

"She is right," Aunt Sunja said.

"It would take us many days to walk there," Heisook said.

Distant gunfire shook the church quarters. Everyone fell silent. Then Grandfather said: "I will make the journey."

Rain began to fall late that evening.

"Sei-Young," Mother said from the doorway, "the official Blue House limousine is here."

I went to the door and saw my chauffeur, Mr. Cha, coming toward me with an umbrella. Behind him, clouds of Communist smoke were rising above an eerie silhouette of mountains. How could we have known when we woke up this morning that the day would end this way?

"Mr. Shin! You are being summoned to the Blue House. Immediately!"

I could not leave the sacred circle now. The world smelled of war, and there was no telling what would happen next.

"My family needs me, Mr. Cha. I cannot go."

"Please. My orders were to come and pick you up," Mr. Cha

implored as the rain beat brutally down on his umbrella.

"You must go," Grandfather said from behind me. Once we both stood in the doorway. A different doorway, a different tragedy, so long ago.

I turned to Heisook, whose face was ravaged with worry. She had already said too many good-byes. Experience had told her that good-byes were forever. And yet, she came up to me and courageously whispered, "Yes, you must go. We will wait for you, Sei-Young."

I quietly promised her, and then everyone, "I will return as soon as I can."

"In the meantime, Father and I will rush home and pack up our possessions," Heisook said.

"No, you must stay here!" Mother reacted, too sharply. She added in a softer tone, "War has just broken out. Two people on the street make an easy target. Please, you must stay."

"I agree with Sei-Young's mother," Reverend Pang told his daughter. Their eyes met in a sad place and swam for too brief a time. Then he turned his attention to me. "We will wait here with your family, Sei-Young. God be with you."

The limousine drove me away from my loved ones. I could hear war coming, closing in on Seoul. The streets were clogged with packed cars and trucks, but mostly with families on foot moving southward.

The hour was midnight. The typically twenty-minute drive to the Blue House was taking over two hours. Rain thrashed against the windows and I couldn't see anything anymore. Why was I being summoned to the Blue House? They didn't need me. My place was in the sacred circle. They needed me. In a different time, during a different war, Father had left the sacred circle, never to return.

We arrived at the Blue House just after two thirty a.m. A swarm of reporters surrounded the limousine. Guards pushed the reporters back. Yelling ensued.

The presidential gates swung open; we drove in. Sun Myung, a young guard, was waiting for me outside the Blue House. We entered together without words. He led me down the hushed main hallway to the President's office. All was oddly quiet. The staff help had obviously been evacuated.

But inside the President's office, feverish conversations were going on between several high-ranking advisors, including Kibung Yi. The room was in a state of panic. The telephone was ringing with one crisis after another. President and Madame Rhee were conspicuously absent.

Mayor Yi ushered me in, slamming the door behind us. "Come in, Sei-Young." He looked at me in a matter-of-life-and-death way and I knew my status at the Blue House had changed. "Listen carefully, our military has no defense against the North Korean soldiers who are rapidly moving south. They are killing our men by the hundreds. Maybe thousands. We desperately need help. American intervention is mandatory."

"I don't understand," I said. "President Rhee announced on the radio that help was already on the way."

"The President had to say something to keep the nation calm. Now, it is crucial that we contact General MacArthur in Tokyo. Do you know who General MacArthur is?"

"He was the commanding general in the Pacific during World War Two," I replied.

"That is correct," Mayor Yi said. "And he is the general who can save us. He has the power to convince President Truman to

send American troops to our defense. But no one here is quali-
fied to try to reach him for President Rhee. No one here speaks
perfect English. I understand from two wise women—my wife
and Madame Rhee—that you do. They tell me you are a young
man of great words. Use these words to get General MacArthur
on the telephone for the President."

"With all due respect, Honorable Yi, our country is in a state
of emergency. The President himself speaks perfect English.
Why doesn't *he* call General MacArthur?"

"It is not protocol for the President of the Republic of Korea
to call a general, no matter what the general's reputation," was
Mayor Yi's explanation.

"May I ask where the President is?"

"In his private quarters with Madame Rhee."

Friday I was a houseboy picking up sweet delicacies, exotic
teas, and prescriptions all over Seoul for the presidential
couple. Today my orders were to contact General MacArthur in
Tokyo. I dialed the overseas operator and asked her to connect
me with the number scribbled on the Blue House stationery.
Men two and three times my age watched me with their
stricken faces. The telephone on the other end rang and rang.

"No one is picking up," I announced.

"Keep trying," Mayor Yi instructed me.

I looked up at the clock. Three forty-five a.m. The telephone
kept ringing. Three forty-six, three forty-seven . . .

Finally, a voice came over the receiver.

"General's quarters."

"My name is Sei-Young Shin," I announced. "I am calling
from the Blue House in Seoul, Korea, on behalf of President
Syngman Rhee. It is of dire urgency that he speak with General
Douglas MacArthur."

"I sympathize with your cause, Mr. Shin," the voice responded, "but I have strict orders not to disturb General MacArthur. I will pass your message on to him."

"Sir, this is a national emergency!" I fired into the telephone. "The North Koreans have invaded our country. All of Asia is on the brink of Communism. It is not only in our best interest, sir, but also in the United States' best interest to help."

"Let it be known that General MacArthur is fully aware of your country's crisis, Mr. Shin."

The telephone went dead. Perfect English could not break official orders. As soon as I hung up, the telephone once again began ringing with one crisis after another. And once again, the room fell into a state of panic.

"You did your best," Mayor Yi said, his face tired and dejected. "Mr. Cha will bring you home to pick up your family. If you choose to leave Seoul, which I would advise you to do, he will drive you to Pusan. President and Madame Rhee will be taking up residence there. After they are safely settled, we will follow them."

That President Rhee was planning to flee Seoul—to leave the scene of the action—surprised me. He was, after all, the President. For a man who just last night had declared that Korea would fight to the end, he was leaving others to man the front while he was hiding in his private quarters, planning his escape to Pusan. I was very disappointed.

I arrived back home in the minutes before dawn. The rain was falling even heavier now and the hope for spotting even a single butterfly—one good little omen—was not possible. Oh, I was wrong! There was Heisook's face in the window; her eyes searching for mine.

Mother and Aunt Sunja had already packed our belongings. Of course, they did not forget my prized possessions; namely, my pine whistle and plaque from Father and my English book from Grandfather.

I did not tell my family about my failed attempt to contact General MacArthur, and they did not ask questions; they understood that my activities for President Rhee were confined to the Blue House. It was now time to head to Pusan. That we were being driven there came as good news to all.

"Mr. Cha," I said as we settled into the limousine, "we first need to make a stop at the Seoul Presbyterian Church."

Heisook was inside the church for no more than five minutes. She came out carrying only her knapsack, packed with few possessions. Her clothing, her silk, and her flute.

The roads were lined with families on foot making the long journey to Pusan. Over the mountainous terrain they trudged.

"Listen!" Grandfather said.

"They are singing!" Mother and Aunt Sunja exclaimed.

"Their voices are whistling through the rain like flutes," Heisook said. Her tone was pessimistic. "Do they really think they will find safety in Pusan? Do we? Is there really any safe place right now?"

"Pusan is considered a safe haven because there's a large military base there," I explained.

"Oh," she responded doubtfully.

Grandfather suddenly hunched over in his seat. Everyone cried out—

"What's wrong?"

"I'm fine, I'm fine," he kept saying, steadying his breath. His face was ashen. "Perhaps I could use some fresh air."

"Mr. Cha," I said, "stop the car for a moment, please."

I helped Grandfather step out of the limousine. He stood in the monsoon, his flesh and bones sagging under the weight of the falling rains. He said he was fine, but he was not fine at all. He spoke to the sky and the sky spoke back.

Then it was time to continue our journey to Pusan.

Pusan was a seaport of fishing waters set against throngs of ragged refugees in the streets.

Heisook stared out the window at countless tents in alleys, at stray dogs and cats and rotting garbage. "What do we do now?"

"We must find a place to stay," I said.

But the search was fruitless. Not a single hotel room in all of Pusan seemed to be vacant. Finally we came upon a boarding-house.

A pair of lifeless eyes peered out from behind the door. "No rooms here, unless you want the cellar."

The cellar was large and dank, home to mice, maggots, and crickets. The stench was overwhelming at first. But at least we were sheltered from the rains and distanced from the war. Over the radio, we learned the terrifying news:

"Communist soldiers now occupy Seoul . . ."

Once we were settled, I went to see President and Madame Rhee. Compared to the Blue House, their temporary residence was modest. Madame Rhee welcomed me in.

"Thank goodness you and your family made it safely to

Pusan," she said, attempting good spirits. "The President will be glad to see you. He was very impressed with your effort to contact General MacArthur."

Madame Rhee led me to the President's office, a small corner room that brought in the overcast day. He was on the telephone, shouting.

"We haven't a single fighter plane. Our military is defenseless without U.N. assistance. We cannot go on being hermits forever! Put that in your newspaper!"

President Rhee slammed down the receiver, then blew on his fingertips until his fury began to cool. "Damn reporters. Like they say in America, you can't live with them and you can't live without them. They're a good source for getting your point across, even if they take unforgivable liberties, those bastards." All his attention abruptly turned to me, and he spoke with such fervor I dared not interrupt him. "The Mayor told me about your attempt to contact General MacArthur. Whether a coincidence or not, the good general called me a few hours later, and now there is hope that Seoul will be returned to us. The United Nations is going to grant us military support. Sei-Young, your readiness to leave your family at a moment's notice for the great cause of your country will not go unnoticed. In fact, I would like to make you my personal secretary. But first I need you to work as an interpreter for the U.S. Air Force. There's a critical shortage of English-speaking Koreans. You will be stationed in Chinhae, thirty miles west of here, as a liaison officer."

Despite my reluctance to take the job, President Rhee had issued his orders. As someone who had spoken out in the name of freedom, it was my duty to obey. I would be leaving in a week's time.

*   *   *

Heisook heard the news that the Americans had come to our aid.

"They're going to drop the bomb on North Korea, aren't they?"

"No," I assured her, holding her close to me. "They would not do that, Heisook."

"And how do you know that, Sei-Young? How?"

"The Russians now have the atom bomb, too. The two powers have an unspoken law which dictates that neither will ever use the bomb again."

She pulled away from me, twisting in agony. "I don't believe in laws, spoken or unspoken. And laws mean nothing at a time of war. Are you the one behind closed doors, making all the decisions? I don't trust the Russians and I don't trust the Americans. My mother is all alone."

What could I say? Heisook was right.

Grandfather's frightening episode on the way to Pusan was merely a warning of what was to come. Three days after our arrival, he collapsed.

Reverend Pang and I carried him to his straw bedding. He was unconscious. My mind blacked out everything except for one thing: Grandfather was dying.

"Wake up, Grandfather," I kept pleading, as I had done once before. That time, he had come back to life. Could the miracle happen again?

Mother nursed him with towels, prayers, songs. My hopes grew dim. Grandfather's spirit was leaving his body, leaving us, leaving me.

"Grandfather, please open your eyes and talk to me," I pleaded.

No movement.

"Please, Grandfather."

If Father were here, maybe Grandfather's eyes would have slowly opened and his spirit would have flown back into his body. But Father was not here, he was as far off as the farthest light. And now, so too, was Grandfather.

In Seoul there would have been a funeral so grand mourners would have spilled into the courtyard. But the war had scattered the congregation. And so, near a church by the sea whose giant bells rang every hour, we buried Grandfather in Pusan. Into the earth with him went his wooden cane, a possession he had held as a symbol of his love for his son, my father. Early that morning Aunt Sunja had planted a magnolia sapling near his grave.

"Every spring it will blossom in unison with the great magnolia tree over little Kwan-Young's grave," she said.

Mother wept. "And together the spirits and the trees will sing."

Heisook held her flute to her lips, ready to deliver a song of mourning, a song so heavy perhaps her fingers would give way to grief. But such a song would not come. Instead, lovely notes floated from her flute, light and feathery as doves in flight.

At a moment of church bells ringing, Heisook looked up at the sky with wide, searching eyes and murmured—

"I will miss my dear friend who is now in heaven, above the stars."

Yes, Grandfather was in heaven. His spirit had flown above the stars. But how I would miss him! For Grandfather was, and would always be all things to me. Dreamer. Thinker. Holy man.

* * *

Defeat for South Korea seemed imminent. Cities fell, one by one. Over the radio came more terrifying news of Taejon, a city approximately one hundred and twenty-five miles northwest of Pusan: *"North Korean soldiers are rapidly making their way south. Eyewitnesses claim that thousands of bodies lie dead in Taejon in swift North Korean capture . . ."*

In Grandfather's death came marriage. It seemed fitting that on the day we buried him, my heart opened up with confession.

"I love you, Heisook. I want us to be together, always. Please be my wife."

Her smile was her answer, soft and serene. "I love you, too, Sei-Young. I am yours forever."

Two days later we were wed. Heisook was a beautiful bride in a plain linen *hanbok* bought at an outdoor market down the street. The way she proudly walked, one would guess she was of royal blood. I was no match for her in the same gray suit I wore to work. I did not even have a diamond ring as an offering of my love.

"Sei-Young, I do not need a diamond ring. I once kept a stone in my pocket as a symbol of my love for Changi. I used to squeeze it, trying to keep my love, my memory of him, alive. But when I gave it up, my love for him only grew. You see, I never really needed the stone. And I do not need a ring."

Our wedding ceremony took place at the same church by the sea whose grounds covered Grandfather's bones. Reverend Pang performed the ceremony, with only Mother and Aunt Sunja in attendance. It was a wonderful day despite the absence of our loved ones. For me that included Eun Ju Chun. Years we spent side by side. So many times I could find him waiting for me on the Steps. Where could I find him now? In my mind, he was still sitting there, waving *Hey, Mr. Egghead, why didn't you ask me to be your best man?*

My bride and I both said, "I do."

Mother's wedding gift to us was a portrait of Heisook and me at our moment of meeting. How she created this moment without being there, and when she painted this moment, were as mysterious as Mother herself. An abstract work of mottled sky and brilliant sun-flecked cherry blossoms; Grandfather was a mere white splash, the flute, a brown wisp. The faces were ours, somehow. Other family members, living and dead, were there, too, on a distant mountainside shaded by clouds and flowering trees.

When I announced my marriage to the Rhees, Madame Rhee insisted on hosting a formal ceremony in the gardens at their residence. She took the liberty of renting a tuxedo for me, purchasing a wedding *hanbok* for Heisook, and hiring a photographer—all with charmed bossiness.

On the appointed date, at the appointed time—noon—Heisook emerged from the shadows and into the gardens, stoically beautiful. Although she said she was honored by this ceremony, she would not fake a smile for the photographer or for the thirty distinguished guests. To do so would be to betray herself, the grief that her brother and mother could not be here. She had said and done things against her will once before and she would never do that again—even for so-called VIPs. Besides our family, among the guests were the President and Madame Rhee, Kibung Yi and Maria Park, and various South Korean and

American generals. Even Professor Stevens attended with his wife, Millie. This time Chancellor Paik performed the ceremony. Heisook and I took our vows again. Afterward, cake and coffee were served.

Later that day when Heisook and I were being chauffeured home, we shared a private conversation.

"Sei-Young, everyone had a lovely time today, didn't they?" she said with hesitance.

"Yes."

"And you? Were you happy?"

"Yes—why?"

"I should have felt happier than I did," she said, staring out. "But I could find no joy in the moment. Everything was too stiff, too formal; nothing was real to me. I kept thinking—*We are already married, why are we doing this?* Is that what life is? Acting in a certain way, knowing the proper manners? The rules of the world make us behave in strange ways, I think."

The next morning I left for Chinhae. I promised my new bride that I would return once a month, but my words echoed of a promise once broken.

"I will earn big money and return before spring's thaw."

Heisook took me in her arms. "I know you will return. Not because of luck or faith, but because my heart tells me, *My husband will return to me once a month.*"

In Chinhae, my assignment as liaison officer was to act as the interpreter for South Korean and American generals as they discussed war strategies against the enemy. Translating tongues was *a piece of cake*—I was picking up American idiomatic expressions along the way—but being stationed in Chinhae was not. In the midst of brutally recorded bloodshed, my monthly visits to Pusan and Heisook's letters were all that sustained me.

My dear Sei-Young,

Time moves so slowly with you gone. I miss you more with every passing minute.

Your salary has afforded us a clean apartment upstairs which we moved into yesterday (no. 304) and food to eat. But most refugees are not so fortunate. Day and night moans of hunger sweep the streets.

Every Sunday morning I buy ten fish from the market. Your mother cleans and salts the fish and lays them out on a bamboo mat in the sun. When they are dried out, your aunt shreds the fish into string-size pieces. Then Father and I take the dried fish shreds to the streets and feed a few hungry mouths. Not many, but as many as we can. It is heartbreaking, Sei-Young. The look in the eyes of the very young and the very old, especially. I wish I could do more "purposeful work," as my mother would say—she does manage to sneak into my thoughts every minute, along with you and Changi. She would be so happy to be here, by our side.

Today it is raining and the faces on the street are more dismal than words can convey. But yesterday was a sun-filled day, so I placed flowers at your grandfather's grave and played for him the song that brought us together.

I save the good news for last. Father recently purchased a furnished house in Seoul, where your aunt promises to plant a glorious garden. It is his wedding gift to us. The man who sold Father the property was desperate for quick money. He sold his house for three hundred dollars in the gamble that it will be destroyed in the war. But it will be safe in Seoul, as you will be in Chinhae, and we will be in Pusan, until our lives come together again.

All my love,

Heisook

When it seemed as though North Korea was just steps away from taking over the Republic of Korea, General MacArthur launched a masterfully orchestrated attack at the port city of Inchon on September 15, 1950, and the war turned around. Soon the ROK reclaimed Seoul with the help of U.N. support. As advancing ROK soldiers pushed farther north into Pyongyang, President Rhee's dream of a united Korea was fast becoming a reality. His zealous voice was often heard over the radio or quoted in the newspapers.

"We must continue marching North . . . We will not stop until we are one nation of freedom!"

Although President Rhee and I shared the same vision for a free and unified Korea, there was something unsettling, almost inhumane, in the way he perceived its realization. He seemed to have a blind spot when it came to the people who were suffering and even dying in the process. Considering the physical torture he had endured as a young man, this struck me as odd. During one of my monthly visits to Pusan, I was summoned to the President's residence. President Rhee sat comfortably in the gardens where he liked to work.

"Sei-Young," he greeted me, "have a seat."

I bowed—despite his protest—then took my seat. "Thank you, Your Excellency."

"Are you and your family well?"

"Yes, very well, thank you."

Rhee basked in the autumn sun and smiled. "Good. Now update me on your mission in Chinhae."

"It is a difficult one, Your Excellency. I find it painful to watch so many young men go off to war, knowing they might not return alive."

His sigh lacked compassion. "The reality of war, Sei-Young—grotesque, but necessary. So we must be strong and put our emotions aside. Otherwise, the country will suffer. Clear your mind of the human sacrifice and see instead our vision for Korea. Our dedicated young men died for their country, in the name of freedom. What greater honor could they ask for?"

A servant appeared with a tray of European cookies and iced tea. How easy it was for Syngman Rhee to fight for a vision while cloistered in a guarded residence of servants and delicacies. We were only thirty miles from Chinhae, but worlds separated us from the camp where the rotting flesh of the wounded promised death without a shred of honor.

And then, just when it seemed that a ROK victory was on the horizon, Chinese intervention in support of North Korea changed history. Once again, the war turned around.

Because more English-speaking Koreans were being recruited into the U.S. Air Force, in March 1951, after ten months of being stationed in Chinhae, I was permitted to return to my family in Pusan. With mixed feelings, I accepted a Bronze Star for my efforts. Others died; I merely translated.

Back in Pusan, I immediately began my new position as President Rhee's personal secretary. Over the course of the next year, President Rhee confided words to me he would never say over the radio or to a newspaper reporter.

"I know American politics all too well, Sei-Young. Since I refuse to be their puppet, they brand me a lunatic. A senile lunatic. This makes them very nervous. But that's quite all right. I like making them nervous. I want them to keep an eye on me and not forget who I am: Syngman Rhee, President of the Republic of Korea!"

As war waged on, in the spring of 1952, President Rhee declared martial law and halted the National Assembly.

"The members of the National Assembly have turned into American puppets, Sei-Young. They will not re-elect me for a second term. My advisors tell me the CIA is pulling their strings. We must campaign for a free election process!"

Was Rhee paranoid, or was it true? I had no answer, but I was learning that politics was a corrupt business, and could probably turn even an honest, well-meaning man paranoid. The truth was, there were many things to admire about Syngman Rhee. There was no question that he had greatness about him. His lifelong commitment to a free Korea was the torch burning in his eyes. But sometimes I suspected the vision had more to do with the name of President Syngman Rhee going down in history than the plight of the commoner. If he passed a man like Father on the streets, would he take note of his tragedy or would he pass him without a thought? The latter, I had to admit. Still, I chose to support the figure who had helped me.

During my tenure as Rhee's personal secretary, I had read and saved thousands of letters from ROK citizens written in support of the Rhee regime. Judging from many of these heart-felt letters, they were penned by common Koreans whose voices had been shunned too long. Were Father alive, his letter would be among these. With clenched fists, Father once cursed the Japanese. Had he survived the Japanese Occupation, he would be clenching his fists in support today.

When the U.N. press descended on the President's office, criticizing his actions for declaring martial law, I used these letters to justify Rhee's position. Cameras flashed and microphones were projected from a crowd of loud reporters. I raised one of many boxes overflowing with letters and declared—

"The people have spoken. Rhee for President in 'fifty-two!"

Newspapers around the world published a photograph of President Rhee at his desk. I was there, too, standing over Rhee and a stack of letters.

Rhee won the election in 1952. I believed I had helped him in his quest for re-election. Later, however, there would be accusations by the opposition that Rhee had rigged the election. Again, I had no answer; nor was I aware of any such activity.

Even if true, I couldn't condemn the man for his efforts. Our first President had the immortal task of rebuilding a nation in the midst of war, and I believed he was the best person for the job at that time. However historians would view this era, they were not there at Korea's moment of crisis.

TWENTY-TWO

1953–1955
Sei-Young

"'. . . to swim across the world . . .'"

ON A HOT SUMMER day in 1953, after three long years of conflict, the Korean War finally ended. But it was a tragic ending. After all the bloodshed, Korea remained divided. That meant Heisook's mother and countless others in North Korea could not see their loved ones across the border. Not now.

President Rhee would not accept this end. He was so close to victory that the loss of the lives—and the prospect of more loss—did not seem to faze him. He wanted to fight until the Thirty-eighth Parallel was obliterated from the soil and Korea was one nation.

At this time I made the decision to leave my position as personal secretary to Rhee and to continue my education. I had learned all I needed to know about politics: It was not my destiny.

* * *

Once I held my little brother's hand as he was dying; once I watched Grandfather being tortured and Mother assaulted. Many things had changed but pain was always the same. Leaving Pusan was a bittersweet ending to the war, for it also meant saying good-bye to Grandfather once again.

The churchbells rang and the magnolia tree spread its young branches over Grandfather's grave. For so many reasons—years of fear, pain, deaths, all the heartache of human life—stoicism had no place here. We wept openly, too hard to even say good-bye.

Then the sound of voices rippling like golden harps reached my ears. It was the sound of refugees filing out of Pusan. Their song awakened Grandfather's sleeping spirit, for I was sure I heard him say—

"Go now, Sei-Young, for I will go with you, waiting to hear the bells of freedom ring across our land."

A military jeep drove us back to Seoul. After crossing miles of war-torn land, we approached the capital city with dread.

Most of Seoul was destroyed. Homes and buildings, including the First Methodist Church, had crumbled to the ground without mercy. We drove through throngs of homeless families and orphans squatting in the streets with no place to go. Recognizable only by its location and one untouched statue, the Seoul Presbyterian Church still stood, although it would require many months of restoration. The house Reverend Pang had purchased for Heisook and me had been spared the worst. Windows had been shattered and the *ondal* floors were ruined. But the house, with its fine red-tiled roof, remained intact.

Heisook was unusually quiet during our inspection of Seoul,

and even of our new home. When I questioned her, she replied—

"I am praying, Sei-Young. For those who survived and for those who didn't. And although this may sound strange to you, I thank God that this is Seoul and not Sinuiju. You see, even though I lived in Seoul for three years, Sinuiju will always be my home. And I cannot imagine coming home to this."

In the early evening while walking alone on the city streets, I witnessed a near-miraculous sight: my old friend staring into the remains of what was once a popular tea house.

"Eun Ju Chun!" I shouted.

Eun Ju howled in disbelief and shouted back even louder, "Sei-Young Shin!"

We shook hands, then hugged. After I told him what I had been doing since we last saw each other, Eun Ju shrugged and said—

"Guess what? I never left Seoul."

"Why not?"

"My mother wouldn't leave her home. And being the devoted son I am, I couldn't leave her. Besides, she's the boss."

Eun Ju's gifts seemed in danger of being wasted in a changing world. I appealed to him to keep in touch with me, jotting down my address and inviting him over. A mere week later, he had taped a letter to our door. Typewritten on official Bank of Korea stationary, it read, "No, I am not Bank president yet, but I will be, Sei-Young. This is my destiny!"

Over the next year, we made repairs to our new home. During that time, Heisook discovered that her marital status no longer allowed her to return to Ewha. Meanwhile I was applying to several fine foreign universities. Reverend Pang had made a wise suggestion.

"Study abroad, Sei-Young. It is a good time to leave our country. When you and my daughter return, the ravages of war will not surround you."

"But what about Heisook? What will she do?"

"I will see another part of the world," she spoke up selflessly. "And maybe I will be able to complete my college degree where we are. Then I should like to become a music teacher."

I was accepted on scholarship to Harvard University in Cambridge, Massachusetts, beginning the winter semester of 1955. There I would study public administration and economics. Our home in Seoul would be loved and lived in by Mother and Aunt Sunja until our return in two years. Reverend Pang elected to live in the Seoul Presbyterian Church, where he claimed to hear his wife's voice in unison with his whenever he prayed.

The night before our departure I watched my wife packing. Lately she seemed content in a faraway sense.

"Heisook, tell me. How do you really feel about moving to America?"

There was no need to gather her thoughts, she simply spoke. "I am packing tonight just as I packed my things one night not really so long ago. Then I was scared. Now I am not. Of course, I am going with you, my husband, who is all things brave and strong to me. But, Sei-Young, I am brave and strong, too, now. I once skated on the Paengma River with Changi and truly believed I was skating in a wondrous dream. That's how magical I felt that day. Safe and protected by my big brother. But it wasn't a dream, it was real. And I was neither safe nor protected—just young enough to believe I was. I must admit that the ten-year-old girl in me tells me not to move from this spot, that if I do, I will get lost and stay lost forever. But I cannot live that way. Whatever happens between the North and South will not change whether I am here or in America. It matters not where I am when I write my letters to Mother—they will remain unanswered. And I am almost grateful that there are no news reports of the condition of Sinuiju. If I heard my hometown was as devastated as Seoul, I could not leave with you. This way, I can still hope. So I go to America wishing things were different—that Mother and Changi were with Father—but I will go bravely and try with all my might to believe that the future will open up to us like a wall of morning glories."

TWENTY-THREE

HEISOOK
Departure

SLOWLY, THE AIRPLANE BEGINS to move. I wave good-bye to our family; they are waving tearfully from the rooftop of Kimpo Airport. I give my last look to Father as I squeeze Sei-Young's hand. A small, hushed part of me has always wondered whether some heavenly force brought me into the courtyard of the First Methodist Church and into Sei-Young's heart. How else could it be explained? And yet . . . Mother and Father's supreme faith still eluded me. Do they ever, even once, question Him as they pray for reunion from opposite sides of the Thirty-eighth Parallel? No, I am sure not.

As the airplane poises for take-off, I am thinking of Changi. The waterfall once told me that he was gone forever. I believed it then, yet that same small, hushed part of me is afraid that I am leaving him behind. It is true that Changi's fate and where-abouts are still a mystery—but at least while I lived in Seoul, we shared the same continent. Maybe he would somehow find me; maybe we would cross paths on a busy street. Like that stone once in my pocket, it was something I had secretly held on to; I could look into passing faces, a crowd, and still carry that wish with me. Yet now I was crossing the seas; I would be so far away from him he might ebb from my memory. The airplane speeds down the runway and his voice rushes into my ears—

"The waterfall tells me that the world is changing and we must change with it."

Though I would have been content to sit on the giant quartz rock forever, the world *was* always changing. And I would change with it. But not my beloved Changi. He would forever remain my big brother, one minute defiantly marching ahead of me up the *san* trail, so proud of the scar on the back of his head, his medal of honor; the next minute sweeping me up in his arms as snow fell around us in patches so magical it hurts to remember.

"You are a silly girl running in the snow. You don't even know where you are going, do you?"

Yes, I do, Changi. Yes, I do.

My thoughts drift to Mother. I will not weep, I will not weep, I am a full-grown married woman. She has no idea where I am right now as the airplane lifts me off the ground. I am going farther from her than she could ever possibly imagine, so far she could never find me. But I remember how she found me once, in a crowd of hysteria, on the day it was declared the end may be near.

"I did not think we would be together on earth again!"

Would we? Would we ever be together on earth again? From the waterfall to across the Thirty-eighth Parallel, to Seoul, then to Pusan and now to America, I was learning that my life was one of journey. And that the lights to heaven had guided me here to this very moment, on an airplane with my husband and the memory of Mother's words—

"I thought we would be reunited in heaven!"

Maybe it was true.

TWENTY-FOUR

Sei-Young
Departure

Over a small mountain village we fly; I look down. A portrait of a peasant family comes into view. I see Father hobbling down the mountain with his rickety cart. I see Mother washing clothes in the river. I see Kwan-Young asleep on her back. How very peaceful he looks. I see Grandfather speaking to the monsoon sky.

I will always be homesick for Nabi, for that mountaintop where even a boy in rags can be crowned by the sun. So much hardship, so much love. So many dreams even as hope perished.

Over the village we pass. The portrait is fading. No, no, no . . .

Sleep well, Kwan-Young! I will always be hyong nim!
Good luck, Father!

No matter where I look out, one face remains clear—

Grandfather's. He is the vital link in our sacred circle and from earth to heaven. He did not live forever as my young heart once believed, but as the airplane thunderously breaks through clouds, his spirit takes up the whole sky.

"Your name is Sei-Young, which means 'to swim across the world.' Someday you will do just that."